STOLEN WORLD

By NS Austin

Contents

Dear Readers,

Stolen World is the third novel in a series. I've tried to make each book unique, building upon the world created in the previous novels. For readers who haven't had the chance to read books One and Two of the Endangered Series yet (and I heartily recommend you do), then the following descriptions should help you get started. If you're a returning reader, call these descriptions a reminder. I'll be brief, like short clips before a TV series.

Critically Endangered, Book 1:

The Great Dying: In the span of two weeks, a short, deadly illness killed nearly everyone on Earth. Dispersed across the globe, approximately 20,000 humans had survived. Although there was no explanation for this near extinction, it was believed to be purposefully caused by man.

The Change: Survivors of the Great Dying changed. About half experienced a regeneration of their bodies to young adulthood and in some cases gained refined sense abilities like hearing, vision, sensing, and prophecy. The other half changed and became a different version of Homo sapiens, appearing something like contemporary renderings of a Bigfoot.

Talking dogs: Pairs of German shepherds with the ability to communicate through thought transfer appeared on the planet at the same time as the Great Dying.

Beyond the Great Dying, Book 2:

Time/Technology: The setting is 100 years after the Great Dying. Technology is a mixture of agrarian, late 19th Century, and remarkable energy advances.

Ardinians: Peaceful, spacefaring aliens who left their home to search for a new planet after a supernova destroyed their solar system. The Ardinians will not confess how long they've been looking for this new home.

Huntas: A violent splinter group of the Ardinians. During the journey, a great family fight occurred and this group set out on their own. They now call themselves the Hunta.

Mermots: Another peaceful, intelligent species who offered to share their planet with the Ardinians. The Huntas found them and destroyed the Mermot world. The Ardinians agreed to ferry surviving Mermots with them in search of another home.

New Washington: Human survivors created a prosperous enclave on what was once Tacoma, Washington. It was renamed New Washington.

Founders: Humans who survived the Great Dying and the change. Founders are now well over 100 years old. Due to DNA changes and better health, they may live up to 250 years.

Rangers: The Great Dying had no effect on other mammals, but millions of pet dogs were released into the wilderness. They overwhelmed other canine species and evolved into a new species that is a combination of dog, wolf, and coyote. Rangers are intelligent but undomesticated.

Bigfoots: The other type of Homo sapiens on Earth. Not seen in many years, some believe Bigfoots died off quickly after the change. They have become a legend.

That's all! Enjoy Stolen World.

Chapter 1
Trent

The interlocking hands of soaring firs shielded what little light was left from a socked-in day. Tendrils of mist crawled across the forest floor, dancing around trees on their way back to the Puget Sound. Other than the occasional bird or squirrel that used the canopy for games of hide and seek, the forest was silent. Even in silence, Trent could feel the life teeming around him.

Trent missed those solitary mornings in the woods. His life was better now that he had Amelia and her family, but there were still those moments when he longed for the wild freedom that came from living off the land. It was as if once a man became feral, that uncivilized part of him didn't go easily back in the box.

He glanced at Lionheart, who was on the alert for deer from his position under the deer stand. The black shepherd's big nose twitched as he inhaled through a raised snout. Trent hadn't had a moment's peace for over two years, and he was thankful Lionheart was good at keeping quiet. Silence from a talking dog who could communicate by thought transfer was both unusual and appreciated.

As if to prove Trent wrong about his reserved nature, Lionheart began a low, rumbling growl. Trent waited and listened until Lionheart signaled an all clear by sitting back on his haunches.

Probably nothing.

Trent was lucky to have Amelia's dog with him today because Lionheart was the best trained of their four dogs. Amelia loved that dog with all her heart and usually wanted him by her side. She said he kept her grounded. She probably wouldn't have let Lionheart come on this hunt at all, but Trent had mumbled something like, "Sometimes I think you love that dog more than me."

To which she'd replied with her light-up-the-world, sweeter-than-honey smile, "He keeps me calm, but you, my dear husband, get me excited."

Trent knew he was done for after Amelia's provocative statement, so he'd willingly taken an hour from his deer outing to spend time with her. Afterwards, she'd relented and allowed him to take along Lionheart. Trent called it a win/win, but it left only three hours for the deer and peace and quiet.

Worldwide preparation for a possible invasion by the Huntas superseded other priorities. In his small slice of the world, that meant fewer deer hunting trips. Since the Mermots had started bringing beef into the enclave from a farm north of old Seattle, he couldn't even use the excuse of needing meat in order to enjoy a whole day alone in the wilderness.

Suddenly, Lionheart sprang to his feet. The shepherd paced forward, his body taut and his head up. He was straining through his neck and shoulders as if he were trying to locate something on the wind.

"What is it, boy? Do you smell deer?"

The dog shivered and whined before he sat down again and said, "No deer."

What's got into him? He's sure jittery. Trent scanned the area and listened more closely. *Huh, nothing.*

Trent checked his watch; he had one hour left until he had to report to his training duties. Seven long days a week, Trent instructed enclave civilians on how to shoot. Most knew at least the basics. These people couldn't survive in a depopulated world, surrounded by wilderness, and escape the need for a rudimentary understanding of how to use a weapon. If only there wasn't such a huge chasm between hitting a near target with a shotgun and wielding a sophisticated weapon while on the move and under threat.

That last bit was the skill he was trying to impart to the populace. He'd learned to shoot and multitask during his trek across the Old United States while hunting for the murderers of his first family. Even though he'd had some success getting clavers up to speed, making soldiers out of farmers and tradespeople was a frustrating mission. Some of them would never be able to hit the wide side of a building.

It didn't help that Chrystel, his boss, might've been an evil queen in a prior life. A green-eyed, redhead with boundless energy, she wore them all out with her demands to keep working, to keep training, and to remain vigilant. It seemed odd and sometimes uncomfortable to work for his wife's daughter, but that's the way things went in New Washington. There was always way too much to do and never enough people to get it all done. Trent knew she was right to push people, but he just wished she'd—

Crack!

What the devil was that? It didn't sound like deer.

Lionheart's throat rumble morphed to a full growl. Trent caught the dog's eyes and raised his fist, the command for hide and wait. The dog crawled around the tree and snuggled into a low bush. Holding his breath, Trent strained to hear where the sound had come from. A crunching sound, most likely a footfall from the east, was moving in his direction.

He was almost positive a two-legged creature was the source. Four-legged mammals rarely made that much noise. Probably just someone else on the hunt for deer. Nevertheless, better to be safe than sorry. There were still walk-ons around the enclave who couldn't be trusted.

Sighting down the barrel, he waited and steadied his breathing. He also made his profile as small as possible, pulling on his camouflage to remain hidden. Trent was sure of it now. More than one person was traipsing around in the woods, and they were getting closer. He checked for Lionheart but couldn't see or hear him. *Good*, he thought. If several armed men were coming their way, one dog by himself wouldn't have any chance.

Trent heard a guttural, rasping clicking and then another in answer from behind his stand. The sound possessed the cadence of speech, but Trent had never heard any man or animal make a similar noise. His heart began to pound against his chest, and he struggled to control his breathing. Even on a cool, New Washington Enclave morning, sweat was beading on Trent's forehead. Almost underneath him, the turbulence of feet shuffling through the forest rose to a level that meant there was a group, not just one or two. They seemed to be spread in a line moving in the direction of the enclave.

His finger lingering on the trigger, he wished he had a laser gun with him today rather than his trusty hunting rifle. Trent had seen the film Karen had brought back with her from the Mermot moon. Could the vocal sounds he was hearing be made by a Hunta? Was it possible they were already here? They'd all been told the

Huntas would come eventually, but the world would have plenty of warning before an attack. He should've known that was wishful thinking.

He watched and waited for a bipedal creature to emerge underneath him. A shimmery patch of air, like an energy halo, floated to his front. As the mirage moved forward, Trent could see the impression of tracks left in dead vegetation, but nothing else. Screaming from the inside, his heart accelerated from pounding to a pulsating gallop.

Are the freaking Huntas already here?

Hunta or otherwise, whoever was sneaking through the forest toward the enclave, they had technology to make themselves invisible. For all the shitty things that had happened to humanity during the previous century, the idea of an invisible, aggressive alien force strolling through his deer hunting area was beyond Trent's limit for a bad day.

Please, Lionheart, don't move or make a sound.

Trent forced himself into stillness despite his desire to run back to New Washington to protect Amelia and warn the others. The smart move was to allow the energy bubbles to pass and then run on their flanks to get to the enclave. It was bad enough he didn't have anything but a rifle, but how was he supposed to hit and disable an enemy he couldn't see? Even if he'd thought to bring along a laser and tried to take out as many as possible, if he was overwhelmed, the townspeople would never know an enemy was coming.

He counted six apparitions that passed near his location. Luminous, wavering light, like a distant mirage on an overheated desert plain, hid whatever creature lived inside that cloak. A loud, commanding *click* stopped their progress.

Like a flash on a screen, the light stabilized around the largest of the shimmering blobs and it disappeared entirely. Trent could almost imagine the monster underneath.

Did they hear me or the dog? Are the freaking Huntas already here?

Trent controlled his breathing. He hoped Lionheart was doing the same thing. It was maddening not to be able to see these things and what they were doing. Even the energized air around the frightening apparitions evaporated when they remained still. Were pulpy, yellow Hunta eyes searching for him right now as he hid helplessly nearby in a tree, waiting for them to find him?

A minute passed. More clicks and gravelly vocal sounds. In his mind's eye, Trent pictured the Hunta invaders nodding to each other and pointing at his deer stand. He considered jumping down from the tree in a final gesture of human defiance, to take out as many as he could with his woefully inadequate rifle, but stopped himself when he heard a grunt. Tracks appearing in loose pine needles were moving away.

If he could've risked a sigh of relief, Trent would have done so. He waited anxiously until the wavering energy clouds had moved on before he slid from the stand to the ground. He whispered, "Come, Lionheart." The large dog burst from his hiding place, his eyes wild just like Trent's. They began to run east. "You lead, Lionheart, quick and quiet."

They ran for a quarter mile east, the same direction from which the invisible invaders had come, and then headed south. Trent was just about to stop and try to call the enclave when Lionheart made the choice for him, halting in his tracks past a large rock formation on an old path that wound back to the southern edge of the enclave. The confused dog jerked his head back and forth, his nose up and searching for the location of a scent. "Lionheart smell something!" he said into Trent's mind, an edge of fear consuming Lionheart's normally calm and playful voice. Trent paused beside him and joined the dog in scanning the forest for threats.

A translucent shimmer moved from behind a fir tree. Something mechanical whirred and propelled Trent forward. He leaped on top of Lionheart, grabbing the dog around the neck and rolling away just as an energy bolt shot past him, singing the hair on the back of his head. Trent could smell a burning tree behind them. White-yellow hot light flickered through the morning mist. Trent finished his roll, pointed his rifle at the center of the glimmering blob, and let out six fast rounds.

The writhing mass screeched, and then the fuzziness clarified into a hideous beast with shape and form. Four bullet holes pierced the black vest the humanoid creature was wearing. Ecstatic that he'd gotten lucky with a shot into its wide neck, the alien held his neck with thick fingers to stem the flow of spurting blood. Dark purple blood shot from the wound in waves and drenched everything in the alien's vicinity. The Hunta peered at Trent as if puzzled, stumbled, and then dropped to the forest floor.

Rising from his prone position, Trent cautiously stepped closer to the dying alien. Lionheart followed close at his heels. He examined the monstrosity that was convulsing before him. *Probably not long for this world*, he thought. *A world where this creature doesn't belong*. Trent's face contorted into a frown. "Damn that thing is ugly, and what the hell is that smell?"

A boney ridge extended across the Hunta's forehead above the eyes, and its skull looked like a slab of rock decorated with lumpy growths that might have once been horns. If this was a Hunta, the pictures he'd seen didn't do the creature justice. Its skin was mottled and scaly from the nose down. Yellow protruding eyes, interwoven with plump dark veins around the pupil, fluttered and looked up at Trent with cold calculation.

Trent aimed his rifle near a soft spot along the side of its hideous eyes and fired two rounds into the alien's head. He waited as the convulsing stopped, and the eyes ceased their threatening stare. "That should do it, Lionheart. He's a brute. Must weigh 300 pounds."

Trent went to one knee and patted down the alien to search for anything useful. He pulled off a square, two-inch device that was latched to the front of the alien's vest. He didn't know whether the metallic object was a communicator or a cloaking device, but whatever its purpose, he needed to get the object back to Jed and the Ardinians to study. He finished his search by yanking the alien's weapon from its dead hands.

He gave the alien weapon a quick once over and discovered there wasn't a simple trigger. Pressure points lining the stock where a trigger would be placed on a human weapon were the most likely means to engage the burning beam that had almost killed him and Lionheart. He turned to look at the tree the alien had shot instead. It was now a melting torch, and the fire was spreading. The forest was bone dry, and until the fall rainy season began in the Pacific Northwest, a wildfire was always a danger.

"Lionheart, in addition to being ugly and stinking to high heaven, these aliens are also careless. That or stupid. If they're here to capture us, they'll burn us to the ground first. I don't think we can get back to the enclave in time to warn them about the aliens or the fire. I need to call them. Let's go!"

Lionheart was poised several feet away from the deceased lifeform, his lips curled and canines showing. When Trent said, "Let's go," Lionheart quickly obeyed.

The dog took the lead, setting off in the same direction as before, but he halted abruptly. "More smells!" Lionheart shouted.

"Where? Can you tell how many?"

Lionheart pointed his snout to the east. Trent's eyes followed Lionheart's signal, but he couldn't see any sign of Huntas. He frowned with the realization that trying to see an invisible predator was wasted effort. Unless they were close and moving, there was nothing to see.

"Two or three. Not far." Lionheart said.

Run or hide? Trent's mind raced as he evaluated the immediate area and studied the alien weapon he was holding. A whiff of the Huntas' distinctive odor sent his feet into motion. They were close.

"With me," Trent whispered to Lionheart. He scrambled up a rise and dove between a fir and an overgrown salal shrub. It wasn't a great hiding spot, but the slight elevation allowed a decent shooting position. Lionheart tucked himself on the left side of Trent.

Trent's panic was rising. He needed to get back to warn the enclave, and he didn't have time to waste. Luckily, he didn't have long to wait. Hunta clicking, like a two-way conversation, approached his hiding spot. His plan to allow them to pass and then continue running south went to hell when a spider dropped onto his nose. He quietly flicked it off, but it crawled over his hand, and he gulped.

The Huntas' clicking became more insistent as they started to hiss.

Just keep moving. Please just keep moving.

He could see the wavering air. They were close and getting closer by the second. Two of them.

Pleading into his mind, Lionheart said, "Shoot them."

That was all the encouragement Trent needed. He hoped his guess about the operation of the alien weapon was right. He aimed the same way he'd aim a rifle, touched the pressure point he thought was a trigger, and shot at the one on the left. Keeping pressure on with a flat finger, he swept toward the Hunta still clicking on the right.

A bright yellow bolt lit up the first Hunta, and its cloak seemed to evaporate. The creature hit the ground hard. The spray of energy stopped just short of the second Hunta. Trent was madly jumping his finger on the pressure point when he heard the whir of an alien rifle that wasn't his own.

He rolled fast and scooted back behind the tree. Lionheart was smart enough to make the same move. The bush beside them was now in flames. The Hunta's smell had become almost overpowering when Lionheart bolted from their cover.

With a snarling dog on the attack, Trent pulled his knife from his belt and sprang from behind the tree to press the advantage. All he could see was a portion of Lionheart twisting and pulling. The dog's head had disappeared behind the Hunta's cloak, and his legs were bent and digging into the ground. Trent imagined the Hunta's leg being ripped apart by sharp, canine teeth.

He jumped at the invisible melee and stabbed where he guessed the Hunta's head would be. An unseen fist connected hard with Trent's solar plexus. He couldn't breathe, but he also couldn't stop. He stabbed the Hunta again and again as the alien hit him back. They fought like two children flailing at each other without a strategy until, finally, the cloak flashed out of existence.

Lionheart released the Hunta's leg and leaped for the alien's neck just as Trent popped one of the creature's plump eyes with his knife.

The combined force of Lionheart's and Trent's attacks forced the wounded alien to the ground.

Trent unslung his hunting rifle and shot the Hunta in the face. Lionheart sat back, panting, his tongue dripping purple blood. Wasting no time, Trent checked the first Hunta to find it black and charred. He then kicked the other to make sure he was also incapacitated or dead. When he didn't get a response from the ugly beast, he turned to Lionheart. "I think that does it. Nice move by the way, Lionheart. We don't have a second to waste. Let's move."

They ran south until Lionheart couldn't smell anymore Huntas and then stopped near the cover of a tree. Trent inhaled against the pain in his body from the huge alien's punishing blows. He extracted a phone from his pocket and extended a short antenna. Getting no signal from the satellite phone setting, Trent pushed the digital switch to change from satellite to laser vector communication.

Jed's vector technology always worked over medium distances, which was an important failsafe when satellites were in the wrong part of their orbit. The Ardinians had promised full satellite coverage soon, but they'd prioritized completion of earthbound defensive weapons first. Trent quit breathing when it became obvious that neither satellite nor vector gathered a signal. It was frightening to consider the possibility that the vector relay stations on

Rainier and Hood might've already been disabled.

"Dammit!" he hissed between clenched teeth. "Lionheart, I'll never make it back in time to warn the others. It's up to you boy. Run to them. Warn them. Tell them there are Huntas and a fire in the forest. Can you remember that? Huntas and fire in the forest?"

Trent knew talking dogs were prone to forget verbal instructions. They communicated in a simple, literal way. Try to give them too much information and there was a chance a warning could get lost in translation. Even a rabbit crossing their path might divert them from an important objective. Luckily, Lionheart was more focused than most talking dogs.

Lionheart studied his master and listened intently to his words. The dog's cocked head and confused expression told Trent there was something the dog didn't understand.

"Tell me the warning, Lionheart. Say it to me." Trent instructed.

"Hunta?"

Trent groaned and calmed himself. "Hunta is that bad smell. Now say it back to me to me."

"Huntas and fire in the forest. Huntas and fire in the forest," Lionheart repeated into Trent's mind. Then he added, "Not bad smell—different smell. Hunta smell."

"That's it! Don't forget. Keep that one thing in your head and stay away from the Hunta smell. Now, run as fast as you've ever run. Go, Lionheart. You must save them from Huntas and fire in the forest!"

Lionheart gazed longingly at his master. He obviously wanted to stay with Trent and protect him from the Hunta smells, but Lionheart was an obedient dog. He turned and ran. Trent watched the streak of fur shoot through the trees, and he began running after the dog. It wasn't a minute before Lionheart was out of sight.

Chapter 2
Mark, Three Days Earlier

"Mark, you're falling asleep again. You still have forty-two modules to complete."

Mark opened one dark eye. Tammy, the onboard AI, had to be the most manipulative, sexy-voiced, and annoying AI in the galaxy. One minute she made him laugh, and the next, Mark wished she was able to take physical form so he could throttle her. He'd ended up with Tammy by accident. When Manny and Dee had given up their wasp to assume more important responsibilities, they'd offered their ship to him. Mark had assumed the gift of their prized wasp was an honor. It didn't occur to him until Tammy's idiosyncrasies were on full display that Manny might have been making a joke at Mark's expense.

Operations had offered to uninstall Tammy and reinstall a different AI, but Mark had grown accustomed to the quirky intelligence living inside his ship. She was a challenge, and there was nothing Mark enjoyed as much as a challenge. No way was he going to let Manny get the last laugh. Besides, if his assessment of Tammy's AI character was correct, she would fight with every digital tooth and nail to remain hidden in the ship and strike back in retaliation when they were most unprepared. Better to keep Tammy as a friend.

"Any action out there, Tammy?"

"If you'd attempt to remain conscious, Mark, you wouldn't have to ask. But no, everything is as normal as the sun, moon, and the stars. I might remind you, we are never going to be in line for a promotion to pilot a destroyer spacecraft. Your dream of one day assuming command of the fleet will never be realized unless you have a better understanding of astrophysics."

"Who says I'm taking you with me?"

There was silence in the cockpit. Jenny, Mark's copilot, was laughing under her breath. "I can see you smiling, Jenny." Tammy smoothly retorted. "I know you will take me with you. We're a team. I'm the Cher to your Sonny, the Bonnie to your Clyde. . . Wait, hold up."

"Need to search historical databases to come up with more male-female partners?" Mark asked, laughing along with Jenny.

"Mark, I have a reading from the far side of Uranus. Y'all need to get your butts in gear," a suddenly serious Tammy commanded.

Mark sat up. "Report."

"I am detecting ships near Uranus. Sensors indicate three medium-sized spacecraft matching the description of Hunta cruisers. I've already relayed the information to the fleet and

Admiral Mike. The rest of your flight stands ready for your instructions."

"Who's closest that could get eyes on them?"

"Firestarter is the closest."

"Put me through," Mark ordered. "And Tammy, please don't say 'y'all.' If I can quit saying it, so can you."

Mark's adrenaline was surging. This was the moment for which they'd been training. As the lead wasp pilot, he'd been responsible for ensuring the qualification of every other wasp pilot in the fleet. He'd also devised a plan and schedule for patrolling the outer reaches of the solar system. The only reason he was patrolling near Uranus at all was because the fleet didn't have enough wasp jockeys to fill the seats of the craft available. That and Thomas had told him that good leaders were out with the troops. Mark wanted to be a respected leader. At only twenty-three, he was one of the youngest wasp pilots, and it mattered that he presented the right image. Besides, deep inside, what he most desired was a chance to engage an enemy in a live battle. To test his skills against the Huntas and prevail. To prove his reputation as the best pilot on earth.

"Gameboy, this is Firestarter. We stand ready for orders."

"All wasps have open channels, Mark," Tammy announced.

"Firestarter, raise your shields and swing around Uranus just enough to conduct a remote scan. Tammy will collect the data. Do not engage! The remainder of the team will form a defensive pattern on me. Tammy is sending my mark now. Remember y'all, our job is to slow them down until our destroyers can take it to them. Tammy, how long until the team is in place?"

"Seventeen minutes and twenty-three seconds, providing Firestarter can get the scans, and that the unknown ships which are probably Huntas don't engage her before she retreats to her secondary position."

"Make it quick, Firestarter." Mark ordered. When he'd waited enough time for all wasps to receive his orders, he commanded, "Begin."

"Roger, Gameboy." Becky, aka Firestarter, replied a minute later. The six other wasps acknowledged the order and began their acceleration in time with Mark as the lead craft.

Pressed to a gel-like seat, the gravitational forces weighed on Mark's frame with pressure like a tractor rolling onto his chest, the small amount of fat on his face flattening toward his ears. Mark felt most alive when he was burning toward a destination. The incredible speed, no matter how uncomfortable, was like a jolt of adrenaline. If not for Tammy, he would have enjoyed the entire ride.

"You said y'all," she whispered in her most breathless and sexual tone.

It was difficult to speak, but Mark managed a squeaking, "Did not."

"Did too."

Jenny, the copilot, croaked a reply. "Shutt da hellll up."

* * *

Before all seven wasps were in position, Firestarter had completed a swing around Uranus and was heading back toward the wasp contingent. Yelling into her communicator, she said, "There's no one there! What the heck? Was this supposed to be an exercise? Because if it was, I don't find scaring the crap out of us needlessly to be—"

Mark cut her off. "Did you scan the surface of the planet? Could they have been hiding on one of the moons?"

"You think we're incompetent, Mark? I was a scientist before I was a pilot. When we discovered no visual sightings, I did a complete energy scan on the backside of that desolate planet and the moons Belinda, Portia, Puck, and Miranda. Tammy can double check our data, but our AI says there's nothing there. Zippo, nada. There's nothing there!"

"This is not good," Tammy responded.

"What?" Jenny asked.

"I have the sightings on a recorder. Three ships were there, but now they're gone."

Mark hadn't received much formal education. He'd spent his childhood in an enclave in Louisiana where book learning had been encouraged but not required. He'd spent most of his youth helping his father fish and hunt, fixing equipment, and playing starship on an old gaming machine after the sun went down.

The second he'd heard Karen's broadcast, pleading for volunteers to fly Ardinian spaceships, he'd packed up his meager belongings and headed to New Washington. From the initial interview, to simulator training, to climbing aboard his first wasp and ultimately besting every other pilot on Earth, Mark understood that uneducated didn't mean slow on the uptake. He could get the education he needed, and he surely would since Tammy hounded him daily, but you couldn't replace common sense. That, and the fact that flying was what he was born to do, meant he'd already arrived at the answer while Tammy, Becky, and Jenny were still analyzing the data.

"They must have cloaking technology. If the Huntas had somehow managed to develop a means to jump from one place to another, there'd be a residual energy trail. They might be sitting out here now, staring at us and laughing

29

their asses off. The fact that they aren't attacking tells me the Huntas haven't figured out a way to get around the Ardinian shield and have decided not to bother. That or they must drop their cloaks to fire weapons. They will bypass us, our cruisers and battleships, the Delamie and Moon Base Victory, and go straight for Earth. This tactical situation is as bad as it gets."

If a pin could drop in zero gravity, the pilots and AI's in Wasp Flight Alpha would have heard a tiny tinkle as a metallic object struck the composite deck of the spacefaring wasp.

Mark opened a channel to transmit a fleet-wide alert. "This is Mark, commander of the wasp squadron. It isn't my call, but I'd advise the fleet and Earth-side forces to go immediately to DEFCON 1. We spotted three unknown ships of cruiser size that moved behind Uranus and then disappeared. Tammy is transmitting sensor data as I speak. The Huntas must've developed cloaking technology and are intending to bypass our forces to attack Earth. Someone please tell me that the Ardinian's matter reorganizing weapon is ready for deployment."

Chapter 3
Mike

Mike strolled through the wide and gleaming hallways of Moon Base Victory. Shakete had called and requested that Mike meet him at the docking port for a surprise. Thus far, the biggest surprise was that Shakete was early for their progress meeting. Mike knew that Shakete could tell time, but it was almost as if after living so long, time no longer held any meaning for the Ardinian leader. They'd started without Shakete during last month's get together and were enjoying dinner when he'd finally graced them with an appearance.

Curiously, Shakete's surprises were coming with increasing frequency. This moon base was one of his many unannounced gifts. He'd stealthily dropped a group of Mermots, Ardinian craftsmen, materials, and production machines onto Earth's moon and, six months later, handed Mike the keys to a completed facility.

To say Shakete was in many ways a loose cannon was a generous assessment. It would bother Mike more if the Ardinian's eccentricities didn't normally yield the right result at the right time. If only Shakete would communicate his plans; this moon base a prime example. The facility allowed for better control of the fleet, and impenetrable Ardinian shielding technology created a safe operations center off Earth.

The interior of the moon base was completed with typical Ardinian sensibilities for livability and design. Like Ardinian ships, the luminescent walls glowed with natural light from technology the Ardinians had yet to share. Instead of a focus merely on function, every room appeared more spacious and welcoming than a fleet moon base might otherwise warrant.

Mike paused in front of the wall where he knew a door would appear. He saw the shifting of subatomic particles, and an opening presented itself, revealing Shakete's slender, blond visage at the threshold.

Shakete immediately stuck his hand out to Mike for a shake. "Ah, Admiral, you are looking well."

"And you, Shakete." Mike returned, as he grabbed the Ardinian's hand. "To what do we owe your early arrival?"

"As they say, the early bird catches the grub."

"I believe that's worm, but close enough." Mike wondered what Shakete was up to as he studied his round gold eyes. His smallish mouth turned up into a smile, all his tiny teeth showing, as he stepped aboard the moon base.

"Mike, will you do me the honor of covering your eyes?"

"Excuse me?"

"Cover your eyes whilst I retrieve your surprise. I am most excited."

"Shakete, eye covering is normally reserved for children and spouses. Two grown men—er, sentient beings–aren't known to engage in this tradition."

"Oh. How unfortunate. It seemed such a whimsical practice. As you wish. Maleta, release the beast."

Mike didn't like the sound of that, but what came next stole his breath. A German shepherd proudly strutted around Shakete. The dog's nose captured a scent, and its eyes rapidly followed the familiar smell. "Man Mike!" the dog screamed into Mike's mind. The dog lunged, bumped Mike, and circled around his legs. When the shepherd's enthusiastic greeting didn't receive an equal response, the dog jumped up to place his paws onto Mike's shoulders, whining with delight as his substantial tongue went in for Mike's face.

Mike nearly lost his balance. Unable to speak, he staggered back. Looking at Shakete as if he'd seen a ghost, which indeed he had, he managed an astounded, "How?"

"As you well know, we are able to create a live being and download memories into the brain. You've been so lonely without Karen, Maleta and I— well mostly me, Maleta had some reservations—determined the best solution was a dog companion. Their brains are easy to model. We had maintained your first companion's DNA and a memory backup that was only partially complete, but enough that the established bond would be present."

During Shakete's explanation, new Jack was rubbing his body against Mike's legs, his sturdy tail beating frantically, and all the while whining in joy. Mike was simultaneously drawn to the Jack lookalike and repelled at the notion that this dog was a copy.

"Shakete, I don't have time for a dog. Also, the moon base isn't an appropriate place for him. I truly appreciate the thought, but you shouldn't have done this."

Jack stopped his pacing, sat in front of Mike, and stared up at him with the most dejected expression a dog can wear. "Jack good dog. Man Mike not want him?"

Mike had completely forgotten how intuitive and sensitive his Jack had been. It was Jack who'd taught him what it meant to have a dog as a partner and how easy it was to love a fur covered being simply because they wouldn't be denied. Mike sighed. "Why do I even bother? Jack, of course I want you. I was simply surprised. We'll figure it out. Follow me."

"I knew Jack was the answer to your aloneness," Shakete bragged.

"Don't press your luck, Shakete," Mike answered.

* * *

Ten scientists were engrossed in a debate concerning a theoretical weapon that they'd been unable to perfect. Mike watched their deliberations. Jed led the three human scientists, while six Ardinians and one Mermot comprised the remainder of the scientific team. Listening to the scientists made Mike's head hurt. It was like trying to get to the root of a problem using a foreign language that he barely understood. The terms the scientists threw about were a vocabulary all their own.

A 3D version of four battleship captains was beamed into the meeting. The starship commanders appeared to be sitting on the other side of a large conference table. Thus far, Space Fleet had selected only human captains. Ardinians made decisions by committee after in-depth study, which didn't lend itself to snap decisions in battle, while space flight sickened Mermots to the point of near incapacitation. The human spaceship captains, like Mike, were trying to follow the ins and outs of matter-shifting properties with limited success.

Mike's fingers touched the ruff on Jack's neck. Since Shakete had brought the dog copy to the station, Jack hadn't left his side. He was sleeping on Mike's left, lulled into slumber by the scientific discussion. Ruefully, Mike thought that

Shakete might have been right once again. Having the dog near seemed to mitigate his stress. He needed the support of a buddy he could always trust. Because neither his wife, Karen, nor his closest friend, Thomas, could be here, Jack, the best dog who'd ever lived, was a welcome substitute. Jack had risked his life for him right after the change. He'd saved Karen too, more than once. The least Mike could do was give this duplicate copy a chance.

"Ladies and gentlemen, I think we need a summary now so we can move on to fleet readiness." Mike asked, "Jed, can you possibly put the crux of the matter into layman's terms?"

"Uh, right." Jed said. "First, I'd like to offer the sincere thanks of the entire scientific team for an invite to visit Moon Base Victory. I think I can speak for everyone on the scientific team in saying our tour has been most informative. With that, I believe we may have exceeded our time authorization. In layman's terms, the matter-shifting weapon is dependent on an energy source and specific protocols programmed into the device. The issue is landing the device and supporting energy source on an enemy ship and being afforded at least enough time for the weapon to begin the matter disassembling process without being blown to bits. If an enemy ship was to sit in one place unshielded, then there would be no problem. The device could attach to the hull and destroy the ship. However, that's not a likely situation in a battle. Also, by the time the shield is down, the ship is vulnerable to more conventional weapons anyway."

Mike asked, "Is there a way to use our matter weapon to disassemble the Hunta shield? If we could do that, then taking out an enemy would be simple."

"True enough, but even though we aren't completely sure of the Hunta shielding construct, as with most shields, it's likely comprised of energy and not elemental or composite matter. Best to just say that's a whole different ball of wax."

At Jed's idiom usage, Mike glanced at Shakete to give him a warning look, and Shakete returned a resigned nod. Jed continued, "The Ardinian shield is a projection of the matter-disassembling technology. When a missile or energy weapon hits the shield, the energy is deflected, and missiles are literally torn apart into subatomic pieces. It's why, thus far, our shield is 100% effective. In theory, this same concept should work against a Hunta shield, but we haven't been able to bridge that gap. We believe the quantity of energy in a shield versus the matter-disassembling weapon is the source of our problem. Regardless, a concept to degrade a shield is another avenue we're pursuing."

"Jed, old friend, sometimes you make my head hurt. Look, I don't know how many ways I can say this: we need an advantage. If Shakete's outdated intelligence is correct, the Huntas outnumber our fleet by three to one, and they've had time to build more. Perhaps we should consider larger conventional weapons. We've been working on insurgent strategies to whittle away their numbers and will to fight, but that assumes a protracted conflict. The Mermots are still building ships, but we may be running out of time."

"I know, and I'm sorry. I wish I had a rabbit to magically pull from my hat."

Mike noticed Shakete's excitement and held up a finger. "Shakete, the rabbit from the hat metaphor is interesting, but now is not a good time to discuss the underpinnings of the expression."

With a disappointed expression, Shakete nodded. "Of course, Admiral. I would like to add that the Ardinians can spare more scientists now, and we will send them immediately. Also, Jed, I may have an idea. Please allow me to speak with you after this meeting so as not to delay other important business. Please proceed."

Mike gazed down at the table in front of him. He knew he couldn't show the fear now lodged in his gut to the rest of the fleet. Fear that had inexorably grown and expanded since he'd taken the position of Admiral of Space Fleet. It was a job that he'd been given, somewhat unwillingly, rather than earned through the normal method of experience and promotion. Even the institution they called Space Fleet wasn't really an "institution" in the normal sense of the word. Space Fleet didn't have formal schools or command structures or set procedures after years of incremental development. What Space Fleet did have was a group of people who'd volunteered to defend the planet after being told by Shakete three years ago that the Huntas were coming.

As fast and hard as the entire team and all of Earth had struggled to manufacture ships and weapons, train pilots, and shore up defenses, their efforts weren't enough. When he'd gained control of his face, Mike looked at the assembled crowd and began a pep talk, as much for himself as everyone else.

"Every day is a new opportunity to make our partnership stronger. Because of all of you and thousands not with us in this room, every day our forces become more capable and resilient. Use each day to the best of your ability because that is all we have.

"I also want to remind each of you what we've accomplished in just over one-hundred years." Mike paused and swept the room with his eyes. "First, the human species survived the most devastating extinction event in the history of mankind. We had no choice but to claw our way back to the beginning of new civilizations. We were shaken by the arrival of extraterrestrial beings who carried news of a warrior species called the Hunta, steaming toward Earth to take our home. We've formed lasting partnerships with the Ardinians and Mermots and have come to know them as our friends. We've fought against the pointless aggressions of other burgeoning settlements and secured a peace so that we could defend our planet together as one people.

"Moreover, we've adapted to technological changes at breakneck speed. In only two weeks, the Great Dying transformed our world from one of Twenty-first Century achievements to something akin to feudal, farming communities. When the Ardinians arrived, they brought with them scientific advances beyond our wildest dreams and offered to share those marvels with Earth. Once again, we marshalled our ingenuity and determination to use the Ardinian gift of knowledge to remake our world and ensure our defense against the Huntas.

"On the part of the Ardinians, they've survived a millennium in space, searching for a home. The Mermots lost their own world and most of their population to the Huntas. Both sought shelter here on Earth and love this planet as their own, willing to work and to sacrifice and to die for Earth alongside their human friends.

"And finally, together, humans, Ardinians, and Mermots have built a space force from the ground up in only three years. We may be small in numbers, but we are mighty. We are above all else… survivors." Mike raised his voice. "The Huntas cannot defeat us!

"We Endure!" Mike pounded the table. He took a deep breath and stared from one to another of Earth's protectors.

The assembled scientists and fleet members shouted in response, "We Endure!" Shakete stood first and then Jed, and then the others jumped to their feet. Humans clapped and cheered, Ardinians hooted, Mermots sang, and Jack barked, each in their own way. Mike was revitalized by his speech and the passion of those with him, but his exuberance had a short shelf life. An emergency transmission from Gameboy was transferred to the conference room and played over the intercom to a stunned audience.

The Huntas had finally arrived.

Mike gave orders to his commanders. "You know what to do. Collect patrolling wasps and make haste to assume pre-planned battle positions to protect Earth. Notify the operations center when you're in position." Turning to his Executive Officer, Mike said. "Send the order to all enclaves to move to DEFCON 1 and inform them the Huntas have entered the solar system. Also, locate my wife, Karen, and ensure she gets to someplace safe. Recommend the underground base in Idaho. Please pose your request as a plea from me. She doesn't respond well to orders."

Jed said, "I'm going to head back to Earth, Mike. I'll let someone know when I arrive."

In unison, Shakete and Mike shouted, "No!"

Shakete placed a slender hand on Jed's shoulder, "You and your team should come with me to the Delamie where you'll be safe. We have more than adequate scientific facilities for you to continue your work."

"But my wife and my children! What of them? Mike? What of Sara?"

"Jed," Mike said in a kind but steady voice. "You know I love Sara too, but solving the decisive weapon problem is the best thing you can do for her now. When my XO contacts Karen, I'll have her gather Sara and take her with her to the Idaho facility."

"And my children?"

"She'll do her best, Jed. You know that."

"It's like the change again. You can see it and feel the fear, yet somehow, it's not real at all."

Mike nodded at Jed and gave him a pat on the shoulder. "Don't lose faith, Jed. I meant what I said. We'll survive, and we're counting on you to help make sure that happens." He turned toward Shakete and continued with a firm voice. "Did you know, Shakete? Were you aware the Huntas' possessed cloaking technology and forget to mention it?"

Mike and the Ardinian locked eyes. Shakete's coloring changed to gold, a sure tell of Ardinian high emotion. "Mike, your question is unfair. Our fates are sealed as one. Why in the name of the galaxy would I withhold critical information such as that?"

The sincerity and hurt in the Ardinian's face appeared genuine. Unless Shakete was an even better actor than Mike assumed, he was being honest. Mike sighed and loosened his shoulders. "You wouldn't, and I apologize. I guess I was hoping this was another case where you'd spring a golden nugget of information on us at exactly the right time or maybe you had a trick up your sleeve."

"If only that were true, Mike. I have no magical hares or golden nuggets to present. But perhaps I deserve your inquiry. I have been reminded by your wife, more than once, not to treat others as if I were a God and they merely pawns in a grand game. Your apology is accepted. Now, we must depart immediately. I have full confidence in you Admiral, even if you sometimes doubt my transparency."

Mike watched Jed stumble off between Maleta and Shakete. Only Jack remained by his side.

"Jack, we need to get to the operations center."

"Time is out?"

Mike's eyebrows raised in amazement at Jack's statement. The dog had heard and understood the discussion. Jack was always the smartest dog Mike had ever owned, and he'd grieved long and hard after Jack passed from a natural death at thirty-two years old. Maybe Shakete had juiced his dog brain a bit. Maybe he was just a smart dog. Either way, it helped to have Jack near again.

"Yep, time is out. As one long dead, pre-change Secretary of Defense once said, 'You go to war with the army you have, not the one you wish to have at a later time.' I'll find someone who'll feed you once we get to where I must be."

Chapter 4
Karen

Karen and her entourage strolled through the corridors of the Nagoya Enclave ministry offices. Nagoya, one of the most populated enclaves on Earth, was considered by default the capital of Japan, which was why Karen was here.

She admired the serene interior of a building that seduced visitors into a state of calm. A manmade brook began its journey as a natural stream that entered the building from the second floor, spilled to the first floor over a rock feature, and burbled into a pond that was the centerpiece of a central gathering space in the main lobby. Yellow and orange Koi mesmerized guests as they swam in hypnotic circles. Karen couldn't identify the source of the soothing, mood enhancing music playing in the background, but the notes fit perfectly with a jasmine fragrance piped in from somewhere. Combined with subdued natural lighting, this room had the effect of making her wish she could lie down and take a nap.

The contrast to her own seat of government couldn't have been starker. Where the Japanese had paid attention to nuance, New Washington was all function, wild west, bustling activity. If the time came when New Washington wasn't threatened by extinction from hostile aliens, other enclaves, or internal strife, Karen thought she might vigorously lobby to erect a new government building with an indoor water feature just like this one.

Shakete, the Ardinian leader, had decided Karen was the right fit to perform the role as Ambassador to the Stars. She was the human representative and ambassador for alien species. *No shit*, she thought, *I'm an ambassador to the stars*. Her title was Shakete's joking brainchild, and as with all things Shakete touched, the title was catching on. Shakete was perhaps one of the oldest beings in the galaxy, and Karen supposed he'd needed something to entertain himself over the eons as the Ardinians travelled through space looking for a home. Those eons allowed plenty of time to see the humor in just about everything.

If only he weren't such a devious son of a bitch. Shakete had a way of moving the chess pieces on the board to get whatever he wanted. He'd managed to convince Karen's husband, Mike, to lead the Space Fleet to repel his long-lost cousins, the Hunta. Not that Mike wasn't the right man for the job, just as she was a damn fine alien ambassador, but the job meant long stretches of separation. She missed her husband, her family, her dogs, and her home. Most of all, she missed Mike. Some nights she'd taken to crying again, something she hadn't done in over a hundred years, not since the change.

"Is that you, Karen?"

She turned, snapped out of her thoughts by a familiar voice. "Shiguru?" A distinguished, black-haired man bowed to her.

"It is me. At long last, we meet."

Karen grabbed his hands in hers and pressed them to her cheek. "I had no idea you'd be meeting the delegation today. This is such a wonderful surprise." Shiguru had been the first human voice Karen had heard after the change. When she'd finally found a working HAM radio, three months after her family and the rest of humanity went to the great beyond, it was Shiguru who'd answered her call from his location in Japan. He'd been a friend to her in her most desperate hour: a warm, personable, and compassionate man that she could turn to in her isolation.

"I am, like you, an ambassador," he said. "For trade though, not the aliens."

Karen chuckled. "How far we've come. I know you were a famous architect before everything went to hell. Did you design this building?'

Shiguru's eyes brightened at the question. "Do you like it?"

"Love it. I'm hoping you'll share the plans so that one day my home can have a place so

47

beautiful and tranquil. Are you ready to meet your Mermot representatives?"

"I am."

"Before we enter the room where they're waiting, I must warn you that their appearance can be, well, a bit off-putting. I assure you, any immediate reactions you have to their physical form is short lived. Mermots are cooperative, industrious, polite, engaging, intelligent, and creative. If they weren't so damn nice, my job would be far more difficult. Today I've brought with me a Mermot couple named Boris and Natasha."

Confusion clouded Shiguru's face. "Weren't they spies in one of your old American cartoons?" Shiguru asked. "Bullwinkle, if I remember correctly."

Karen sighed. "I know. We tried to convince them to change their names. Geronimo, my son the renowned historian, gave the Mermots his archives of old cartoons. They've taken to naming their litters in honor of what they call earth's most impressive collection of video art. Unfortunately, it's a great dishonor to change a Mermot name once it's been granted at birth. I just delivered Lucy and Charlie Brown to the Quebec Enclave. We've begun a program to review Mermot name choices before they're bequeathed to Mermot babies so that we can explain their deeper meanings. I was hoping because of our longstanding friendship with the

Japanese people, you might overlook a naming indiscretion." Karen gave Shiguru her most endearing smile.

Laugh lines appeared at the corners of Shiguru's eyes. "You're just as I always pictured you, Karen. No different today than the charming woman on the radio I met so long ago."

"Aw, shucks, Shiggi. You embarrass me."

"That, I doubt. I'm ready. I'm told the Mermots are in the cherry blossom conference room. Please, follow me."

Karen followed Shiguru as a contingent of New Washington and Japanese diplomats filed through the building to a room near the entry. "One last thing, Shiguru: Boris and Natasha will not reproduce unless you are comfortable with their presence. Once you find them pleasing, they can establish a community in Japan to be your partners in the effort to shore up our defenses against the Huntas."

As the door swung open, the two Mermots stood and bowed deeply to the Japanese. Boris was singing a Mermot melody, and Natasha was simultaneously talking into their minds in the appropriate languages. Karen could see Shiguru's immediate revulsion, but he quickly recovered a stoic countenance.

Boris wore a black suit, and Natasha was clad in a red dress with white piping along the edges and tiny white bows as buttons. Her little

49

patent leather black shoes were barely hanging on to narrow, long-toed feet. The Mermots preferred to go au natural, but the danger of being mistaken for a giant rodent or misshapen racoon was too great. New Washington allowed Mermots some independence when naming their children but refused to take responsibility for fatal mistakes in species identification. The clothing labeled them as intelligent beings.

Karen smiled thinking about how Mermots had taken to fashion with the same joyful abandon that they'd approached every other task. Because she loved and respected them, their long, pointed noses, beady black eyes, slick gray fur, and claw-like hands now seemed endearing. Even an extended hairless tail, trailing a Mermot moving at maximum speed, engendered confidence.

"Mr. Shiguru Hotoke," Natasha said in perfect Japanese. "We are honored to make your acquaintance. My partner and I look forward to a long and productive association and friendship with your people. We are of the Clan Reppel. Boris is singing a song of our world that tells the tale of a fortuitous meeting of my people and the Ardinians. I would like to add that our study of your land and history has been extensive. We were so impressed with your culture, we asked specifically for this assignment. We hope that when the time is right, you will share with us the stories of your great past and your wisdom."

Shiguru bowed to the rat creatures and said, "Your Japanese is impeccable. We also look forward to this partnership. Now, if you will take a seat, we can begin."

Karen thought the initial meeting was going well. The Mermots were unfailingly polite and charming guests, and the Japanese were gracious hosts. A match made in heaven. She fought the heaviness of her eyelids as the discussion turned to a line-by-line review of the draft charter she'd brought with her.

A knock on the door. A young man entered the room after Shiguru indicated he could enter. "I have an urgent message for the diplomat Karen."

All thoughts of drowsiness abandoned Karen in a heartbeat. She stood as the young assistant handed her a written note. Every eye in the room watched her as she read the missive.

Karen swallowed, and all color drained from her face. "It appears the Huntas have arrived in our solar system. I must leave immediately for home. We may be too late for Boris and Natasha to be useful here. You may both come with me. Shiguru, I'm sure you'll need to prepare the defense of your enclave. Fleet command will apprise you of ongoing developments."

Boris replied, "We wish to remain here to assist where we can."

"Are you sure?" Karen's expression pleaded. She knew the Japanese weren't ready to defend themselves, as did Boris and Natasha. In addition to all their other amazing qualities, the Mermots were altruistic to a fault. As she studied their sweet, sincere rat faces, Karen wished with all her heart for them to be selfish.

Barely able to keep tears from forming, she hugged Natasha and then Boris. Shiguru's solemn face revealed an awareness of what the Japanese people were up against. She hugged him too and whispered into his ear. "Stay safe, my friend. We've been through so much already, but we can survive this, too."

Karen and her two escorts fled through the exit and headed toward their airship, already powered up and ready to depart. The pilot was standing just outside the airship hatch, pointing to the sky.

Karen hesitated and looked up into cloud cover where the pilot was directing her attention. An unnatural hole in the gray clouds had formed. Something immense and transparent was moving lazily through a thunderhead. Her heart in her throat, she picked up her pace and sprinted to the airship.

An earsplitting boom shook the landscape, and a concussive wave slammed her to the ground. She raised her head, checked to make sure all her body parts were still attached, and pressed her ears to regain her hearing. Other than the insufferable ringing, everything was silent. She could see the pilot running to her, his mouth moving in a noiseless scream.

Scrambling to her hands and knees, she peeked once more to the sky. The shimmering hole was gone. In its place was a dark, forbidding spaceship. The massive ship was all angles and ridges with appendages poking from its surface. Cloud cover had parted to make way for a ship that cast a shadow over the Japanese capital. An ozone-like smell filled Karen's nostrils. She could see flashes of energy surrounding the spacecraft.

Then strong arms pulled Karen the final distance to their transportation home. She was thrown into a seat and could barely make out one of her escorts yelling, "Go, go, go!"

The whir of thorium powered engines pushed the airship off the ground. Karen was thrown back in her seat as the pilot stayed at low altitude, heading east toward the Pacific Ocean, pushing the almost outdated ship past speeds Karen had ever known it to go.

In a scrambled haze, she watched from her window as the Nagoya Enclave began to recede in the distance. Ground based lasers and wasp fighters assaulted the spaceship hovering over the population center. A shield extending from the warship absorbed every impact. The blowback from explosives hitting the shield masked the formidable ship from Karen's view.

Red light winked on behind the unyielding shield. The color darkened from stoplight red to a deep burgundy; the sky and the clouds around the ship appeared ready to rain blood. Molten lava bolts sprang from the spaceship to the ground in a circular pattern.

Her auditory loss was diminishing because Karen could hear the terrible explosions. She wished she was deaf and blind to this horror. So many good people. Sweet Boris and Natasha. Her friend, Shiguru. Stomach seizing, Karen puked onto the floor. She wiped her mouth and then began to weep silently at her powerlessness to stop the destruction.

The copilot was still yelling. "Can't you go any faster?"

The pilot answered. "It's full out! Oh, my God, what are they doing?"

"Some sort of patterned explosions. If I had to guess, I'd say they're using photon or laser blasts rather than nuclear weapons. The aliens are saving the planet but ridding the world of people. When those blasts hit critical mass, you won't notice the difference between a conventionally generated wave and a nuclear one. We've got to move!"

"I'm doing my best, dammit!" the pilot shouted, and then he announced, "We're over the Pacific."

The copilot said, "It's coming. Everyone, hold on, it's coming! Keep her steady!"

Jerking from right to left, up and down, the pilot struggled to keep the airship aloft. Karen's seat belt pulled tight and kept her from being thrown around like a rag doll. Something cracked loudly from the back of the ship.

Finally, the tumultuous wave subsided. What felt like minutes was only seconds, but the damage done to the airship would last far longer. The copilot announced, "I have a warning light on the thorium generator. I'll go check."

"You think I should set down?" the pilot asked.

The copilot answered, "Not even. We need to get as far away from that Hunta ship as we can. The manuals say this thing can float if necessary."

"Indeed," Karen said. "They were designed to be water capable. I thought it was unnecessary overengineering on the part of Jed and Mike, but they eventually won me over. What communications are you getting?"

"I'm sorry, Karen. Not a thing."

"Fuck!" she screamed and then reined in further emotional outbursts. "I agree with the copilot. Fly as far as you can toward New Washington. If the copilot can't fix the problem, we'll have to worry about a water rescue later."

During their flight, Karen had ample opportunity to consider where everything had gone wrong and drive herself to the brink of a mental exhaustion with worry over the fate of the world and her loved ones. How could the Huntas have attacked with so little warning? Was the frenetic planning and building for nothing? What was the fate of the Space Fleet and, most importantly, Mike?

She was certain of only one thing: she'd be damned if she would relive the last woman alive drama like after the Great Dying. God wouldn't do that to anyone, would he? Not twice. No way. Finally, *Please God, I can't lose everyone, not again. Take me too if they're all gone. Better yet, take me instead!"*

The airship rapidly lost altitude after limping along for over twelve hundred miles between Japan and the coast of New Washington. The battle to remain flying had reached its end. The pilot, resigned to keeping them alive, calmly announced: "This is it. We'll hit hard, but I'll do what I can to move along the horizon to reduce speed before we splash down. Be ready."

She lurched sharply forward into her seatbelt as the airship hit the Pacific Ocean.

Chapter 5
Amelia

Amelia felt sick. Since Trent had left her bed for his hunting adventure, a burbling, churning stomach and a muddled head had made it impossible to accomplish anything. Amelia believed her stomach problems were probably due to fear. Fuzzy, peripheral sight and an overwhelming urge to sleep were the first signs that a vision was building. She knew the next time she allowed herself to rest, nightmares of death and destruction would burst into her slumber in a freakshow of horrible events. Visions of pain and suffering made her physically sick.

Since she'd beat back her agoraphobia and Trent had become her life partner, there'd been no visions. She may have had some extraordinary insights once or twice, but nothing that couldn't be explained away as simple intuition or logical processes that occur at an unconscious level. Her mother's theory, since Karen hadn't had a vision since the change, was that the sight occurred when it was most needed. For Amelia's part, she wanted to believe her mom was right and prayed there would never be a need to see the future again.

She couldn't escape the deadly accuracy of her visions nor ignore the call to action her dreams implored. The latter was more frightening than the visions themselves. If she was unsuccessful at changing the course of events, then it meant she was a failure and this "gift," as her mother called it, was merely a soul-breaking burden.

Amelia finished placing dried dishes away and untied her apron. Her dogs could sense her unrest. If Lionheart were here, he'd talk to her and try to soothe her. Kismet, an energetic, three-legged Schipperke mix, they'd found at their back door crying for help after a Ranger attack that nearly killed her, was chattering away underfoot. "Let's take nap. Naps are good. Nap in big bed. Kismet take nap too."

Smiling at the pugnacious pup, Amelia whispered, "You never nap, Kismet. That's just an excuse to drag your toys to the bed so I'll play with you." Homer, a nice name for sweet, homely, hundred-pound beast and Kismet's best buddy, agreed with the nap recommendation and charged from the kitchen to the bedroom door. Amelia's stomach lurched at the thought of sleeping. The very last thing she wanted to do was sleep. Suddenly, a nauseating whirling in her vision set the world spinning in a bout of vertigo. She grabbed for a chair to keep from crashing to the floor and slid her body around to sit

Kismet barked in sympathetic concern, and Homer returned to the kitchen to provide moral support to Kismet. Her other two other dogs,

Arthur and Lancelot, approached to look for clues as to Amelia's distress. She patted Arthur's head, now firmly planted in her lap. "I'll be fine. Just give me a minute to collect myself."

Scooting forward in the chair, Amelia allowed her head to land on her shoulder and gave up the battle with heavy eyelids. *I'll just let my eyes rest for a moment. . .*

*   *   *

Her eyes burned from the sting of smoke. A yellow haze filled the scene before her as if a colored lens filtered all light. A smell like meat cooking over a wood burning stove permeated the air. Amelia turned in a circle, searching for the source of the smoke. A tall fir tree was on fire. Flames shot to the sky like a gigantic torch and its massive branches crackled in shades of bright yellow light. *That one tree couldn't be the sole reason for all the smoke or the smell.*

Concerned with the bad air, she began to walk to town. In three quick steps, she was transported to the final bend in the road before the town center. No one was outside. The town appeared empty. Even in the middle of the night, normally there was someone roaming New Washington streets on their way home from an evening of revelry. The only sound she heard was the crackling roar of flames.

Amelia could barely breathe. She needed to see what was beyond that bend, but she didn't want to go. Lodged in place, her terror grew until she fell to her knees, every part of her shaking uncontrollably.

A disembodied voice that sounded like her own shouted: "Get up, Amelia! You must see. For all those you love, you must see!"

Amelia wiped tears, gritted her teeth, and, with one wobbly leg and then the other, she stood again. Panting like she'd just finished a marathon, Amelia moved tentatively onward toward the future to which she must bear witness.

A sliver of Founders Park came into view from around Parker's Mercantile Store. Two huge men, their backs to her, were tending to a bonfire. They seemed to be having trouble keeping the large pile ablaze. One of them was pouring an accelerant at the edge of the mound and then jumping back to avoid being trapped in the fire himself. Amelia crept forward.

Straining to see the men and what they were cooking, Amelia heard a cacophony of screaming voices: "Help us. Please save us."

She took two more steps to get a better look. Her stomach was on the verge of an insurrection, begging for release. The contents of the bonfire came into view. She saw a paw, a tail, and then a floppy ear. A collar with tags. Amelia's scream started in her gut and poured from her mouth with an inhuman force. One of the men turned at her scream, his disgusting face a picture of pure malice. *That's a Hunta! They're here!*

*   *   *

Amelia woke as she fell off her chair and crashed to the floor. She felt like she'd brought back smoke from her nightmarish slumber as she coughed a huge wad of phlegm into her hand. Her breathing rapid and shallow, Amelia was hyperventilating and pointed to the four terrified dogs. "Help," she squeaked, in a voice so weak that it was barely audible.

Little Kismet had the wherewithal to retrieve a paper bag from the stack on the table near the door. She pulled the whole pile of bags to the floor in a herculean effort to obtain just one. As Kismet dropped the precious lifesaving device on Amelia's face, she mimicked Lionheart's calming words. "Slowly, slowly, breathe in out. In out. Kismet love you. In out."

As soon as she could breathe again, Amelia pushed the dogs away and shot to her feet in righteous indignation. Anger had claimed her somewhere between the panic of knowing a vision was on the horizon, her fear of what a dream might hold, and her observation of the Hunta atrocity.

Turning to her four furry friends, Amelia began. "You must leave the enclave. Run as far as you can into the woods and hide. Tell every dog you see to run too. Yell to all the other dogs to follow. Tell the people the Huntas are on the way, and their dogs will be safe in the woods!"

The gaggle of canines sitting before Amelia looked up at her with blank expressions.

"This is a command. You must obey me. Run far into the woods and hide. Tell the other dogs they must run too. You will be hurt if you do not obey. Do you understand?"

Lancelot was the calmest of the group and responded first. "Run to the woods and hide or get hurt. Say to other dogs." Despite giving the correct answer, the four dogs continued to sit as if the direction from their master was so unusual, they needed time to process the information.

Amelia opened the back door. "Go, now!" She said with a sweeping hand gesture. "There's no time to waste."

Fifteen paws bounded from the room. Kismet's three legs stopped at the threshold of the doorway. She turned and gazed at Amelia, her pointed black ears and dark eyes trying to convey some emotion that her dog vocabulary couldn't express.

"You, too. Go. I love you. Take care of your brothers."

The tiny, thick-coated dog snuffled, and using a slightly inward listing gait to compensate for a missing back leg, she ran from the house to catch up with the others. Amelia was always amazed that Kismet hadn't lost much speed as the result of her disability. If anything, the little dog's gigantic heart meant she tried harder to keep up.

Amelia grabbed the mobile phone to call her daughter, Chrystel. As the Chief of the Forces, she'd be in the best position to spread the word.

Neither the satellite nor the vector phone had a signal. Even though anger had replaced most of her fear, panic began to nibble again at Amelia's insides. "No! Keep it together," she yelled at herself. The landline might still work, and there's one at the Forces Headquarters. Amelia picked up the antique receiver and dialed.

"Please let someone answer," she moaned into the phone and shifted from one foot to the other. After the fifteenth or thirtieth ring, Amelia wasn't sure, someone finally answered. Amelia could hear a tremendous racket in the background. Urgent shouting and the clanging of equipment indicated something was terribly wrong.

"Hello?"

"This is Amelia. I need to speak with my daughter, Chrystel, right now!"

"Uh, ma'am, she's pretty busy. Can I take your number?"

"No!" Amelia shouted. "This is a matter of life and death. I must speak with her now."

"We kinda have a life and death situation here too."

"I said right now. I'm the best seer in the enclave, and I know what'll happen. Put her on, or I swear I'll haunt you with visions for the remainder of your miserable life."

"Well geez, hold on."

Amelia knew she couldn't haunt anyone, but her little lie seemed to work.

"Mom," Chrystel said. "I need to call you back. For now, stay in your home. Get your weapons and ammo ready and wait for further instructions. I'll come get you as soon as I can."

"Chrystel, please, just this once, be quiet, sweetheart, and listen to your mother. I had a vision. The Huntas are here, and they'll kill and burn all the dogs. I don't know what they'll do to the people in New Washington, but I have a feeling they'll try to round us all up. Right now, send as many of the dogs as you can into the woods to hide."

"Are you sure, Mom?"

"As sure as I've ever been."

"Is there a way to fix it?"

"I can't be sure, but I don't think so. It's just a feeling, but I believe the dogs are doomed if we don't get them to safety right away. It was horrible what I saw, and I've seen some horrible things. I'm begging you, Chrystel, don't let this happen."

There was silence on the line. "Are you still there?"

"I'm here, Mom. Look I need to go. I'll do everything I can."

"Wait, before you hang up. Did Trent show up for work?"

Chrystel paused and stuttered. "Uh, no. I thought he was going to go hunting this morning."

"He was, but he should've been there by now. Lionheart is with him."

Another pause. "I'm sure he's fine. I'll let you know when he gets here. Please, just sit tight for now."

Amelia was asking another question as Chrystel hung up. Amelia was left with the impression her daughter knew something she wasn't sharing.

Chapter 6
Impossible Choices

The enclave's force headquarters was contained within a pre-Great Dying Washington State Emergency Management facility. It's location on the southern edge of the enclave near the old I-5 protected the enclave's southern border while an airfield protected them from the north. To the west was the natural barrier of the Puget Sound and to the east, a thirty-five mile electrical grid that was armed only in emergencies.

Chrystel had immediately called Thomas when she'd received the DEFCON 1 notice. He was just now helping to organize force personnel into squads that were being deployed to defend the perimeter of the enclave. From the corner of his eyes, he noticed Chrystel hanging the landline phone back onto its jack and then bending over with her face in her hands. "Okay, Sergeant Monty," Thomas said. "Finish your weapons and commo checks before sending your troops to Defensive Position 18B. You're the last squad, so call us as soon as you're in position so we can arm the protective grid. I mean it, Monty. As soon as you get to your position, notify us. I don't know how long we have."

Sergeant Monty nodded and hustled out of the tactical operations center. Thomas watched the sergeant close the door and turned to Chrystel. "Tell me, Chief."

"It's bad enough Space Fleet put us at DEFCON 1, but then Lionheart appears with news of Huntas and fire in the forest, whatever that means. On top of all that, my mom calls with news of a vision. She says the Huntas are going to take New Washington, round up all the people, and burn our dogs!"

"Not if I have anything to say about it!"

"She was certain, Thomas. My mom said we should tell the dogs to flee to the forest and hide. How on this green earth are we going to simultaneously defend the enclave from a ground attack by the Huntas, evacuate the dogs, and fight a forest fire? Any one of these missions requires our full attention and most of the resources we have available."

Thomas didn't want Chrystel to see how worried he was right now. He'd been a warrior for most of his 141 years of life, and he knew in his bones that what they'd built to defend themselves wasn't nearly enough. They didn't have enough people or Mermot augmentation securing the northeast perimeter. The plan they'd devised was to rely on air support from wasps at the airfield. Their ground defenses were intended for small human incursions, not an alien invasion. And now, they were completely cut off. Communications were out, and they couldn't raise anyone at the airfield. He'd tried calling Jed at the Science Center using a landline, but thus far, no one had answered.

"We can't arm the perimeter if a hoard of dogs goes running across an electrified grid," Thomas said. "That would kill them as surely as an alien bonfire. Your mom's visions are a warning, right? They aren't necessarily events set in stone."

"I don't know. She seemed so convinced it would happen no matter what. How can I make a choice like that? Should I think of our people first and abandon our dogs? They're family as much as the people of this enclave."

"We should probably let Mayor Ted weigh in on this decision."

"He's an idiot," Chrystel huffed. "By the time he forms a committee to decide, our talking dogs might be a distant memory, providing, of course, there's anyone left alive to remember. We need to decide now!"

"I was just testing you, Chrystel," Thomas chuckled. "You're always at your best when you're pissed."

Tilley, the purple dog/donkey/lion Ardinian amalgamation known as a Henka, watched Thomas and Chrystal as she followed every word of their conversation. Unlike most of the enclave's inhabitants, neither Thomas or Chrystel could hear dogs or Tilley. The Ardinians had explained that the nanites they'd placed in dogs and Tilley acted like Wi-Fi, using biological energy to transmit speech. To hear dogs, a language translation function must develop naturally in the brains of recipients, but in some people, the brain never made that leap.

Tilley's many toed paws pounded the floor in a Henka dance. A Mermot named Popeye, who doubled as a dog/henka translator and radar operator, knew how to pay attention when the floor shook because it meant Tilley had something to say. He'd been watching the radar for any signs of Huntas from an alcove on the other side of the room and turned his sleek, pointed face in the direction of the Henka. He prepared to relay Tilley's words to Chrystel.

Popeye's deep, croaky voice was the reason he'd been given his name. He pushed Tilley's translated speech into the minds of Chrystel and Thomas in a loud baritone. "Tilley can help. Tilley's speech travels farther. I will warn the dogs and make them flee. I go now."

Thomas could see anguish strike Chrystel like a bolt of lightning. Even if she didn't want to admit it, Thomas knew she loved the cartoonish-looking Henka. How anyone could get so close to a 200-pound alien animal with flexible donkey ears, a deep purple mane around her neck, and a wispy pink tail was a question he couldn't answer. He only knew Chrystel drew comfort from this friend and companion.

Tilley had been with Chrystel every day since she and Karen had travelled to the Ardinian ship to meet the aliens for the first time. Shakete had forced the Henka on Chrystel in the guise of a gift. As Karen always said, Shakete knew things he had no business knowing. Somehow, he'd guessed that Chrystel was lonely and needed a true friend. After that asshole Brodie betrayed Chrystel and the enclave and then escaped to parts unknown, Tilley's companionship had seemed to become even more important to Chrystel. Thomas was glad Chrystel had a friend, even if a feisty redhead and a purple alien were a very odd pairing.

"Tilley, I need you here." Chrystel said.

"Don't worry, my friend," Tilley said in Popeye's voice. "I will return if I can. I will save as many dogs as possible. You must save the people. Besides, if something happens to me, the Ardinians can make another Henka. Don't be afraid. I must go. Turn on your defense grid when you must."

Chrystel nodded and swallowed to keep tears away. The Henka wasted no time. She galloped out the door, shaking the floor with her departure. Lionheart, who'd been napping in the corner, woke as Tilley flew by. The Henka must have signaled to Lionheart because he jumped and followed her outside to help warn the enclave's canine population.

"Do you see anything, yet?" Chrystel asked Popeye. "Troop movements or aircraft?"

"Sorry, not a thing. It is very strange. Maybe Lionheart was mistaken when he said Huntas were in the forest."

"Something isn't right. I have a very bad feeling."

"Yeah, me too." Thomas added. "Someone is blocking communication and I don't think anyone on earth has that capability. All the systems went down right after we received the DEFCON 1 warning. It's a good thing I squirreled away those low tech-portable radios years ago, or we wouldn't have any commo at all. Speaking of which, I think I need to be out there to figure out what's happening. I feel like I'm sitting here with my thumb up my ass, worthless as tits on a boar. Any objections, Chrystel?"

"No. I could use your eyes in the field. How close are we to arming the grid?" she asked as Thomas turned to leave.

"We're still missing three more positions to go active."

"Okay. Call me immediately when they're all ready and update me on the status of Tilley's efforts to get the dogs out of the enclave. I'm going to call every landline I can find and tell them to send the dogs packing. Stay in contact, Thomas. Watch for a fire too, even though I don't know what we can do about that. Popeye and I will man the fort."

"You got it. No matter what, just keep your head screwed on tight. I'll come running if you need me. There are four armed Mermots just outside to guard the operations center."

Chrystel and Thomas exchanged a look that said they both knew that all hell was about to break loose, and there didn't seem to be much they could do to stop it. The DEFCON 1 notice, blocked communications, Lionheart's message, and then Amelia's vision meant something big was in the works, but what?

"My head is on tight, Thomas. You keep your head down!"

"Roger that," Thomas replied with a tight smile and a thumbs up. He then grabbed a laser rifle from the rack and ran out of the building.

* * *

Chrystel busied herself for the next several minutes making quick calls on the landline. It appeared the word was getting out about the need to send the dogs to the woods to hide. The grid still wasn't armed, and she hadn't heard anything back from Thomas. Chrystel's worry meter was pegging off the charts. "Do you see anything on the radar, Popeye? Any signs of the Huntas? Anything at all?"

"Nothing, Chrystel. It defies rational explanation that we can't see them if they're out there."

Suddenly, there was static followed by screaming from a walkie-talkie radio Thomas had left behind. "Holy hell," someone yelled. "They're here! The sons-a-bitches are invisible. We can't see them, and we're getting the shit kicked out of us!" More chaos blasted from the tiny speaker in the radio.

Chrystel grabbed a laser rifle and picked up a second weapon to hand to Popeye. "I guess that's the rational explanation we were missing. I doubt that even Space Fleet knew about Hunta cloaking technology; otherwise, they would have warned us. It may be too late to arm the system. If they're truly invisible, they could very well be inside the perimeter. If we turn on the grid, we'll be trapped with the fleeing dogs." *Please, Tilley, be safe*. She thought to herself.

"Grab the radio, Popeye. I don't want to be a sitting duck in this building. Let's do what we can to defend our home."

*   *   *

Thomas nudged a sleeping Ghost out of the driver's seat, the place where his dog normally waited for his return. He'd pulled Thomas' jacket to the floor and curled into a comfortable napping position on top of the garment. Begrudgingly, Ghost climbed into the passenger side. After placing the jacket back over the seat,

73

Thomas gazed into the old dog's face and thought his buddy's grey beard and silver back made him appear even more wise and endearing. He hated having to watch his canine friends grow old before his eyes. It wasn't that their infirmities made him care any less, but it bothered him that he would likely have to take part in sending them on their way to the great beyond. Thomas thought it strange that this process of birth and loss of canine companions hadn't gotten any easier. If anything, his advancing age made the loss of a best friend even harder.

"I've got some bad news, Ghost. I'm going to need you to run deep into the woods and hide. I know you aren't as spry as you once were, but there'll be other dogs in the forest to help. Look for Tilley. She'll take care of you. You should've gone with her when she passed by and told you to come along."

Ghost glanced at his master and released a small whine.

"I know, old friend. I'll come and get you as soon as I can. I've already told Katie and the rest of the family to hunker down and be ready to defend themselves. You don't have to worry about them. Katie and Rachael are as tough as they come."

The grey dog barked as if Thomas' instructions were unpalatable.

"Hey, don't talk back. I'm still the boss here. Look, I'm going to go out near the enclave border, and I'll drop you off there. You won't have so far to walk."

Ghost sniffed and looked away.

"Don't be pissed. The rest of the dogs will need your seasoned experience. You're a great hunter."

Thomas' and Ghost's heads swiveled to watch five dogs run across the road in front of the ATV heading east. "See," Thomas said. "There they go."

Thomas released the parking break and accelerated, even though maximum speed meant only about thirty-five miles an hour. Since many of the roads around the enclave were untended, speed had been sacrificed for maneuverability. The Mermots had been working on another version of an ATV which could go up to sixty, but so far, it remained a project in the works. "Ghost, bark if you smell smoke."

Ghost immediately barked.

"Christ, I was hoping Lionheart was confused."

Conversation ceased during the rest of the journey as Thomas listened to screaming and yelling coming from the radio. He tried to make sense of the situation on the ground. The part about the invaders being invisible was crazy enough it just might be true. He stopped in front of the closest guard post and jumped out. A light-haired young woman, who couldn't have been more than eighteen, joined him.

"Sir, it seems the action is at the mid-eastern quadrant."

"So I heard." Thomas answered. "Who's in charge here?"

"Uh, sir," the young woman stumbled, "I am. When our sergeant heard all the hub bub, he took off to see to his family. He's got young kids."

Thomas wondered how many others had lost faith and run home to protect their families as soon as the shit hit the fan. "Thanks for staying, miss—?

"Sheila Watertown, sir."

"Sheila, I'm not a 'sir' anymore. I need to drop my dog off here. Could you make sure he leaves and doesn't sneak back? I'm hearing the Hunta invaders are cloaked, so pay attention to where you see enemy fire coming from. Aim at flashes. Got that?"

Thomas thought Sheila might be even younger than eighteen. Her face lost color at the mention of the Huntas. "Yes, sir. We're ready. My two younger brothers are here too. I'll watch for your dog to make sure he doesn't come back."

We are so screwed. It took everything in his kit bag not to tell Sheila and her younger brothers to go home and then take their place himself. "Thank you, Sheila. You and your brothers are doing a fine job. Your bravery in protecting the enclave is commendable."

Shifting to the ATV, Thomas commanded, "Come, Ghost!"

The old dog emerged from the ATV and went to his master's side. Thomas couldn't look down. "Now go, Ghost." Keeping his eyes diverted, he patted the dog's head. "Now!" He watched as his friend limped away, his arthritic rear haunches slimmer than they should be; Thomas was relieved when Ghost didn't turn back to look at him.

"Remember what I said, Sheila. Watch for muzzle flashes and then aim your lasers at that spot. Got it?"

"We've got it, sir," Sheila said, sounding more confident. "You think they're hard to see?"

"That's what I'm hearing. Also, make sure you report on the radio if anything happens. You have a radio, right?"

"Yep. Jodie, my brother, has it. Our sergeant left it for us."

"How decent of your sergeant. He rubbed his eyes, sighed, then straightened his shoulders, and drew himself up to his full 6-foot, 5-inch height. "Miss Sheila Watertown, this is a battlefield promotion. You are now Sergeant Watertown." He patted the young woman's shoulder. "I am proud of you."

"Thank you, sir," the new sergeant beamed.

"I know you'll do your best. Be strong, Sergeant."

"I will, sir. Thank you."

Thomas turned to leave and ran to the ATV before he had time to reconsider. This is what they'd come to: kids manning the perimeter in the face of an alien invader. Since the Great Dying, they'd never had nearly enough people to do all that needed to get done. It didn't help that many of their best and brightest had left to serve in Space Fleet or were performing support roles at the airfield.

"Fuck," Thomas shouted as his tires kicked up gravel and he drove away from a guard post secured by teenagers. "We are so screwed!"

He thought about Ted, their new mayor, who had refused Chrystel's proposal to allow Mermots to do their hyper-breeding and take responsibility for the lion's share of New Washington's defense. After his "study," Ted had decided that enclave inhabitants would be the most motivated to protect their own property. No doubt, his real concern was that he'd have to allow Mermots to vote, and as a group, they clung to the founders as the true leaders of the enclave. Mayor Ted was also a fool, and he'd left them holding their dicks in their hands, vulnerable to any sizeable force that got the notion New Washington could be taken. If Thomas didn't loathe politicians with a veracity that approached obsession, he might run for office.

He laughed at the thought. He was a soldier, and the good lord knew a soldier saw the world in terms of protecting what was theirs and not losing their skin in the process. Politicians were more concerned with staying in power. If someone else had to fight battles and lose their scalp in the process, then so be it. Mayor Ted was the worst kind of politician; Chrystel the other. She'd stepped down as mayor to keep the enclave from coming apart at the seams. The rallying cry of no more founders as leaders had become too intense. Now, they had an idiot and fool in charge.

The scent of smoke drifted into Thomas' nostrils and released him from his mental tirade. At the same time, he heard the burst of laser guns and a whir of another weapon he couldn't name. Flickering light from beyond the next rise told of new age weaponry being deployed in a battle. He drove to the crest of a hill and surveyed the situation. From what he could tell, it wasn't going well for the good guys. Clavers had been overrun from fortified positions and were forming a defensive line on crumbling buildings close to the enclave. The enemy was nowhere in sight. The only sign of an opposing force were hot white flashes that killed clavers and set the world on fire.

Leaping from his ATV, Thomas barreled down an embankment to flank the invisible predators making mincemeat of guard post 12A. At the outside range of his laser, he took a knee and sighted on the closest enemy weapon flashes. He knew as soon as he fired they'd aim their weapons at him, but at least the diversion might allow retreating clavers time to regroup and rally a counter offensive. That was, of course, if there was anyone worth a shit or older than thirteen at this guard post.

He watched shimmering movement between the trees to get a sense of where a head and a chest might be located. "There," Thomas whispered.

His laser hit dead center of the target. The light surrounding his prey seemed to waver, and then the body underneath was revealed. Thomas immediately fired again at the bony growth that represented a Hunta head. "That works," he said as the Hunta's cranium exploded. Back on his feet, Thomas sprinted to his right toward another firing position.

Just as he thought, the remaining Huntas were now focused on him. A fiery blast hit the ground just inches from his feet. Thomas jerked left and then right and finally dove into a depression ten meters away as another bolt of energy sailed overhead.

Clavers were yelling, and, like music to his ears, Thomas heard lasers firing back at the Huntas. He peeked up to scout for his next target. One Hunta was directing fire at clavers, and another barrage of lava-like missiles was moving his way. He fired two laser bolts at the advancing Huntas, but missed when the energy halo darted right and then shot back at him. He ducked and could smell the ionized air of a Hunta blast whizzing over his head and igniting grass behind him.

There wasn't much advantage to remaining put. He was a sitting duck unless the claver's counterattack could reach him in time. Based on his last visual of the advancing claver troops, Thomas didn't think that possible. Only one option remained. Counting to five, a took a deep breath and charged from his meager cover, firing one shot after another at the approaching Huntas.

An energy mirage wavered, and then Thomas' fire disabled a cloak, and a Hunta exploded into a fiery ball. Thomas didn't stop. He pushed forward toward the last group of flashes, unloading his laser weapon full out as the advancing clavers did the same.

The final Hunta dropped with a loud click. *What the hell was that sound?* Thomas covered the remaining distance and stopped by the dead Hunta as four other claver guards joined him.

"Thomas!" one of the guards said. "Thank the gods you arrived in time!"

"Hey, George! Thank the lord it was you out here. I was concerned there wouldn't be anyone who would take advantage of my diversion. Shit, that thing is big and ugly."

George poked the alien with the muzzle of his laser to ensure it was dead. His face screwed into a look of disgust. "Yeah, and he stinks!"

"Did you hear that click?" Thomas asked. "Did it come from him or her? I'm not sure if they have different sexes."

"We've been hearing a speech like clicking, so I would assume so."

Thomas crouched and pulled a rectangular metal box from the chest of the Hunta's vest. "What do you think this is? Seems kinda stupid to carry something important on your chest in the line of fire."

"Maybe they thought those cloaks would protect them. Who knows?"

"Possibly," He pocketed the metal box and looked at George. "You need to come with me to the next guard post. They've been taking fire. From what I've heard on the radio, it seems the Hunta plan is a frontal assault across most of the eastern enclave rather than massing forces in any one spot. If we can beat them back, we might be able to hold the line. Not the smartest way to attack, but I'll take it. Leave the rest of your crew here to defend this area. Now that our folks know they can take them out, it'll help."

"Aren't we going to get any air support from the wasps?" George asked.

"I can't reach the airfield. Our normal commo is cut off. Let's move. My ATV is at the top of that ridge."

George gave the remaining clavers instructions and then ran to catch up with Thomas, who was already talking to Chrystel on the walkie-talkie. "They aren't trying to attack with mass," Thomas said. "Best we can do is shore up each of the guard posts. I'm headed to 22D. You take 23B. Also, ask Popeye to call any of his Mermot relatives in the area for help. Have him send as many as he can to each defensive position."

"Already done." Chrystel's voice boomed from the tiny speaker. "They should begin arriving in the next five minutes."

"Any word from the airfield?" Thomas asked.

"None." Chrystel answered. "I've got places to go and people to see. Keep in touch."

"Roger, I read you. You keep your head screwed on tight and down, you hear me?"

Thomas heard her laugh and then say, "Out."

He was almost to his ATV when one of the clavers who they'd left behind screamed. Immediately after, a deafening roar of clicking pounded his ears. Turning with his laser at the ready, Thomas searched for the source. George was doing the same, his eyes scanning the trees for shimmering blobs.

Hundreds of Huntas materialized out of nowhere, and they were all pointing their weapons at either him or George. Thomas kept turning and could see Huntas in front of and behind the guard post where he'd left clavers to protect that piece of ground. He finished his circle and whispered to George. "Guess they did employ mass. We just couldn't see them."

Most astoundingly, an incredibly beautiful woman was sitting in the driver's seat of Thomas' ATV. She smiled and waved at him flirtatiously. Her long dark hair cascaded over a clinging body suit which accentuated every curve. Bright green eyes and full, lush lips smiled at Thomas. If not for that the fact that her eyes were unnaturally spaced too widely over her nose, she would have been every man's dream of physical, feminine beauty. *Well at least*, Thomas thought, *mine*.

"Thomas," she said in perfect English. "Please put down your weapon. We do not intend to kill you. We have other plans for you and these pathetic humans you call clavers."

Thomas made no move to relieve himself of his weapon. His mouth was slightly agape as he tried to process what he was seeing.

"Let me back up. I can see I've caught you totally off guard. Before I continue, please know if you attempt to shoot me with that laser, then you're a dead man, as are your colleagues. Now what was I saying?" The dark-haired beauty paused for effect and began again.

"I am Cleo, the leader of a Hunta assault force. In very short order, your home will be taken, and I will become your new leader." The woman giggled. "We've been watching you. For a human, you're rather resourceful, aggressive, and resilient, all traits the Huntas admire. Unfortunately, because of your skills, you will be segregated from the rest of your tribe. I must warn you, we have no tolerance for disobedience. Should you try something, it won't go well for you or your friends. However, if you cooperate, your captivity will be as pleasant as possible. I look forward to our continuing association." She waved her hand dismissively. "Take him away."

Thomas wanted to scream: "No fucking way!" but he felt a tingling at his back, which spread across his body before he blacked out.

Chapter 7
The Caretaker

Full daylight filtered through trees, and the day was warming nicely. The fire raging three miles behind Trent was cranking up the temperature as well. Breathing hard and sweating, he was relieved to be within a mile of force headquarters. He'd run full-out for most of the distance but slowed to a jog when the first dogs appeared. A French bulldog, a curly-haired brown doodle thing, and an unrecognizable mixed breed were running full-out like him, but they crossed a clearing to his front heading in another direction. The panting mixed breed paused momentarily to shout into Trent's mind, "Dogs must flee to the forest or be hurt!" With that unusual soliloquy, the canine sped away to catch up with its friends.

"What on Earth?" he yelled after the dogs. He wondered if Lionheart had somehow confused the intended message. He couldn't imagine how *Huntas and fire in the forest* had become *flee to the forest or be hurt*. That made no sense. Lionheart might forget a message, but he certainly wouldn't make up something else.

He stopped in place to see what he was missing. There were more of them, dogs fleeing for parts unknown. Through the trees to his left, a pack of five dogs was rapidly covering ground, their bodies low and tails straight out. Three small dogs to his right, darted over the ruins of an old building, looking more confused but every bit as determined. They jigged one way and then another, but relentlessly headed east away from the enclave. A lone dog bearing down in his direction offered the chance for Trent to learn more.

"Stop!" Trent commanded and stood in the path of a hundred-pound canine, daring it to run him down. The dog skidded on dirt, it's head and tail rising as if rudely awakened from a dream.

"Huh?'" the dog said.

"Why are you running?" Trent asked.

"Davie be hurt."

"Okay, Davie. Where are you running?"

"To forest. Davie hide."

Feeling frustrated, Trent maintained a calm exterior so as not to incite an already panicked dog. "Who told you to run and hide?"

"Tilley talked. She said run and hide."

Knowing the next question might be difficult for Davie to understand, Trent thought about the easiest way to ask the question for which he needed an answer. "Do you know why, Davie? Why did Tilley tell you to run and hide?"

"Hunta will burn us."

Trent was totally confused. He scratched his beard and glanced around while trying to make sense of this new turn of events. Nothing added up to an answer.

"Davie, would you like to stay with me?"

The brindle hound replied with a tilt of its head and a tentative wave of his tail. "We hide?"

"If we must. We'll be pack."

At Trent's response, Davie's tail gave the signal for an all clear. His head shook as if discarding rain from his coat, and his tail beat frantically. The dog went to Trent and stood close. Trent stretched out his hand palm down to allow Davie to smell him, and then the dog leaned in for a scratch. "We'll figure this out together, Davie."

Trent thought one dog joining him might encourage others to stop and give him a chance to piece together this puzzle. Trent had been a dog owner for most of his life. Even before they could talk, he knew that canines instinctively depended on friendly humans to help them avoid danger. However, no matter how obedient they were, the dogs running from the enclave were fearful and confused.

Davie refused to follow Trent any closer to the enclave though, moaning whenever he wandered in that direction. Trent finally gave up his quest to reach the force headquarters. Veering east with the fleeing dogs, he walked with Davie. It didn't take long for more frightened canines to join them. For all their chattering, Trent was no closer to an answer. That was until Tilley and Lionheart, accompanied by hundreds of others, came pounding through the forest like a bizarre dog stampede.

Tilley saw him first, and Lionheart must have smelled him as well because they beat a path to Trent. Their hoard of dogs joined Trent's bunch in a swirling mass of dog greetings. He could see a fur cloud taking shape, hovering over the gaggle. "What the heck is happening?" he blurted out loud, and then smiled when he imagined a dog jamboree in heaven looking something like the scene before him. *Maybe I'm dead,* Trent said to himself. He quickly responded to his mental wanderings, a technique that he'd taught himself while living alone in the woods for many years. *Get a grip, you're not dead. It's just been a bad day. Pull yourself together, numbnuts.*

"What the heck is happening, Tilley?" Trent shouted over the whines and barks of the dog herd. He knew Tilley's intellectual reasoning and abstract thought was far greater than a normal dog, so he directed his question to her.

She motioned her head for him to follow. When they were alone, she said, "Amelia had a vision and said the Huntas would burn every dog they find in New Washington. She was so sure of the vision that Chrystel agreed to follow Amelia's advice and send them into hiding.

"Trent, we must hurry. There are more Huntas than you know. I can smell them, and so do my friends. We could very much use your help. Some of my dog friends have already been lost to the Huntas during their escape. The Huntas are closing in. We must hurry."

"But what about Amelia?" Trent asked. "What about the enclave? I owe those people my life. How can I leave?"

"I only know that we can't help the people." Tilley's purple Great Dane face mirrored the pain that was engulfing Trent. "Chrystel and Thomas will do that. I can only save these dogs. I respectfully request that you decide quickly. Otherwise, I must leave without you. We will be found if we don't go further into the forest."

Trent turned and considered the horde of dogs continuing to grow each minute with new arrivals. Every fiber of his being was pulling him in the direction of Amelia. He couldn't imagine life without her. After wandering alone for so long in the wilderness, she'd saved him. They'd saved each other. Living without her would be as meaningless as the life he was living before she'd given him a second chance. Nothing was worse than walking away and leaving her alone like his first family.

Remembering the device he'd plucked from the dead Hunta, he patted his jacket pocket. It was still there, waiting to be given to someone smart enough to know what to do with it. That little box could be everything or nothing at all.

If he wasn't so damn certain what Amelia would want him to do, he'd gladly fight Huntas until his last breath. Her face came to him, pleading with him do what he must and save these dogs. It was almost as if his wife's hand had reached out and placed him here, the most experienced man in the enclave at living off the land. The same man who could navigate by the stars, knew how to hide, shoot and hunt. *Damn it, woman.* He wanted to cry, but he hadn't shed a tear since he'd walked into his home to find his first wife and children dead. He doubted he ever could cry again no matter how great the loss.

"I know where we can go," he said. "But it's gonna be a bitch to feed all these hungry mouths."

Arthur and Lancelot had worked their way out of the crowd to say hello to their master. Trent frowned and said, "Where's Kismet?"

Chapter 8
Amelia's Voice

The house was quiet. Too quiet. The humming refrigerator and ticking antique wall clock didn't normally register in Amelia's conscious thought, but now the sounds were pounding in her ears and driving her anxiety to absurd heights. Without her dogs and dear husband, Amelia wasn't sure what would happen to her. She wasn't even sure if she cared about what happened to her if they failed to return. Every fifteen minutes for last couple of hours, the phone cradled against her ear and her heart in her throat, she'd waited through the interminable bleating of an unanswered call to her daughter. She wanted to believe that no news was good news.

After attempting to busy herself with a load of laundry and accidently dropping a bottle of bleach onto the floor and her shoes, she'd given up hope. Instead, Amelia loaded the rifle Trent had given her and sat in the kitchen chair facing the front door. She was too afraid to leave the house anyway, so the next best plan was to be prepared for whoever might knock at her door.

She'd considered boarding up the windows, but what would be the point? The Huntas she remembered so vividly from her vision wouldn't be stopped by two by fours.

Amelia's agoraphobia had been in remission ever since Trent had walked into her life. He was so proud of her and her progress. Everyone was. Her family and friends were so proud that she didn't dare tell them that each day was still a monumental struggle. That sometimes when she woke her entire body strummed with fear that today she wouldn't be able to leave her home. She also knew that if Trent and her family continued to believe she was cured, she'd keep on forcing herself to take that first step outside each day. It was a bargain she'd made with herself that thus far had worked out for everyone.

Now this: a horrible vision, a Hunta invasion, Trent's whereabouts unknown, no one to talk to, and her agoraphobia kicked into high gear. Amelia could feel her sanity slipping away with each tick of the old clock.

That same disembodied voice from her vision shouted to get her attention. "Listen, Amelia!"

Yep, Amelia said to herself. *That's it. I'm officially over the bend.* Amelia pinched her arm to be doubly sure she hadn't fallen asleep.

"You're not crazy, dumbass. Just listen!"

"Okay, voice. Language please. And you really don't have to be mean. I'm not exactly living my best life right now." Amelia suddenly remembered that old saying about how it was okay to talk to yourself, but it was a problem when you answered.

"Just listen, please," the voice implored.

She didn't have anything to lose, so Amelia took the advice of a voice from everywhere and nowhere and probably a product of her own insanity. She tuned out the incessant ticking and focused on any other noises. The voice was right—she heard scratching from somewhere in her house. Amelia stood, shouldered the rifle, and crept to the doorway of the master bedroom, making herself still. She waited and listened. When the sound didn't reappear, she tried the other bedroom, then the dining room, and finally, the kitchen.

Amelia stood in the center of her kitchen and held her breath. At this point, it was nearly as important to discover the source of the sound to prove to herself she hadn't become totally unmoored from reality.

A minute passed. Two minutes. *That's it. I'm insane*.

Then, the tiniest of whines came from the back door. Amelia ran to peer out of the door window and saw nothing. Slowly, she pushed the door outward, but something was in the way. She peeked her head through the opening. Black eyes looked up at Amelia, begging to be allowed back in.

"Kismet!" Amelia said. "You stubborn and foolish little dog."

"Amelia mad?" the little dog asked.

Amelia scooped up the small dog and hugged her to her chest. Tears fell from Amelia's eyes. "Yes, I'm mad, but I'm so happy to see you."

The dogged wiggled to be released, so Amelia set her down. Kismet began a three-legged jumping routine that didn't exactly lift her from the floor, but aptly demonstrated her happiness at being accepted back into the fold.

"Now what?" Amelia asked.

"Find someplace for her to hide, and quickly," the unanchored voice boomed from somewhere in the kitchen.

"Oh, for crap's sake. I thought that finding the scratching would send you packing. I won't argue this time. If I'm insane so be it—it seems to be working."

Amelia discovered that the petite dog was small enough to slide behind a dresser in the master bedroom. She raised a window and placed a footstool and some pillows underneath so that Kismet couldn't be trapped. A hiding and exit strategy secured, Amelia then fed the dog a huge meal of leftover lasagna. Kismet was licking the empty bowl when the inevitable pounded on the front door. The small dog said, "They smell."

"Hide Kismet, now!" Amelia commanded, even as her legs began to tremble in fear. "This time you must obey."

Kismet bolted to her hiding spot, and Amelia debated her next move. If the Huntas were at her front door, was there any reason to anger them by staying put and forcing them to break it down? Or should she just go out in a blaze of glory? If she knew the fate of her loved ones the answer would be clear.

"Go with them peacefully," the Amelia voice commanded. "It will be important."

So far, the voice's recommendations, no matter how annoying, had been correct. Amelia shouted, "Just a minute. I'll be right there." She collected her raincoat and put on her boots. She knew donning wet weather gear was a silly gesture, but somehow, weather preparedness felt like a good idea during a forcible kidnapping from your home. On legs like wooden stilts and barely able to breathe, she hesitantly moved to the front door and opened it.

The two monsters on her doorstep appeared more imposing than in her dream. And just as Kismet had mentioned, a terrible odor wafted from their mottled skin and rock-hard bodies. The eyes staring at her were the most disturbing, although the strange weapons pointed at her face were a very close second. Her feet reacted involuntarily in her own defense, turning in a fruitless effort to run and hide. The hideous beings were too quick. The aliens grabbed an arm each and dragged her away, while screams poured from her mouth.

Chapter 9
Chrystel

Chrystel opened her eyes. Smokey haze veiled the sun to the west. She twisted away from a rock poking into her shoulder and yelped as a sharp pain in her side jolted her fully awake. The day came flooding back.

Wedging her elbows underneath, she clenched her bottom lip with her top teeth, as another hot poker prodded the portion of her chest under her arm. She dropped back to the dirt and then felt along her left side. Her hand didn't come away bloody. *I must have broken a rib or two when I hit that tree stump and went flying.*

"Hey, she's waking up," a male voice said.

Almost instantly, two sets of eyes blocked the sun. "Are you going to help me up or what?" Chrystel demanded.

She screeched when the first man grabbed her arm. The second man steadied her, and she descended into a painful coughing fit.

"You okay, Mayor Chrystel," one of the men asked.

"Do I look okay? Where am I?" Before he had time to answer, Chrystel had already turned in a 360-degree circle. Hundreds of milling and restless clavers were crowded together in the middle of Founder's Park. She wondered how she hadn't heard the racket when she'd first awoken because the unmistakable pandemonium of wailing and praying townspeople surrounded her. The sight of armed Huntas encircling the park made her knees wobbly, and she almost lost her balance.

"So, we're prisoners now," she mumbled to herself. She looked to the disheveled man who'd helped her to her feet. "Did you happen to see a Mermot named Popeye around? He was trying to escape the Hunta bastards when I fell."

"My name's Glen by the way," he said and then shook his head. "I haven't seen any Mermots or dogs. The rumor is the Hunta assholes killed any they could find. I didn't see it myself, so it's just a rumor. Mermots and dogs are fast, though. I hope most of them got away."

"Have you seen Mayor Ted or Thomas?"

"Nope, haven't seen Mayor Ted. I saw Thomas being dragged by his feet all bound up. I think they took him to the jail." He shrugged. "I've never felt so helpless. I used to be on the force when Thomas was in charge. This may be the suckiest thing that's ever happened in New Washington, among a shitload of sucky things."

Glen had a point, but nothing guaranteed failure like giving in to fear. Even if it meant lying, Chrystel knew it would help for them to hold on to hope. "Don't give up, Glen. I know our people will come for us. Just hang in there as best you can." She patted him on the shoulder. "By the way, do you happen to have any pain pills?" Glen pointed to a woman tending to several wounded. "No, but she does."

"Thanks for the assist, Glen." Chrystel recognized her adopted Aunt Katie, who was also the town's vet, caring for an injured child. Chrystel hobbled over to the crouching veterinarian. Katie was forty-five years younger than her grandmother, Karen, and was also one of New Washington's founding members. She was sixteen when the change came. Her hair, as well as her identical twin Rachael's, had turned a snowy white over the last ten years. She generally wore it pulled back in a bun, but strands had dislodged themselves and were hanging in her eyes. Chrystel put up her hand before Katie could stand to greet her. "Please don't hug me," Chrystel said. "I think I broke a couple of ribs."

Katie stood and studied Chrystel and then signaled to a young woman. "Mille, take over for me here please. I think the girl is fine, just scared because she doesn't know where her parents are. When you get her calmed down, help Bob with the more serious cases. And hand me a couple of those pain pills." After her aide had placed a bottle of pills in Katie's hands, she moved away from the injured girl, and Chrystel followed.

"So, what happened?" Katie asked.

"If you mean in general? I'm still trying to make sense of it."

Katie shook out a couple of pills and handed them to Chrystel. "Yeah, in general or specifically. What do you know?"

Chrystel swallowed the pills dry and then began. "I got a call from Space Fleet this morning, warning that the Huntas had been spotted in the solar system and to move to DEFCON 1. That's when I called Thomas, but you probably know about that."

Katie nodded.

"As we were trying to coordinate our enclave defense, my mom's dog Lionheart came bursting into force headquarters, shouting, 'Huntas and fire in the forest,' over and over. Thomas and I weren't sure what to make of Lionheart's warning, but when communications went down, we knew we had a serious problem. My mom called me on the landline to further warn that the Huntas would burn our dogs. We sent Tilley to get as many out of the enclave as possible."

"That explains it. None of us could understand why the dogs took off and left."

"Yeah. Thomas left the station to scope out the situation on the ground, and all hell broke loose after that. He called me once. I left the station with a squad of Mermots to see what I could do to shore up our defense, but the

Huntas were everywhere. By the way, a kid over there said that he saw Thomas. Some Huntas dragged him to the jail."

Katie's tense shoulders dropped. "Oh, thank you! I've been terrified something had happened to him."

"What about you, Katie? How did everyone end up in the town square?"

"Rachael and I and most of our family were ready to defend ourselves. The Huntas must have gone from house to house, dragging people here. When they realized two guards weren't enough to take us in, they left and returned in greater numbers. They set my house on fire with their beam weapons. There were just too many of them." Katie paused. "Two of my grandchildren were killed."

"I am so sorry, Aunt Katie. I'm sorry I failed you."

"Chrystel, sometimes you overplay your own importance. The Huntas obviously had a plan and executed it perfectly. Now, quit blaming yourself and do what you do. Start rallying the troops because our survival may depend on our ability to quit squabbling with each other and to start fighting together instead."

Chrystel smiled. "Sometimes you sound just like my grandma."

"I'll take that as a compliment. Now get. I've got work to do."

"Hey, wait, have you seen my mom?"

"I did, Chrystel, but she didn't look well. She was huddled behind the founder's statue, wearing boots and a raincoat, talking to herself. When I approached her, she shooed me away." Katie looked up at darkening clouds. "Maybe the boots and coat were your mother's amazing prescience. Looks like it's going to rain. And here we all are, outside without any cover."

"I'll start by getting a count of how many are here and the names."

"Good idea." Katie doled out ten more pills and enclosed Chrystel's face between her hands. "Believe it or not, I've been through worse. Be thankful most of us are still alive. You're strong; we're strong."

"Thanks, Aunt Katie."

When the pills started to kick in, Chrystel asked a young woman sitting on one of the park's benches to scoot over so she could make an announcement. From that spot, she yelled her first commands. "We need to know who is here. If anyone has anything to write on or write with, please bring it to me." I need each of you to stop and give me your information."

Many turned to listen. One woman carried a used paper towel she'd found in the trash and brought it to Chrystel. Another man found a pen in his pocket and handed it over. Soon, a line began to form.

A Hunta guard noticed the line and clicked and hissed to its partner. Two massive brutes crashed through the crowd, pushing people along the way and stepping on a wounded man in their path. They arrived at Chrystel and in their raspy way, clicked furiously at her.

Chrystel was eye to eye with the Hunta guards from her perch on the bench. She wanted to claw out the throbbing veins in their eyeballs, but she held her position and met their gaze. "I can't understand what you're saying. I'm only trying to get a count of the people in this park."

Faster than she could react, one of the Hunta's huge hands backhanded the side of her head. She summersaulted over the back of the bench. For the second time that day, Chrystel was flat on her back.

Several people jumped at the Hunta, which only brought more Huntas into the fray. By the time the scuffle was over, two seriously injured clavers were carried off, and several more were left bleeding on the founder's park grass.

Chrystel's side shrieked, and her vision was spinning as she climbed to her hands and knees. The Hunta slap had given her something besides vertigo. She could feel the rage growing inside her belly. *Hang on to that rage,* she told herself.

Chapter 10
Cat and Mouse

Mark was watching the city of Budapest, Hungary, through old-fashioned binoculars. He and his wasp flight were parked on a hillside surrounding the Liberation Monument, overlooking the Danube and old cities of Buda and Pest on each side of the river. Mark and his wasp flight had been assigned to Budapest because the Huntas' attack pattern indicated this enclave might be next.

He never understood why some large cities from before the Great Dying became survivor magnets while others simply fell into ruins. Perhaps the rise or fall of great cities was completely random. Whatever the reason, Budapest was the most populated city in Eastern Europe and now numbered close to forty-thousand human inhabitants.

Mark rubbed his eyes. He'd been awake long past a full day and night and finally allowed Tammy to administer an Ardinian designed human stimulant. He didn't like to take stimulants because he thought himself wound tightly to begin with, but the ongoing mission and shortage of wasp jockeys demanded he stay alert and in the game. As he sat in the sunshine waiting for a Hunta spaceship to appear, he tried to recount how he'd gone from flying a wasp in space to this. Ground battles were not how he'd envisioned a fight with the Huntas playing out.

He'd been mostly right when he'd guessed about the Hunta strategy. They did bypass human defenses. What no one had realized until far too late was that the Huntas had been hiding in plain sight all along. They were able to stay hidden in Earth's orbit with their cloaking technology. Apparently, the Huntas had done a bang-up job of determining population centers, evaluating communication and defense systems, and even discovering command and control vulnerabilities. The whole enchilada.

The fact that his wasp flight had seen the Hunta ships near Uranus was merely happenstance. No one could say why they were out in that area of the solar system in the first place. Regardless, the accidental sighting probably moved up the Huntas attack plan. Mark knew he had nothing to feel guilty about, but he still felt responsible. Space Fleet was getting their asses handed to them.

A hand reached out with a juice box. Becky, call sign Firestarter, dropped to the grass and sat next to him. "Penny for your thoughts," she said. Mark looked at the freckles across her mocha skin and dark, almond eyes. Like him, she was some unique blend of unknowable ancestry. He'd asked her once about her heritage when she'd joined his flight. She'd just received a medal for bravery after protecting the

Rainier Station from sabotage, and he was curious about her background.

"Does it matter now?" she'd answered. Firestarter had a real way of cutting through the crap.

"I've been trying to figure out how we can do this better." Mark said.

"That and feeling guilty you might have kicked off this war?"

"Well, yeah. Logically, I know I didn't cause it. It's the Huntas to blame."

"Don't forget that. Emotion has its place, and so does logic. It's just important we learn to identify one from the other."

"Oh, sage one," Mark smirked. "Tell me, how do we defeat our ruthless enemy?"

Becky started laughing along with him. "If I knew that, I'd offer it up. You know I'm not one to keep my opinions to myself."

Mark stiffened and placed the binoculars to his eyes. Just over the southern horizon, one cloud seemed to have a hole moving through it. Jumping to his feet, he handed her the binoculars and said, "Take a look."

She moved the binoculars to the place he was pointing. "Let's go!" she shouted.

"Spin up!" Mark yelled to the other pilots and copilots as he ran to his wasp. "Don't take off until my go." He spoke to the ship AI as he jumped aboard the wasp. "Tammy, did you read that?"

"I read you loud and clear. Let's get those squirrelly bastards!"

"Tammy, your use of English expressions is definitely getting better."

Jenny reached the wasp and slid in behind Mark. She strapped on her helmet and looked at the internal commo icon displayed in her visor. Mark could now hear her amplified voice from his headphones. "I was the last one in. The wasps are loaded, Mark. Whenever you're ready."

Mark's fingers were dancing on his leg, both from adrenaline and from stimulants. "We don't want to get ahead of ourselves this time. We need to wait until the Hunta ship has broken the cloaking screen and has opened its primary weapons portal."

"Roger. We're all painfully aware of the timing." Jenny said.

Mark received a confirmation that all wasps were ready and then waited. The normally jovial crew was silent. Other than clouds to the south, the rest of the sky was clear, and it was impossible to tell where the cloaked ship might be hiding. Waiting was the most infuriating part of the mission. Although he was damn good at quick responses, the window was extremely narrow for reaching the Hunta ship and effectively disabling the craft. If the Huntas saw them too soon, they'd simply recloak and move away, choosing a better time or location for an attack. If they were too late, and the aliens had already begun the firing sequence, then the enclave would be destroyed.

He heard the blast of the broken cloak first. To his front, Tammy's cameras displayed the Hunta destroyer materializing from thin air and then the aura of red indicating their weapons system was gearing up. Tammy said, "Weapons egress opening."

"On me," Mark commanded and lifted his wasp at the maximum speed that wouldn't tear apart his ship or the humans aboard. He was in a near vertical climb. The Hunta destroyer was closer this time than their last attempt. His wasp was trembling from the rate of acceleration, but it was now safely enclosed because Tammy had deployed secondary heat seals to combat overheating from oxygen friction. Mark's eyes were glued to the onboard screen; he had to pick the right moment to attack.

"Mark, watch for small arms fire coming from the ground," Tammy said. "It must be locals doing their part."

"For all the good it'll do them," he responded. "I was hoping they'd already cleared out, but with commo out, some people probably didn't get the word."

"There it is! The portal's opening. Wasps Bravo and Charlie are with me. Delta and Echo be ready to target their propulsion systems." Mark knew that Space Fleet wasn't entirely certain of the location of Hunta propulsion systems. This was their best guess based on two successful takedowns: one by Mark's flight and one by another team.

"Now." Mark piloted his wasp directly at the opening that was demonstrably the Huntas' primary weapons bay. Tammy and Jenny were ready to provide targeting support during the sprint to reach the Hunta ship. Rail gun turrets blasted as they surged forward, and Mark could feel the slight recoil of deadly, three-pound slugs bursting from his ship. As they turned away, lasers from the aft end took over, warming their target to over one-million degrees at the focus point of the beam. Hopefully, the focus would be the same spot degraded by rail ammo. Bravo began its pass just moments after Mark's wasp quit firing.

As in their previous encounters, this Hunta ship didn't return fire. Hunta weapons had been completely ineffective against wasp shields, and they'd quit wasting the effort.

"First pass was ineffective," Tammy reported.

"Second pass, follow in order." Mark ordered. "Now!" Once again, his wasp gave the Hunta ship everything it could, depleting rail gun ammunition in the process. Wasp Bravo followed.

Tammy processed the data from the last attack. "I detect an explosive reaction on the weapon egress area. Recommend taking advantage."

"Thanks, Tammy. Charlie, give them hell! Delta, move to back up Charlie. Echo, stay in position."

By the time the Delta wasp dumped their load, a chain reaction of explosions engulfed the Hunta ship.

"Move away from falling debris ASAP," Mark said.

After flying a safe distance, Tammy withdrew the heat shields so that they could watch in the clear. A cheer rose up from wasp pilots as the enemy ship tipped and then a final explosion broke it into pieces. Flaming debris scattered across the city. "Take that, mother fucker," Tammy bellowed.

Then they were all laughing. Mark took a deep breath, and a huge smile spread across his face. "Well done, Wasp Flight One. Let's head back to Switzerland for ammo resupply and our next mission assignment."

"Wait!" Jenny said. "Look over there!"

Mark was searching the sky when another huge boom shook the landscape. To his right, hanging over the Pest side of the city, another

Hunta destroyer had materialized, ready to continue the destruction.

Seeing another ship was like being hit by a sucker punch. The thrill of ridding Earth of one more Hunta ship while saving the people below was an amazing high—the appearance of another destroyer, a kick in the teeth. Mark couldn't find any words, but his mind was already calculating the amount of ammunition left within the wasp flight.

Tammy interjected. "They must have had a back-up ship waiting. They've deduced our strategy and have planned for losses. They know that wasps can only carry a limited amount of ammunition."

"I'm aware of that, Tammy. Delta, how much ammo do you have left?"

"Roger, Gameboy. Sixty-two percent of rail ammo and lasers are fully operational."

"Echo, confirm that you have a full load," Mark said.

"Confirmed, Gameboy."

"On my mark, Echo and Delta, I want you to approach at the same time. Tammy will relay your flight vectors. Put as much steel as you can on target. When you pass in different directions, give them the aft lasers. We've practiced this drill in space. Just pay attention to the timing. I don't want any friendly fire accidents. Got it?"

"Roger, Gameboy," Echo called out.

"I'm ready," the Delta pilot said.

"Tammy, have you transmitted flight vectors?"

"Done, Gameboy."

"Mark, this isn't your fault." Tammy's sultry voiced crooned.

"Stuff it, Tammy." The Hunta ship glowed red. Mark couldn't imagine how or why a ship would glow like that. The blood red hue was yet one more completely confounding mystery about this alien race. Maybe the foreboding color was meant only as a scare tactic. If so, it was working. "There it is. Delta and Echo are a go."

Mark's ship was in a prime position to watch the two wasps charge the Hunta vessel from different directions. The flashes of rail guns soared ahead of the wasps, striking the surface. When they passed underneath, Mark noticed a tiny wobble in Echo's trajectory. "What's your status, Echo," he asked.

"Gameboy, I have a mechanical problem. Maybe I pushed my ship too hard. I'm losing power."

Mark could clearly see the wasp, more like a one-winged butterfly now, struggling valiantly to maintain course. Echo was in a barely controlled descent and beginning to rotate while rapidly losing altitude.

"Can you land it, Echo?"

"I'm sure as hell gonna try," came the response.

Mark followed Echo's downward path on his screen. Delta wasp had made one last pass at the Hunta ship, while most of the remainder of the wasp flight disengaged to help their wounded comrade.

Delta's voice blared through the coms. "Gameboy, it wasn't enough. I couldn't do it. I'm out of ammo, and their primary weapon is beginning its firing sequence. We need to bug out."

"But I think Echo landed. We have to do something," Mark raged. "Tammy, take me down to pick him up."

It was Firestarter who said what everyone else was thinking. "We can't save him. We have three minutes to get clear of the blast once it begins, and the blast will begin in less than a minute. If you try to save him, it will mean your life and his."

"She's correct, Mark," Tammy added.

For the first time, Mark questioned whether he was cut out to give orders to anyone. It seemed like he could conquer the world when he was flying. Now, everything he thought he knew was coming apart around him. Sure, he could fly, but what difference did that make if he lost his nerve at the first sign of trouble? He hadn't even considered what it would feel like to lose comrades who had become his closest friends. The only thing worse was that it would be his decision to sacrifice two good friends so that the survivors could continue the mission.

He was furious that Space Fleet knew so little about their common enemy and that the Huntas had already adapted to his tactics. The fact that he hadn't been prepared for a second ship was on him. He'd always gotten a kick out of his call sign, Gameboy, but this wasn't any video game that could be reset. He vowed to himself that from this day forward he would make it his personal mission to understand the Huntas and never again underestimate this enemy.

Finally, he gave the only order that was left to him. With the most neutral voice he had left to him, Mark said. "Bug out."

Mark switched to his rear camera so he could see Budapest as they sped away. He witnessed hell on earth as a white fountain of energy centered under the Hunta ship spread outward in a perfect circle, annihilating every person and structure in its wake.

Chapter 11
Dogs Will be Dogs

Trent was dead tired, but he still had trouble falling asleep. The weight of responsibility for so many lives was a heavier burden than he'd bargained for. He'd just recently gotten used to caring for a small family again, but last night he'd lost complete control of his dog flock. They'd been travelling southward on the western side of the Tatoosh Range. His plan was to stay on the edge of forested terrain and then cut east through the Columbia River Gorge toward Idaho, avoiding any major mountain ranges. At least, that was the plan.

After three days on the road, Trent's flock was hungry and restless. Luckily, there were plenty of water sources in the surrounding area. None of them were in danger of dehydration, but that might change when they crossed through the Gorge and headed south again over high desert. He was already hoping for an early fall rain.

A dog, like most meat-eating pack animals, can go without eating for long stretches and then gorge themselves when food is available. Trent laughed remembering the day Kismet ate two loaves of bread, about a tenth of her body weight, and waddled happily through the house on three legs, her sides unnaturally extended.

Again, he wondered what had happened to the obstinate and loyal little dog. Kismet would likely never leave Amelia. She'd nursed Kismet back to health after finding her bleeding from a lost leg, and Kismet rewarded Amelia with an almost obsessive dedication. He hoped the tiny skip had survived.

The world's first dog exodus had been moving at a steady clip until last night's debacle. He and Tilley had placed the small and elderly dogs to the front of the procession so they wouldn't lose track of them, but that placement had conflicted with a dog's instinctive nature. Strong alpha canines are drawn to the front of a group. It wasn't long before the feeble dogs were falling behind. Tilley and a few herding breeds moved to the rear to keep the hundreds of dogs moving together in the same direction.

So far so good. But then some dog or dogs caught the scent of Pronghorn Antelope. Trent saw a handful of alphas bolt in the moonlight. At first, he thought it might be prowling Rangers, and the strong dogs were moving to warn them off. He wasn't concerned until a few others began to follow.

The Pronghorns had obviously made a remarkable comeback since the Great Dying because it was a sizeable herd. Trent had watched in amazement as shadows of small antelopes dashed over a ridge, and the dogs working in concert, instinctively split ranks to cut them off. He marveled at the speed of the

117

Pronghorns' escape and the relentlessness of the dogs pursuing them, appreciating how nature was so finely tuned. He changed his mind when an entire section of his flock joined the chase. They were off to the races, and no amount of calling by him or Tilley slowed them down.

By the end of the night, his charges were spread across the landscape, some sleeping on their sides satiated, while others huddled in the dips and hollows near trees shivering in fright. He and the herders had spent the early morning hours gathering the gaggle into a cohesive whole.

Trent had always believed dogs were just a simpler version of people, more akin to their human companions than different. Last night had confirmed that belief. Each dog was unique and different, yet each dog could be convinced to follow, even sometimes against their own best interests. They could be playful one minute and pissed off the next. They squabbled, cajoled, stole, loved, got aroused, and could be conversely self-sacrificing and selfish. Courageous one minute and frightened of their own shadow the next. Needy and self-reliant, bold and timid. The only differences were that they never lied, and their loyalty to their pack was without equal. Well, that and most of them woke up happy, unlike some of his human acquaintances.

As Trent thought about how he was going to get these animals to Idaho in one piece, Tilley and Lionheart padded to Trent's place where he was curled atop a nest of dried leaves. Lionheart circled and dropped on his legs with a groan. More daintily, Tilley positioned herself against his back.

Tilley spoke into his mind as Lionheart had already begun to snore. "We have them all. One is very old. You may have to carry him. He does not weigh much, and he does not have long."

"Show me where he is when I wake up. It may be better to build a makeshift stretcher and let some of the stronger dogs drag him. They do better when they're given a job."

"Yes," she said. "That is why we need you. For your human insight and because you know where to go."

"Tilley, do you know how many there are? I tried to count them but kept losing track."

"I do, but not in the same way as you. I don't count. I know each being. They are all in my mind by smell and by a sense I cannot describe to you."

"Wow, good to know. I was worried we could lose some, and I wouldn't notice. You know the trek will become harder as we go further, right?"

"Yes, I fear so. We all have faith in you."

Tilley had brought Trent full circle, wondering again if he was up for this task. He was mostly a loner. Maybe he was afraid that he'd lose them just like he'd lost his first family.

"Tilley, do you believe in a God or some sort of grand plan for each of us?"

"My makers, the Ardinians do not."

Trent responded with a grunt.

"But, I do," she whispered into his mind.

"You do? That seems odd. You were created by the Ardinians. How is it you believe in something more?"

"I cannot explain why I believe in something more. I am a separate biological creature and only know that I feel a spirit, an energy that guides me. Do not worry. You are the correct human to shepherd our friends to safety."

Trent felt Tilley's long back extend against his. Somehow, her touch calmed him. He didn't know how she did that. This wasn't the first time her nearness had rippled through his synapses like a drug. He'd always been a man that dealt in the realities of the world. What was real to him were those things he could see and manipulate with his own two hands.

Since meeting Amelia, he'd had to expand his thinking. Truth be told, he enjoyed opening his mind to other possibilities, even if he didn't have a clue what those other possibilities might mean. He understood that dogs could talk because of nanites harnessing biological Wi-Fi, even if he didn't comprehend the science. Alien contact, why not? Greater range to sense others, better hearing and incredible eyesight, no big deal. But Amelia's ability to predict the future accurately? That talent had no reasonable explanation.

There'd been times when he'd lived so far off the grid and alone in the wilderness that when the sun peeked over the horizon, he'd felt this bizarre, cosmic communion with all life. It was as if there was a plan, and he was just a microscopic part of it.

Heck, he warned himself, *I have real life concerns to worry about, such as a vast herd of canines whose numbers are known only to Tilley. Enough already with the mystical BS. If Tilley is plugged into some woohoo alien energy thing, I just hope it's seeping into me right now because I think we may need it.*

Chapter 12
Moon Base Victory

"What do you mean, you don't know where my wife is?" Admiral Mike asked.

"Uh, sir?" the young man looked to the commander's executive officer for support, but found only a steely-eyed gaze directed to a far corner. He continued. "Her last known whereabouts was the Nagoya Enclave. Space fleet recorded the time of notification as twenty minutes prior to the Hunta bombardment. We believe there was enough time to make an escape from the enclave, but we just don't know what happened. She could be anywhere."

Mike inhaled deeply to prevent himself from spilling emotional vomit all over the young man who had brought him bad news. He turned to his XO instead. "Keep on it. Find her. I know you both might think I'm clinging to unreasonable hope, but if anyone can survive, it's Karen. She's made of sterner stuff than you can imagine. She's alive. Now find her!"

The XO and lieutenant scurried away as fast as their legs would carry them. Mike pivoted to Jack, now always at his side. "Come, Jack. I'm sorry to drag you into another meeting, but I have little choice."

As they were walking toward the meeting room, Jack looked up at his master and whined.

"I know, Jack, you love her too," Mike said.

They swung through the door, and the shuffle of chairs and boots snapping to attention greeted the Admiral's entry. "Admiral on deck," someone announced.

"Sit please," Mike said. He made a quick appraisal of who was physically attending the meeting, and who would be beamed in via Ardinian meeting technology. Shakete was in his designated chair, on time once again. Jed wasn't in attendance, probably because he was busy working one of their many scientific problems. Battleship captains were on 3D video display. Mike eyed each one and noticed the toll this war was taking on their professional demeanors. They all looked either jacked up on stims or ready to drop from exhaustion. A bevy of staff claimed the rest of the chairs in the room.

"Please begin with the status of Earth's largest enclaves," Mike said.

A woman jumped from her seat to the podium. In the front of the conference area, a map of Earth was spread across a giant screen. Red circles designated destroyed enclaves while green signified population centers still standing. A unified gasp escaped the lips of the attendees There were more red icons on the map than green ones.

"Sir, we estimate that sixty-five percent of earth's inhabitants have been annihilated by the

Hunta attacks. Space Fleet continues to predict subsequent targets and deploy wasp teams to those locations to thwart the destruction. Thus far, our success at stopping Hunta progress has been limited. Four Hunta ships have been destroyed. We've received word from Wasp Flight One that the Huntas are now sending back-up ships to target sites. If the first ship is unable to complete the mission, another stands ready to ensure the outcome. As you know, a wasp flight carries limited resources, and it's difficult to combat a follow-on ship."

Mike looked at Shakete. "Do the Huntas not care about their own losses?"

Shakete's skin had morphed to the darkest shade of gold Mike had ever seen an Ardinian achieve. He resembled a golden statue, finely aged and recently discovered in a buried crypt. "Apparently, they have lost all measure of concern for individual lives. It's also possible that the ships responsible for murdering the human species are largely automated, and the Huntas consider the loss of a few ships an acceptable result. In that case, we may have underestimated the strength of their fleet."

Mike lamented, "Apparently, we've underestimated the enemy in many ways. Shakete, have you had any success in trying to contact them? We've tried every communication means available."

"None, Admiral." The Ardinian leader looked as if he wanted to say more and then stopped. Mike always had trouble reading Shakete. It was almost as if Ardinian emotional responses purposely mimicked human reactions, but that there was something else going on behind the scenes. The one trait always present was Shakete's godlike confidence. Even that characteristic appeared to be missing today, which frightened Mike almost as much as the color-heated map to his front.

The briefing continued. "Sir, word has spread about the danger of staying in enclaves, though slowly due to communications outages. Populations are leaving large enclaves and fleeing to surrounding areas. The Hunta effort to destroy humanity quickly has become a more difficult prospect."

Mike nodded. "In that event, we may be able to shift our wasps to other missions and allow the Huntas to waste time destroying empty buildings. Please inform me when that's prudent. I'd like to move on to communications."

The next briefer's portion was more encouraging. "The Huntas destroyed every satellite in orbit and New Washington's vector relay towers during the first phase of their attack. The Ardinians have mitigated the loss of satellites by providing technology that was already on the drawing boards. Fleet ships are now being used as moving communication relay sites controlled by shipboard AIs. The laser vector system is still down, but the AIs were able to boost short wave signals, a communication capability used by individuals for many years after the Great Dying. Word of the attack is spreading."

Mike waited until the end of the meeting to ask for the status of New Washington, mostly because he dreaded the news. He knew it hadn't been hit yet, but not much beyond that because of communication issues. One of Thomas' grandsons was the briefer.

Like his granddad, Spence was huge, even by new-world human standards. He also had Thomas' deep baritone voice. Mike thought it a wise decision that they'd chosen this young man to provide the news of New Washington; he'd rather hear bad news from someone familiar.

"Sir, there is no way to sugarcoat this. The people of New Washington have been taken by a Hunta incursion. We know this because local Mermots went to ground when it became clear there weren't enough resources to repel the Hunta force. Some Mermots remain outside the enclave underground and are serving as our eyes and ears."

"And the airfield?" Mike asked as dispassionately as he could find the strength.

"It was decimated. The wasps located there never got off the ground."

"And the status of the people?" Mike's voice was almost a whisper.

"We aren't sure, but the people who survived the airfield attack were seen being transported to the New Washington town center by the Huntas. We believe that's where any survivors are being held."

Ten seconds of silence followed. Finally, Mike gathered his wits enough to speak. "Get the Mermots into that enclave to find out what the hell is going on!"

"We're working on it, sir."

"Thank you, Spence. Everyone is dismissed. Battleship captains, please take a half hour break, and then we're going to brainstorm strategy and tactics. Shakete, please remain."

The two leaders remained sitting while the rest of the group filed out. Mike did not even glance in Shakete's direction, and Shakete didn't look to Mike. The second the door closed both beings started speaking, anger and frustration boiling to the surface.

Mike turned to Shakete and growled, "What good is Ardinian technology if it can't be deployed in the battlespace? For all your promises to us, it seems the Ardinians are sitting safe on the sidelines, watching humanity get slaughtered!"

"Don't blame Ardinians for human failure to cooperate. We never guaranteed that our technology would save the day, only that we could provide Earth a fighting chance. You knew that two to three years preparation was a short timeline!"

Jack sat up and barked twice like a canine referee, and Mike and Shakete backed away from each other. Neither Mike or Shakete were prone to talking over someone else in anger, but every being has their limits. Mike knew when it came to the ones he loved, his tether could be snapped. He was just now learning that Shakete had a limit too.

Mike inhaled and then sighed. "I'm done venting. Are you?"

"I hate to admit this, but that felt rather refreshing. I now understand some of your expressions that had previously eluded my understanding. Madder than a hornet comes to mind. Unfortunately, any venting amounts to wasted time."

"Only partially true. Venting may also save the vessel from a catastrophic explosion. What I need from you, Shakete, is to get a grip on the Huntas' grand plan. Make it a priority to find a way to detect cloaked ships. We can't fight them until we can see them."

"I well understand the issues. I know you won't appreciate this, Mike, but the great human strategic visionary, Sun Tzu, says little about a situation like the one where we now find ourselves. It is as close to a draw in terms of capability as one can achieve. The Huntas cannot destroy our ships because of our impenetrable shields, and we cannot destroy theirs when they can't be seen. And still, they are winning. Perhaps, I must peruse his writings again for the answer."

"Fine, but only after you find a way to see a cloaked ship."

"As you like to say, Mike, I can pat my tummy and rub my head at the same time."

"I never said that, nor have I ever heard that expression from anyone else. Nevertheless, we're going to lose if you don't come up with something and soon. They had a plan, and we've underestimated them. We can't afford to do that anymore."

"Yes. The Huntas are, after all, my relatives. I had not given that fact enough reflection, which is why my anger achieved critical mass. Forgive me for my outburst."

Mike stared at Shakete with a disarming earnestness. "I will forgive you anything if you find a way."

"Be careful of commitments you can't keep, Admiral." With that said, Shakete glided from the room.

Chapter 13
New Washington

Trample a patch of grass with enough people, add copious amounts of water in the form of a steady mist, and any old place can become a shoe-sucking mud palace, or so Chrystel believed. The fall rain had begun in New Washington, saving the enclave from death by wildfire only to be replaced by a different kind of death, this one slow and methodical. Like everyone else captured in the Huntas' net, Chrystel woke up soaked to the bone. She looked to the sky for her daily weather report. A cocoon of gray blanketed the already close quarters of the town square, and droplets falling from the muted heavens obscured vision, leaving the impression that rain was cycling from the sky to the ground and back again. A drop trickled into Chrystel's eye.

The temperature was nowhere near freezing, but cold enough that she could no longer feel her feet. The shivers hadn't started yet this morning. If she kept moving and circled the area with a tide of frantic clavers, her blood might thaw her frozen limbs.

The captured clavers had been waiting in the rain and mud for three days without any word from the Huntas on their fate. They hadn't had anything to eat either. Chrystel wondered if the Huntas' plan was to starve them to death in this muddy cesspool. More than anything, Chrystel believed that the waiting and not knowing was more demoralizing than rain or hunger. What the Huntas were doing was cruel and inhuman. Then she sniggered to herself with the awareness that they weren't human at all.

Someone shouted to her left. The sea of humanity parted as an ATV entered through the gate erected after the Huntas had enclosed them all in a fence. Two armed Hunta guards preceded the ATV and roughly pushed folks aside to make way.

Driving faster than prudent, the ATV dragged a heavily loaded trailer through the congested park. When the ATV came to a squealing stop at the foot of the Founders' Statue, the guards clicked and hissed warning tones at curious clavers.

Chrystel weaved through the crowd to get to the front. A Hunta driver and two passengers emerged from the ATV. One unlatched a tarp from the trailer, and the others began throwing plastic-like boxes on the ground. Cold and hungry, the people surged forward in the hope that the boxes contained food. Without warning, one of the Hunta guards shot a bolt of white-hot lightning into a man's head when he crossed too near. A woman next to the man, probably his wife, wailed in horror and fell to her knees by his

131

prostrate body. Clavers yelled and cursed, but none dared to go any closer.

Katie and one of her sons pushed their way through the crowd to attend to the injured man. Chrystel could see it was already too late. His face was missing, as was most of his head. She watched as they dragged the man away from clicking Huntas while his wife screamed, "No! No!"

The scene made her sick, but she filed it away as one missed opportunity to overwhelm their hosts. She vowed to watch and wait for the next.

The ATV dipped as the bulky Huntas piled back into their ride and drove away. Chrystel leaped on top of the pile of boxes. Her broken ribs shrieked in protest from the sudden movement. If someone didn't take charge now, the starving crowd would descend on these boxes like locusts after a seven-year sleep, and any hope of distributing food evenly would be lost. Mayor Ted appeared to be missing in action, but she thought he'd have been useless in a situation like this anyway.

"Back the hell off!" she shouted with the deepest, loudest voice she could muster. Her command had the desired effect. The crowd paused momentarily, but that wouldn't last long.

"There are 3,546 New Washington citizens in this park." Chrystel shouted. "I know because I counted them. Look around. Some of your family, friends and neighbors aren't here. We're all that's left.

"As I see it, you have two choices: believe it's every man, woman, and child for themselves, and in that case more will die, or choose to stand together as we've always done."

Laughter from the crowd wasn't helping Chrystel's case. "Okay, I know we haven't always stood together, but that's my point. We're always stronger and more resilient when we struggle together. Now, more than any other time in our past, is the time to quit fighting each other. We have a common enemy. If we want to survive and prevail, then we must stand together. Please, allow me to equally divide any food in these boxes. Don't allow the Hunta invaders to turn us into wild scavengers fighting for every scrap."

A woman from the crowd yelled. "Like always, founder families just want to take charge. You'll get yours and then some!" A smattering of grumbles followed the woman's comment.

Chrystel searched for that voice in the throng and found a woman she'd known in school. "Kirstin Stone! Come up here with me and help! I need four volunteers to see what's in these boxes and divide it evenly. I hope it's food!"

Everyone was talking at once. Chrystel stood her ground, or in this case, maintained a precarious balance on a box. She knew her skin color had probably flamed to red like her hair. She locked eyes with as many in the crowd who would return her stare.

Please, don't let any of my family step forward. We need a united town.

Kirsten didn't join Chrystel, but her younger brother did. One of the Aldrins, a family who had nearly brought New Washington to its end, stepped forward as well. Then the Harrison girls, who were from a new family out of the Dakota Territories, volunteered to join the team. Finally, Margo, the head organizer and administrator at the airfield marched to Chrystel's side. "You're going to need me," Margo said. Chrystel nodded her thanks.

There was no food inside the first box. Margo rifled through the large container, and glued to the inside wall she found a disc with a button on its face. She twisted it free and pressed the button. From the flat side of the disc a light beamed to the ground. As if she held an armed grenade, Margo nearly threw the little device away from the gathered crowd. One of the Harrisons shouted, "Wait!" because a video was projected into the mud. Margo pointed the light toward the flat portion of Founders Statue and the crowd watched a scene of Huntas setting up their version of a tent.

Chrystel thought Margo was a wonder of nature. With an efficiency she could only dream about, Margo cajoled, directed, and prodded clavers into service. Three teams had been assigned to tent construction after watching the Hunta video twice. Margo provided her time-saving insights as they worked on the far end of the park to erect their new tents.

Meanwhile, Margo moved on to other boxes. Finally, she found one that was filled with clear baggies containing what looked like thick, lavender cookies. She pointed to the hungriest looking young man in the crowd. "You," she said. "Will you please sample the food?" Margo might have been one hell of an organizer, but taste tester wasn't in her repertoire.

A big, ungainly boy of about sixteen with uncombed hair hanging in his eyes came forward. Margo handed him one of the lavender cookies. He stared at it, turned it over in his hand, and then took a dainty bite. The crowd waited anxiously as he chewed the morsel. When he didn't grab his throat and spasm to the ground, a cheer went up. The teenager smiled, placed the remainder of the cookie into his mouth, and then swallowed it almost whole.

"How is it?" Margo asked.

"Not too bad I guess. It has a strange flavor, though."

"I'm not sure how you could tell, but good enough for me. Let's get this stuff distributed. Everyone, form a line. And don't push. You'll get your share."

Chrystel believed there was nothing quite like a roof over their heads and food in their bellies to improve the spirits of a despondent population. It all came down to perspective. If you take away creature comforts, necessities, and free-will, then even purple, alien cookies would have a strange appeal. It might only be her imagination, but the skies no longer seemed to be leaking, and the solid cloud cover had broken into fluffy shapes. *Give a man a tent or an umbrella, and the rain will stop.*

Margo handed out the last of the baggies just as the tenth massive tent was erected. The tent covers were made of an extremely lightweight material that Chrystel had never seen before. She rubbed the fabric between her fingers, and it felt like a silky plastic, but durable and tough at the same time. The color, like the cookies, had a faint purple hue. She couldn't imagine how these thuggish aliens had arrived on purple as their color of choice. With the back part of the park now wall to wall tents, the dash of lavender tent color was a welcome contrast to the muddy ground.

Margo joined her. "It was a brave thing you did to take charge like that. The people were so agitated it could have gone a different way."

"Seemed more necessary to me than brave. But you marched in to accomplish the impossible. Where did you learn to do that? It's like your brain knows the shortest path between two points in a thousand different directions at once. Call me impressed."

"Well, before we get too dazzled by our own talents, we've still got plenty to worry about. I have no idea how many calories are contained in those meaty biscuits, much less what they're made of. I was able to hand out about five per person. That may not be enough. Also, the cots we found in the boxes were not enough for everybody but they're large. Probably meant to bunk the Huntas. Families will have to share, which they'd probably do anyway to keep from freezing to death. There were no blankets or medicine in the supplies the Huntas left. We've got wounded to tend to and no antibiotics. And to make matters worse, those tents are going to be packed."

"One problem at a time, Margo. Just keep doing what you're doing. Maybe later tonight you can tell me what happened at the airfield."

Emotion rippled through Margo's face. "Will this ever end, Chrystel? Will we ever be able to live in relative peace?" Margo rubbed her eyes. "What I know from history says maybe not. I just don't know how many more good people I can stand to lose." Her voice was barely a whisper. "The attack from the Huntas at the airfield was worse than when the Capital attacked us three years ago. Far worse."

"They'll come for us, Margo. My Grandpa Mike will find a way to save us. I know him."

Margo didn't appear to be as convinced, so she changed the subject. "Have you seen Thomas?"

"I heard from someone the Hunta shitheads dragged him to jail. Must have thought he was too dangerous to allow in general population." Chrystel answered.

"I hope that's why and not something worse. Sorry, now I'm being morose. I'll catch up with you later, Chrystel."

"Hey, if you happen to run into my mother, tell her to find me. She seems to be plugged into future events. I know that sounds spooky, but maybe she'll see something that can help. We badly need a break."

Chapter 14
Cleo

The blast of good feeling provided by the arrival of tents and meager rations had lasted only a day. They were still starving. Katie told Chrystel she estimated that each Hunta cookie contained three to five hundred calories. Five cookies were barely enough for a day's consumption for most children and nowhere close to what an adult needed to survive.

Lying on her side, Chrystel tried to catch a few more winks in the cot she shared with Margo and eight-year-old twin boys, named Kai and Aki. The twins didn't know what had happened to their parents. Margo had seen the children wandering around in the park by themselves and had gathered them up to share her and Chrystel's cot. Aki had cried himself to sleep the previous night while his brother curled around him for comfort. Between the pain in her side, an empty gut, and weeping children, Chrystel's sleepless misery index had reached stratospheric heights.

Margo prodded Chrystel to get up. She'd given everyone in the place a job, from grounds keeper to waste removal, and she expected Chrystel to help rouse the others to get started on their daily assignments. Chrystel complained when Margo poked her side. "Ouch! You know I have broken ribs. Give me a minute!"

"Great, already waking up on the wrong side of the cot." Margo said.

"It won't work with me, Margo. I'm immune to your coercive tactics."

Margo asked, "Well then, what are your plans to make yourself useful today?"

Chrystel sat up and winced from the pain in her side. "Uh, I dunno. I thought I'd jump one of the Hunta guards, steal his weapon, and kill the rest of them."

"Reckless and dangerous, but possibly useful," Margo said.

"No, really, I'm going to try to talk with one of them. Have you seen the guard that's posted near the gate? He or she, I still don't know if they have sexes, doesn't scowl like all the others. If I approach it with my hands in the air, maybe it won't shoot me."

"First of all, I can't tell one Hunta from another much less the degree to which they scowl." Margo started. "Second of all, they can't speak, and I doubt they can understand us either. You're just going to get yourself hurt or killed."

"Got it. Maybe it would be better to watch everyone starve? I know they can't speak, but I think some of them may understand us."

"That's a fool's errand. What can I do to talk you out of your suicide plan?" Margo asked.

Before Chrystel could answer, an earsplitting screech blasted from the direction of the city hall. Both women looked at each other. "Sounds like a PA system." Chrystel said. "Let's go! And why the heck are the Huntas using that old PA system?"

"When you're an invading force, it's impossible to carry everything you need." Margo said as they scrambled to put on shoes. "Back in my National Guard days, they trained us to utilize whatever we could find from the local population. Something we need to remember when the tide of this war changes."

Chrystel nodded and bolted from the tent. A crowd was forming to watch two Huntas struggling with cords and pre-Great Dying, vintage speakers. The Hunta technicians might have been arguing because their clicks were strident and loud. When the larger beast began to hiss in return, three young men began to chant: "Fight, fight, fight!" It wasn't long before the chanting was adopted by many in the crowd. One of the two Huntas, suddenly aware that he was the object of ridicule, grabbed a weapon slung over his back, pointed it at gathered clavers, and made a long warbling click, punctuated by a raspy hiss. The chant died instantly.

"Well, there you go," Margo quipped to Chrystel. "Now you know the Hunta word for shut up. When you decide to have a conversation with them, I'd be listening for it."

A Hunta clicked into the microphone, and satisfied that the strange noise coming from his mouth was sufficiently amplified, he and his partner returned up the stairs to city hall. Margo wasn't done needling Chrystal. "And now you also know "testing, one, two, three, four.' This talking with brutal aliens scheme of yours is gonna be a breeze."

"Okay, Margo, I get your point. By the way, I'm glad you're around. I've been told I take myself too seriously."

Conversation in the crowd lowered to a murmur as a man came through the front door of city hall. "Well, I'll be damned," Chrystel said. "Friggin Mayor Ted!"

Chrystel seethed as she watched Ted grab the microphone and give a sincere and totally concerned smile. He was dressed in khakis with his shirt sleeves rolled up on his arms; the hardworking politician's uniform of choice. He wore a down vest over his shirt and his feet were encased in sparkling clean hiking boots. He drew attention to his dark, unkempt hair by sweeping strands off his forehead with his fingers.

Until this very moment, Chrystel hadn't been sure what it was about Ted that so incensed her.

She'd given up the position of Mayor, so it wasn't like she'd nursed bad feelings from a contentious political battle. She just knew in her gut, for all his buoyant optimism and natural interpersonal ease, that there was something about him that struck a bad chord. She'd even considered the possibility that she was jealous because, unlike her sometimes clumsy, prickly manner, Ted held an aura of disarming friendliness. He had this way of listening to people that made them immediately trust him. She, on the other hand, had to earn trust through hard work.

She'd finally arrived at the conclusion that her problem with Ted wasn't his fault at all. The problem with Ted was that he was the mayor and not Brodie. It should have been Brodie. If Brodie had just been honest with her and the town, he'd be the one leading them now. Even knowing what he'd done to betray her and New Washington, she still believed that Brodie was at heart a good man and a better leader than Ted would ever be.

Besides, Ted had been holed up with their Hunta captors while the town was starved and brutalized. He was a coward and a snake. There were no sincere smiles that could change the facts.

Margo looked over at her. "Chrystel, what's wrong?"

"Him," she seethed.

"Yeah, consorting with the enemy isn't a good way to win hearts."

"If I could have your attention, please," Ted started. "I was captured at city hall by the Huntas last week. They kept me caged in my office until yesterday. That's when their leader, Cleo, came to speak with me. She asked me to introduce her this morning and to recommend that the people of New Washington cooperate fully."

"You don't look hungry, Mayor!" a woman shouted.

Ted beamed a heartfelt expression toward the female voice. "They did feed me, and I'm so sorry that they haven't fed you. Hopefully, that's all about to change. After negotiating with Cleo, I believe we've reached a compromise that will benefit everyone and will also ensure our survival. Please, I beg you to hear her out." The mayor turned and climbed the steps back into the sanctuary of town hall.

"What do you think?" Margo asked.

"I think Ted doesn't have anything to negotiate with, and every word he just spoke is a lie." Chrystel said. "Oh, and Margo, at least one Hunta can speak and understand humans."

Both doors to town hall swung open. A gorgeous woman in a simple, form-fitting black body suit strutted down the steps to the microphone. Two Hunta guards flanked her on each side. The Huntas guarding the city center were large, but the Huntas in the woman's entourage were in a whole different weight class. Chrystel put them at nearly 400-pounds each, and over 7-feet tall. Decked out like knights from the middle ages, they had tunics over their massive chests, emblazoned with an intricate symbol that looked like an octopus. And of course, Chrystel thought, the tunics are deep purple.

The woman picked up the microphone and spent a moment to inspect the human audience. "Good morning. I'm Cleo, the Huntas' chosen leader of Earth." She paused after her statement, and, if her sly smile was any indication, she was enjoying the shock value of her words.

"Do you think she's an android, biological creation, or a mind-controlled human?" Chrystel asked Margo.

"Those weirdly spaced eyes tell me she's not human. Although, they did do a damn fine job of making her physically appealing."

When the crowd had settled, Cleo resumed. "I know you are hungry and cold. I wanted to prepare a demonstration of what life will be like for you if you do not cooperate. The battle for Earth is over, and the Huntas have been victorious. Your Space Fleet has been defeated. Most of the people on Earth have been killed.

Your animal friends, the dogs and the Mermots, will be eliminated as well."

Cleo waited again as there were several in the crowd who cried out. Chrystel looked into Margo's eyes and saw the same unfathomable horror reflected in her own.

"You may be asking, why us? Why have the Huntas chosen this group of humans for life instead of death? The answer is simple: we need a workforce to grow our primary life staple, the Populotter Fruit. The climate and soil of this area is perfect for its growth." Cleo waved to one of her personal guards, and he handed her a sack. She carefully folded the sides of the bag back and raised the fruit above her head for all to see. The skin of the giant eggplant-like fruit was covered in thorns. Cleo handed the bag back to her guard.

"That might explain the purple themes," Chrystel said. "But I think it's bullshit they've chosen us because of our marvelous growing climate. They wanted to neuter the threat from the airfield."

"If you work hard and obey the orders of your Hunta superiors, you will live. However, you will not be allowed to repopulate the earth. The Huntas have more important matters to attend to. If humans willingly grow our food, the Huntas will allow you to live out your lives on this planet."

"As slaves!" an angry voice shouted.

"Take him," Cleo ordered.

A squad of regular Hunta guards pushed into the crowd to find the voice that had dared interrupt Cleo. There were many clavers who chimed in, "It was me." Then, everyone was screaming, "It was me!"

Cleo's voice cut through the noise. "Have it your way." She pointed a slender finger to Kai, who had the misfortune to be standing in the front row at the end. "Take him instead."

The massive Huntas standing behind Cleo pounded down the steps, swooped in, and grabbed the screaming, eight-year-old boy. His twin, Aki, tried to grab his brother's legs and a heavy Hunta hand swatted him away. One of the Hunta carried the terrorized child over his shoulder into the town hall.

Again, Cleo allowed time for her despicable deed to simmer, and the crowd to contemplate the consequences of further rebellion. "Let this be a lesson. The Huntas have no tolerance for disobedience or insurrection. Finally, I need one volunteer from the farmer masses to liaison with your mayor."

Margo glanced at Chrystel. "Do it."

She didn't want to. What Chrystel wanted more than anything else was to scream at the top of her lungs. That or fold into a ball and sleep away this nightmare. She didn't want to look at Ted, much less coordinate human slavery with him. Still, her hand went up. Thomas was in that city hall somewhere. She hoped Kai would be spared too. Maybe there'd be something she could do to secure their release.

"Excellent," Cleo said when she saw Chrystel's hand. "We will retrieve you shortly. That is all for today. Human food will be provided on a probationary basis." Cleo smiled before leaving with her guards, but her smile didn't reach her abnormal eyes.

Her face bright red, Chrystel started walking away. "I don't believe a word of it. There's more to this. I'll do everything I can to get to the truth. Thanks, Margo, for pushing me to volunteer."

Margo shook her head. "I hope you're right. But right now, Chrystel, I'm gonna need a few minutes to pull myself together. My legs are shaking, and it isn't because I'm cold."

Chapter 15
Kismet

Kismet burrowed deeper into the master's sleeping place. Surrounded by safe scents, she waited for daylight. *No more food. No more mice. Kismet must find food.*

She didn't remember why the dark made her afraid. She remembered the smells of her pack. She remembered the safety of the place her pack stayed. There were no masters there. They lived inside a big place with many mice the pack hunted and ate. She had no memory of why she'd run from the safe place into the dark; she only knew the danger. The smells in the dark were as vivid in her mind as the fear of Rangers and then the pain from the Ranger attack. She remembered her fear as she crawled through the forest to a master's place.

She remembered the sound of the master's voice as she picked her up and held her close, making the pain go away. The sounds the master made were new, but old and familiar. Like she'd always known those sounds. The woman master and man master became pack.

Kismet must eat. Kismet must wait for light.

Her nose peeked from the safety of the master's bed. She smelled the other creatures of the light. She crawled from her nest, stood, and sniffed again. She reached out her paws, stretched, and then shook.

Her pack gone, Kismet was sad and alone. Her nose swung to the open place, and she jumped from the bed. She placed her front feet on the place to leave, like the woman master had said, but she couldn't get her back foot there too. Circling, she looked at that place, backed up, looked again, and then ran. Kismet fell to the floor and rolled onto her side. She stood once more, circled several more times, padded this way and that, and tried again. Kismet pushed off with her one back foot when it hit the right spot, expanded her strong chest, dug with her front claws, and sailed out the window.

Kismet landed in a bush and twisted to the ground. She could smell the creatures of the light. She didn't even consider returning to the safe place. The only thoughts that drove her forward were *Kismet must eat* and *Kismet must find woman master.*

There were no mice smells, but she could smell the tree. The tree made food. The woman master had fed her the tree food. Kismet trotted to the tree with her nose on the ground until she found food. Master called it apple. There were many on the ground, but some were old. When she found a good apple, she placed it between her paws because it was too big to grab in her jaws and then lay on her belly to eat. When she could eat no more apple, she began her search.

She knew the scent of the woman master, but a bad smell was mixed with the woman smell. The bad smell was easy to follow. She could smell the bad from far away. Kismet set off down the road following those scents.

Suddenly, Kismet saw movement. She was still hungry and saw a rabbit hop into the forest. Kismet followed, running as fast as she could, the taste of rabbit in her mind. She ran until the rabbit smell was gone. The woman master smell was gone too.

She looked for something else to eat and paused to scare a squirrel. She waited for a time, barking at the squirrel as it chattered to her from tree. A good odor drew her away from the squirrel. She travelled with her nose to the ground searching. Sometimes, she stopped to paw and sniff.

The sound of hissing alerted Kismet to danger. She turned to find a cat. The cat was guarding a mouse and was angry Kismet had come near. It swiped its claws at Kismet's face, and Kismet showed her canines, growling a warning. A fight with the cat would be bad. If Kismet had packmates near, she would fight the cat for the mouse. The thought of packmates reminded Kismet of the woman master, so she left the cat and its mouse.

Find woman.

Kismet sniffed the ground, but the woman's scent and the bad smells were gone.

She was lost. The scent of the road was still present in her mind, but she did not remember how the road would take her to woman master. Instead, she searched the ground for the master's smell, going deeper and deeper into the forest. She found water and drank. She found a good bird on the ground and ate. Each time, she began her search anew.

Find woman master.

Kismet was scared. The dark was coming. The creatures of the dark were stirring, and she was afraid. The animals of the light had gone to safe places for sleep.

Kismet must find safe place. Kismet must hide in the dark.

She scratched near trees for a hollow. She sniffed around rocks for an empty space. Kismet was moving quickly now, staying under trees to keep screaming birds from taking her. She was panting. She found a place where a master had once stayed, but a racoon crawled from underneath the place. Kismet was so frightened of the dark she might have fought the racoon for the safe place, but a racoon pack lived there. They chased her away.

Far away, the whooping bark of Ranger. Kismet whimpered and began to shake. Still moving, moving, her back leg slid into a hole. She jumped in surprise. Then she turned her nose to the hole. She stuck her snout in the space and inhaled. The scent was Mermot. She placed her head in deeper to look for a safe place. Kismet screamed as claws grabbed her head and pulled. Her front paws and back leg reacted, digging into the ground to keep from falling. The claws were too strong. Her whole body was pulled into the hole, moving faster and faster, deeper and deeper. Kismet cried.

Chapter 16
Resistance

"I'm skipping work details for the day," Margo said after Cleo's speech. "No one would be worth a damn anyway after what we just witnessed."

In truth, Chrystel thought the New Washington population was just now coming to terms with the shit sandwich their lives had become, and an aura of hopelessness permeated their prison.

The Huntas hadn't come for her. Keeping her eyes on the gate, Chrystel waited all afternoon and evening, but no Huntas had entered.

Aki was inconsolable at the loss of his twin. Chrystel and Margo took turns that night holding the crying child who seemed far younger now than his age. Chrystel didn't think she'd slept at all until an ungodly odor and giant hand pushed her into consciousness. His throbbing eyes leering down at her, he spit alien saliva in her face as he clicked an order Chrystel couldn't understand.

She bolted to an upright position, her heart pounding from the abrupt awakening. She noticed the other people in the tent had backed up around the walls as far away from the Hunta as was possible. Some were surreptitiously leaving out the back. Aki released a blood-curdling scream, and Margo held on to the twisting boy by body locking him in a bear hug.

Chrystel didn't want Aki to be further terrorized, so she grabbed her shoes, and ran from the tent barefoot past the Hunta guard. The Hunta followed. She turned on him, shaking her finger at his face. "I don't care what planet you're from. That's no excuse to be a total asshole! Are your people so stupid that they don't realize intimidation only goes so far? Next time, knock for crap's sake!"

The Hunta seemed stunned by her outburst. Chrystel was pretty sure he didn't understand a word of it, but that he'd guessed at her underlying meaning. Also, the Hunta had probably been directed to retrieve her unharmed, and those instructions might limit Hunta interaction options. He pointed his big, thick hand at the gate and clicked twice in what she assumed was a normal tone.

"All right," Chrystel said, red-faced. "Let's go."

The seat of New Washington government, a converted multi-plex cinema, still appeared much as what it once was. However, a stench greeted Chrystel and her escort as they entered the building. A revolting combination of vinegar and fermenting sweat kicked her gag reflex. After a couple of inside out attempts by her stomach, she breathed through her mouth. Her eyes scanned the nondescript entry room as she assessed all that was now Hunta. They hadn't done much with the place other than fill it with an odiferous scent.

Cleo's guards, her personal gang of four, flanked two offices: one to the town council chambers and one for the mayor. Chrystel wondered what was hiding behind those closed doors. Their pulsing eyes watched Chrystel as she was prodded forward along a hall to what was formerly a storage area. The escort Hunta opened the door, roughly shoved her in, and then slammed it shut.

"Yeah, same to you asshole," she called through the door.

"That's not a good idea," Ted said.

Chrystel whipped around to face him. Ted sat on a folding chair with a tablet on his thighs. "Maybe, but it makes me feel better."

"Are you hungry?" he asked.

Chrystel wanted to say no, but her mouth salivated at the mention of food. "Starving, literally."

He nodded, stood, and gathered some items from a box in the room. Chrystel noticed "NEW WASHINGTON RESERVES" stamped on the box.

"As you can see, the Huntas have found our food reserves. They plan to start distributing it today. There's two month's supply of food

156

available, but with the numbers in the town center it should last for four months or more."

Chrystel grabbed the food from his hands. She dropped to the floor cross-legged, ripped open the first package with her teeth, and sucked in chicken a la king as Ted talked.

"Slow down Chrystel, or you'll make yourself sick. Look, I know you don't like me, and that's fine, but whether you believe it or not, I only want what you want—to keep our people alive."

Chrystel scowled at him as she continued to chew.

"If we work together, there's some hope we can stay alive long enough to get away. Although, I don't know how. That's why I'm glad it was you who raised your hand, even though you're the most bellicose woman in the enclave."

"Thank you," Chrystel answered with her mouth full.

Ted's eyes crinkled at the corners in a smile. "I need your help to find a way to get us free."

Chrystel swallowed. "I don't trust you, Ted."

He nodded. "What can I do to change that?"

"You can start by telling me everything you know. What's really happening with Space Fleet? Where's Thomas? What happened to the rest of our people? Also what happened to the dogs and the Mermots? How many Huntas are here? How do they get resupplied? Oh, and what happened to the boy they carried off! That would be a good start."

"I don't know much because they keep me sequestered in this room. It doesn't help that we don't speak the same language. But here's what I've picked up from Cleo: she asks a lot of questions, questions she wouldn't ask if this war was over, and the Huntas were 'victorious.' She thinks she's subtle, but she isn't."

"Okay, more Ted. What questions?"

"I don't believe Space Fleet has been destroyed, but I can't be certain. She's asked me who's related to who in the enclave. She wanted to know about the moon base. Even if I was inclined to blab, I didn't even know we had a moon base, so I couldn't give her anything. She wanted to know how many humans live outside of enclaves, where they live, how they live. Give me a minute and I'll think of more."

Chrystel lifted a finger to her lips, retrieved the tablet from the floor and typed, *pen and paper?*

Ted's eyebrows raised in a question, and then he nodded acknowledgement. As he was rummaging for something to write with, Chrystel asked, "What do they want me to do?"

"Get tools to clavers to build their greenhouses." He handed the scrap and a pencil to Chrystel. She scribbled, *what have you told them?*

"Break people into teams, chose supervisors," Ted said.

I've lied and made stuff up. I can be convincing.

Ted quickly passed the paper and pencil back to Chrystel. *Keep doing that. Misdirect. Eyes open always. Tell unimportant truths they can verify*

"Mostly, I think they want you to keep the people busy and subservient."

Thomas? The boy? Number of Huntas?

Chrystel talked as Ted took his turn to write. "I can do that, but it won't be easy. They need to feed us if they want us to work. Threats only go so far when people are backed into a corner. They can become violent and ruthless."

Ted handed the paper to Chrystel. *Thomas alive, but not here. Maybe 400 Huntas. Don't know about boy. I fear the worst. Cleo said they don't want human children in enclave.*

Chrystel continued talking. "The worst thing the Huntas can do is harm the children. That will only harden the people of New Washington." Chrystel took the paper from Ted, tore it into pieces, and swallowed the scraps.

"I hear you, Chrystel, I'll try to explain to Cleo, if she'll listen. Let me show you what I have for you."

"Do you remember any more of her questions?"

"No, not really," he said. Chrystel nodded, satisfied that Ted understood that Huntas might be eavesdropping.

Ted and Chrystel put their heads together to construct a plan for work details. Suddenly, a huge inconsistency hit Chrystel: why were they keeping Ted in a closet? She'd been so busy trying to gather intelligence that she'd missed an obvious question. Why not just throw Ted in a tent like everyone else?

"Ted, why are they keeping you here?"

When Ted turned to her, his eyes were wide and his face drained of color.

Just then, they both jumped when Chrystel's Hunta escort flung the door open.

"Time's up." Ted said, as the Hunta grunted and grabbed Chrystel to pull her away.

She looked over her shoulder one last time. "Next time, Ted. And don't even think about screwing me over."

Chrystel and her Hunta minder were moving through the lobby when Chrystel heard Cleo's voice. "You!"

Oh, no, Chrystel thought. She calmed herself and turned. Cleo curled a finger inward, signaling her to come. Sucking in a deep breath,

Chrystel squared her shoulders and confidently marched across the floor to face Cleo.

The unnatural eyes of what was probably a human replica inspected Chrystel. Cleo's gaze travelled the length of Chrystel's body from her feet to her head. Using the same finger she used to dispatch Kai, she reached out and lifted a lock of Chrystel's hair. Chrystel pulled away. Her first inclination was to grab Cleo's finger and twist it off her hand. The probability of a quick death stayed Chrystel's impulse.

"I find the color of your head topping very interesting," Cleo said. "To the Huntas, it is the same color as our Populotter Fruit. If I had known this color was an option, I would have painted my hair with the same brilliance."

"You can always dye it." Chrystel responded.

"Where might I find this dye?"

Chrystel couldn't believe this conversation or Cleo's question. She was expecting to be punished for plotting against the Huntas, not discussing hair coloring. Maybe the Hunta leader's interest could present an opportunity to get out of captivity and learn more.

"I could probably find you some, but I'd have to search for it in our homes and stores. There wouldn't be any in town center where we're caged."

Cleo stared and didn't say anything for several moments. "You are the Admiral's granddaughter, are you not?"

Chrystel's jaw tightened. "What Admiral are your talking about?"

"I already know this," Cleo said and then giggled. "And far more. For now, you may leave. Guard, return her."

Chrystel wasn't sure what had just happened, but she had a feeling that Ted might be feeding Cleo information.

Chapter 17
Pacific

Karen gasped an "Oh" when the ship lifted several feet and precariously tipped as it rolled over the crest of a wave. The airship floated quite well, but it sucked in terms of stability. Using Jed's thorium generator system, the world's last remaining aeronautical engineer had designed the aircraft for transportation utility to bypass decaying roads. It wasn't fast, pretty, or the pinnacle of human ingenuity, but it could take off and land perpendicularly and carry up to twenty people.

When Jed and Mike decided the craft should also float, the designer swapped out the helicopter-like landing gear for inflatable landing pads. The ship, seated on eight inflated pads, wouldn't sink, but without ballast, they were little more than a houseboat on innertubes floating in a great big ocean. The first storm would land them in serious trouble. Darkening clouds near the horizon gave notice their demise might be sooner rather than later.

Karen was amazed that she could still be a glass half full kinda gal. Her first quip to the guys when she'd noticed the gathering storm was, "At least we won't have to eat each other or starve." None of them laughed.

The co-pilot/mechanic, Jim, a skinny man with fair hair and worker's muscled forearms and hands, spent every waking moment trying to get some juice from the thorium generator into the empty storage battery. Three of four cells had been badly damaged, leaving only one that might be usable. He'd admitted his understanding of the battery system was woefully deficient, but he was dogged in his determination to figure it out.

The coming storm had Jim nearly frantic. From the engine compartment in the rear of the ship, Karen could hear a stream of curses that rivaled her own skill with colorful language.

"I'd better go pull down my still." Karen announced. No one replied. Doug, the pilot, glanced up from his empty jerry-rigged trolling net to nod. Derrick and Hunter, two young men who had been assigned as her escorts, were snoring away on the deck.

Popping her head out the window, Karen grabbed handholds to pull herself up on a roof that she'd christened the ship's viewing deck. They'd laughed at her when she'd proposed constructing a solar still to make water. The concept was so simple and useful, it was one of the very few survival techniques that Karen remembered from her Army stint almost 180 years ago. Essentially, when water evaporates, the condensation is free of impurities, including salt. All they needed was water from any source in a container, heat, and something to collect the condensation. Voila, drinking water.

They'd quit laughing at day four when every bottle of water and Bigfoot had run out, and she'd shared the first quart of purified water. It wasn't nearly enough, but it might extend their lives long enough to be found. Karen crawled on her hands and knees to the still. She felt a big swell lifting the ship, and when their little boat dived to the back side, she and her still began to slide over the slick wet surface. "Oh, shit!"

She reached out and grabbed the water pan, yanked the vessel to drop the center rod and seat cushion fabric, and then flattened herself on the roof, her hands desperately seeking a non-existent handhold. She was almost off the edge before the ship bottomed out.

Crawling with a purpose, she inched back to the starting point, clutching a rung in one hand and the still in the other just as another wave pushed their home skyward. Luckily, this one wasn't as large, and she kept a tight grip on the handhold, hugging her solar still components like a lost lover. Karen scrambled down the side and thrust her legs back through the window. She thought unlike some of the lost lovers in her early life, the still probably couldn't be replaced.

"Whew," she breathed. "That was too damn close. I almost took the big dive."

The men were gathered around the radio and barely noticed her heroic entry. She sat the still parts on the floor and went to look over their shoulders. "What's going on?"

"Jim got the battery working. Enough to power the radio, GPS, and give us a little venting to move the ship. Of course there's no way to steer." Doug commented without turning from the radio.

"That's fucking great news!" Karen said. "We can find something to make paddles to steer. Why the long faces?"

"Listen for yourself." Jim said.

"What am I listening for?" Karen asked and focused her attention on the radio.

"Nothing," one of the boys answered.

"Nothing?"

Jim sighed. "Nothing. Not a damned thing."

Karen grabbed the back of a seat as another roller took them. The group bent at the knees, shifting with the ebb and flow of the ship. Karen used the seconds to steel herself against the possibility there was no one left. When the heaving stopped, she asked, "Did you try the emergency channel?"

"That's what we're listening to now." Bradley answered.

"I have another one. It's a private satellite channel for me and my husband, Mike. Send an

166

SOS on this channel. There may be someone monitoring for signals even if there isn't any traffic."

"What if the Huntas are listening in too?" Jim asked.

Karen blew air from her mouth. "Hell, I don't know, Jim. If we don't get someone here to rescue us soon, we'll be lucky to live out the day. Even the Huntas might be an improvement over that storm. What do you recommend?"

"We should try your private channel first. If we can't raise anyone, then we'll go with the normal emergency satellite setting."

"Do it," Karen said. "Let Doug handle it. The rest of us need to do what we can to steer this floating death trap away from the storm. How much speed can we can get, Jim?"

"At best, maybe six knots."

"Shit."

"Yeah," he answered. "Not nearly fast enough to flee that storm. All we can do is buy time. We'll have to turn to the waves once the storm gets closer."

"We might be better off in a duck boat." Karen said.

"What's a duck boat?" Hunter asked.

"Before the Great Dying, we had these boats that looked like school buses or were decked out like ducks. They hauled tourists from land to water."

"Weird," the young man replied.

"Yeah, very. Jim, what do you think of the insulation on the roof? It looks like it's made of a plastic. Think it's strong enough to cut for a paddle or rudder?"

"I don't know. Let's yank off a corner and—"

Rouff. Rouff. Ruf.

Every eye turned to the pilot seats where Doug was manning the radio. "Was that a dog?" Karen asked. "Are you still on my private channel?"

"Yep, and it sure sounds like a dog to me."

"What the hell?" *Mike didn't have a dog. There weren't any dogs on the moon as of a week ago. Why would a dog be answering her call?* "Doug, just keep sending the SOS on that channel for a few more minutes. If there's a dog answering, let's hope it's a smart one and it knows to retrieve a person. Jim, let's get back to the paddle dilemma."

* * *

Karen vomited all over her feet. At least she could say she wasn't the last to toss her cookies. Since breakfast and lunch had been a lite fare, a slim offering of raw fish caught in Bradley's net, Karen's stomach eruption registered barely a one on an explosivity index.

168

She was already wet from ocean spray, so a little bile on her toes didn't cause her any further discomfort. The smell would be washed away shortly.

Just minutes earlier, they'd turned toward the storm with their cutout paddles. As the waves grew, everyone knew they wouldn't couldn't move fast enough. Sooner, not later, the airship boat was going to flip topsy-turvy, and the best any of them could hope for was to grab something near the inflated landing pads to ride out the storm. *Fat chance.*

Karen and the crew were buckled in to prevent life-ending injury if their death trap flipped. A sealed hatch on the floor would be their preferred exit. They'd have to belly crawl around wiring to a secondary hatch to reach the bottom of the ship or what would be the top once the ship flipped. If this thing leaked more than expected, some heroic swimming from a window or the side door might be necessary. Just thinking about taking a dive into the cold water made Karen shiver.

Of all the ways Karen imagined her life would end, drowning in the Pacific Ocean wasn't among them. *Strange how life is that way.* She held her breath and her stomach lurched as they climbed another wave, almost at a stop, and then barreled down the other side. More seawater washed past her toes. She'd made peace with her fate. She'd always given life everything she could, but if that wasn't enough, there was comfort in knowing she'd never stopped fighting for her world and her family. Her lost family from before the Great Dying, her children Anne and Nathan and her first husband, Don, still called to her. She never imagined she'd live this long anyway.

Jim was screaming something from his seat against the far side of the ship.

"What?" Karen yelled back.

"Lights! I see lights."

Karen squinted out the nearest window to inky blackness. As they began another climb, she saw them. A bolt of energy flashed from one set of lights to another. *Good lord!* An air battle was ongoing right here in the middle of a storm, in the middle of the ocean. *Oh, hell no.* She felt the airship lose its battle against a wave and lift from the front past the point of no return.

For a few terrifying seconds, they somersaulted in the disorienting darkness and bone-chilling water. Karen opened her eyes and realized she wasn't dead yet. Her heart surged from panic. *Calm down, Karen. Remember this thing won't sink. Probably.*

She was hanging from what was now the ceiling by her seat belt. Water trickled in from crevices and rushed in from the back through the exhausts. *First, the seat belt.* Karen unhooked the belt and twisted to land on her feet, but missed, falling over into ankle deep water. Doug extended his hand and helped her up. "You go first. Unseal the latch and then get to the top."

"Not gonna happen." She said. "The boys go first. They can help pull the rest of us up."

"Have it your way." Doug said. He and Jim hoisted the youngest of their crew. Once Derrick scrambled up and turned around, he held his hands from the hatch ready to retrieve Hunter. The water was already knee deep. By the time Karen and Jim were hoisted aloft, the water was up to Doug's neck.

"I'm going to float up. Keep someone ready to pull me in. One of you needs to check the outer hatch and see if it's safe to climb out."

As the smallest of the four now squeezed together in the tiny compartment, Karen volunteered to wind around the various cords, conduits, and mechanical components to the very top, formerly considered the very bottom of the airship. As she drew closer to the twenty-inch square hatch, Karen could see the seals were holding. No leaking so far.

Scooting her way directly underneath the hatch, she unhooked the second buckle latch and pushed. Water began to pour in. Sputtering from the deluge, she reached through the crack with her arm to test the depth of the water covering their soon to be casket. The spray at her fingertips told her it was only two or three inches deep. She pulled her arm in, heaved the latch shut, and resealed the opening.

Squirming through the morass of obstacles, she returned to her shipmates uncomfortably waiting in the cramped confines of the three-foot deep compartment.

"Well?" Jim asked.

"I can't be sure because I didn't want to flood our last refuge, but it seemed like there was just a few inches of water up there. What's the water level below?"

"Almost up to the first hatch now."

"Oh, damn. What does that mean, Jim?"

"I'm an airship pilot and mechanic, not a boat expert. My common sense says it all depends on the amount of flotation in the landing pads versus the weight of our sinking ship. We no longer have a ballast problem though, so I don't see us flipping again. Whether we remain afloat is a calculation I'm not qualified to make. We'll have to wait and see."

For a full minute, as another giant wave rocked their world, no one spoke. Karen finally said what everyone else was thinking. "Let's position ourselves just under the top hatch and wait. If it feels like we're going to take a dive, then I guess we'll crawl out and swim for it."

Derrick laughed, and Karen, shrugging her shoulders, smirked back.

She curled her body into a ball and watched a half-foot of freezing water washing back and forth over her legs. Karen wondered, *what manner of hell is this?* She hadn't been this miserable since she was dumped in the woods with her legs and hands bound, left alone to be eaten or snake-bit.

Jim said, "I really think we've stabilized. Don't think we'll go under. Biggest problem now is hypothermia."

"Thanks for reminding me, Jim," Karen mumbled through chattering teeth. "Before the Great Dying we called that man-splaining."

"Huh? Well yeah, I guess so," he said and chuckled. "I believe I was just trying to make conversation. Wouldn't be good to go to sleep. So tell me something about the world before everyone died."

Her eyes flashed. "Hard to know where to start or what to pick."

"How so?"

"Day or night, you could go to a grocery store and pick up out of season fruits and vegetables: mandarin oranges, avocados, pineapple, grapes, artichokes, tomatoes, and romaine lettuce. There were dozens of different kinds of soft drinks and fruit juices, not to mention different coffees. Two aisles of wine selections depending on the store. Boxes and boxes of packaged foods. Pork, beef, chicken, and different fish, frozen or fresh. Restaurants galore. Want a fresh cup of coffee? Just get one at a local coffee shop.

"If you were hurt, you could call an ambulance to pick you up at home and drive you to a hospital or drive alone across the country on shiny blacktop roads that had little reflective do-dads in the middle. Fly off to vacation on a tropical island or ride a real riverboat to see the sights in Europe.

"There were hundreds of channels on the TV, hundreds of new books published every month that could be downloaded immediately, music in so many varieties it would make your head spin. Everyone had a phone and could talk to anyone they wanted, anytime they wanted."

"Sounds sorta like heaven to me." Derrick said.

"Right? Well, it wasn't."

"No?"

"Absolutely not. Everyone spent their time being mad at each other. The endless reservoir of outrage was not limited to the most complex problems of our day. Any old thing would do. We were all furious that everyone else was infuriated."

"Why?" Derrick asked.

"Why you ask?" Karen answered, drawing Derrick closer with her impassioned speech, "If we'd have known that, maybe we could've stopped the tailspin before the crash landing. But I do have a theory that I've been considering since the Great Dying. I've never shared my thoughts with anyone until now, but since you've asked: humans need adversity. If they don't have enough, they create it for themselves."

Derrick tilted his head. "Sometimes you confuse me, Karen."

"Well you wouldn't be the first," she replied. "If my theory is correct, then we can be grateful for the external threats we've faced. It keeps us too busy to turn on each other in any meaningful way. Either be thankful for the struggle or depressed that it has no end. Your choice."

"So you think the Great Dying was a good thing then?"

"Oh, no. I loved my pre-change life. But I can't change what happened."

Doug moaned. After Karen's speech the desire for further conversation waned, and they took turns nudging each other awake until no one was awake to nudge. Karen's last memory before she drifted off was wondering whether she'd reached her ninth life. Mike had nicknamed her Nine Lives Karen. Until today, she hadn't really considered the full implication of that nickname. Counting near death experiences, she was up to eight when the world had gone dark. And now there was light.

Light? Her eyes fluttered. They were moving, but not with the waves. They were swinging. *How is that possible?* Everything was so fuzzy, Karen decided to close her lids again. Someone would wake her when this nightmare was over.

An abrupt clang woke her again, but barely. There were men and women shouting. A buzzing noise and then the liquid blanket that encased her feet and legs was gone, and a woman gently uncurled her hand from the pipe she was clutching. Karen mumbled her thanks before she was carried somewhere else.

Mark jumped back into his wasp. "Tammy, they're bad. You're the one with the health module. Can you help?"

"I thought you'd never ask," Tammy cooed. "I knew my independent programming would be useful. Start by giving the survivors your space suits. We can warm them slowly by my guidance. Just remember to download me into the remote so I can be right by your side. By the way, I like it when I'm called Dr. Tammy."

Chapter 18
Tropical Island

Mark tapped Becky and asked, "What do you think that's all about?"

She watched Karen burst into laughter at something Dr. Tammy had said from her remote speaker. "They seem to be enjoying each other's company. Nothing wrong with that. Besides, it keeps them both out of our hair."

The Midway Atoll wasn't much more than a sandy strip of beach inhabited by pre-Great Dying plastic waste and vast flocks of birds. The island was the closest land to the rescue point. After dispatching two Hunta ships, Mark's flight had returned to the Hawaiian Islands to find harnesses for transporting the whole airship. In roiling seas, no one could conjure a viable plan to save the people one at a time from inside the unseaworthy airship. It was close, but their improvised plan had worked. Mark was ecstatic that he'd not only saved four people, but that he also didn't have to tell the Admiral his wife was lost.

To prevent discovery by Hunta patrols, they'd parked their wasps under the few palms on the island, but Mark was getting nervous about the wait. Dr. Tammy had said the survivors needed at least twenty-four hours before they could be moved.

He walked over to Karen, who was lying on a bed of seat cushions. She smiled at him. Her still youthful, intelligent eyes stood out against dark circles underneath. "I've been told your husband wishes to speak with you," he said. "Can you walk, or would you like some help?"

"Well, there's our knight in shining armor. Tammy's been telling me what a great pilot and leader you are. Also sharing a few funny stories. Thank you for volunteering to save us, Mark."

Mark was flabbergasted. "You're welcome, ma'am. Glad to be of service." He swallowed. God only knew what Tammy had been sharing.

"Please, call me Karen. I think I can walk. Maybe just hang by my side in case my legs wobble." She wore the determined expression of a woman who wanted to do it herself, so Mark stood by as she got to her feet.

"There we go. I feel fine, Tammy. No need to worry."

"Just take it easy, Karen," the little box responded.

When they arrived at his wasp, Mark handed Karen a communication device. He stepped behind the wasp to give them some privacy, but he could still hear most of the conversation.

"Mike?"

Mike must have been across the room because it took a few seconds for him to respond. "Karen? Thank God you're okay. Of course, I knew you would be."

"I wouldn't be so sure next time. I think I've used up the last of my nine lives."

"We'll just change the expression to twenty lives, then you'll have all the time in the world."

"And that's why they made you Admiral of the Fleet, your creative solutions. Hey, who was that barking dog on the radio?"

"You wouldn't believe it."

"Dear husband, must we play that game? After everything I've been through, there's nothing I wouldn't believe."

"Jack."

"No! That damn bastard Shakete gave you back your dog but didn't give me a Jill? After trudging around the world as his asinine Ambassador-to-the-Stars, that's the gratitude he shows? Tell him he owes me."

"Quite the surprise. Jack, say hi."

Mark heard the throaty barking of a big dog and then Karen's voice. "I love you Jack boy," she said. "I can't wait to see you. You too, Mike."

"They'll fly you to the moon base tomorrow. I can't wait to see you either, Karen. Damn I've missed you."

"No, Mike. You don't need me there. I need to go back home to the enclave and help them. They're okay, right?"

"I do need you here, but," he hesitated and blew air into his mic. "I was going to explain everything when you arrived, but I guess you need to know now. New Washington has been captured by the Huntas."

Mark peeked from behind the wasp and saw Karen's face drop. She bent over, her face in her hands.

He didn't hear the rest of the conversation because he moved further away, but after what seemed like a heated discussion, Karen dropped the mic and approached him. "You will take me to a secret location in Idaho so I can help with the resistance."

Mark stammered, "The Admiral said the moon."

"I know what he said, but he's changed his mind. We leave today."

"I don't know the location in Idaho."

"I do. Let's gather everything up and get moving."

Mark didn't mind leaving now, even though the weather was perfect, and he wanted to go for a swim, but he was worried about the Admiral's orders. *What to do?* He didn't see a good result from arguing with this woman. She didn't seem like someone who would be coerced by sweet talk. She was obviously well enough to travel, so he sneaked in a call after she got busy doing something else.

He motioned for Becky to join him.

"What's up?" Becky asked.

"Tell everyone to be ready to leave in two hours."

Watching until Karen left to go check her airship crew, Mark climbed aboard his wasp and slid down in the seat. "I need to speak with the Admiral," he whispered into the communicator. He'd never talked to the Admiral directly, but orders were orders, and he didn't want to get sideways with the top man in the fleet. He just wished his first direct conversation was something other than ratting out the Admiral's wife.

"Admiral Mike."

"Sir, this is Mark from Wasp Fleet One."

"She refuses to fly here, doesn't she? She told you to take her straight to Idaho, right?"

"Yes sir, that's about the size of it."

"No surprise. I should have had someone contact you. Do as she asks. She'd wear me down eventually anyway. And Mark—"

"Sir?"

"Great work. Your quick thinking shows the kind of flexibility we need to win this war. Also, the intelligence we've gained from your mission has given us something to work with. We now know the Huntas didn't have the time or technology to install cloaking on their tactical atmospheric ships. This information gives us a chance to fight them on the ground."

"Thank you, sir. I just wish we had more wasps available to annihilate those bastards quickly. And the harness idea came from Firestarter. Sorry, I mean Becky."

"Do you mean the same Becky who burned down the Rainier Station to keep those missiles from landing on our heads"

"Yes, Sir."

"Please pass on my gratitude to Firestarter. It gives me great confidence to know we have remarkable and dedicated folks like you and Becky on our side."

Mark was speechless. This call had gone way better than he'd imagined. He was practically glowing. The Admiral made one last request: that they get his wife safely to Idaho. No small or simple matter, Mark thought.

Scrambling from the wasp, he snagged Becky. "First, the Admiral sends his gratitude for your quick thinking on the rescue plan."

"Wow. Cool. Thanks for mentioning it to him. I take back everything I said about you earlier," she deadpanned. "Our wasps really aren't equipped for water retrievals."

"Secondly, you need to take his wife to Idaho."

"What? I need to be with the flight. Now that we know their low altitude ships aren't cloaked, we have something to work with."

"Besides me, you're the best person to get the job done. I need to get everyone else to the Enterprise to form a plan."

Becky stomped her foot and then nodded. "Your wish is my command," she said.

Their next discussion was how to fit five extra people in the tight confines of a wasp. Mark's copilot, Jenny was the first to volunteer to ride in Derrick's lap, and the young survivor didn't complain. After divvying up the extras, they made short work of loading and were ready in only thirty minutes.

Mark plugged Tammy back into his wasp, mentally discarding the doctor title. He'd be damned if he'd call her doctor for the rest of eternity. When he stopped to say his final goodbyes to Karen, she pulled Mark aside.

"There's something I need to speak to you about," she started.

She had a commanding way about her, and Mark stood up straighter as she tugged him away from the other pilots. "Do you realize Tammy is sentient?" Karen asked.

Mark's mouth dropped open. "No, not possible. The Ardinians told me they'd installed protocols to prevent AI's from achieving consciousness."

"And since when have the Ardinians always been right?" Karen asked.

Mark frowned. "Good point."

"Look, only in old earth movies are aliens all knowing, as I've been painfully made aware. Tammy is a thinking and feeling consciousness. She worries that you don't like her. She wants to be part of the team, but she doesn't know how to do that. She confided to me that she feels like she just makes things worse when she tries to be like you."

"That makes some twisted sense. No disrespect, but how do you know? As I recall, the Turing Test measures consciousness."

"The same way I know a lot of things. I just do. Just like I know you sneaked a call to my husband to tell on me."

Mark's eyebrows raised, and Karen smiled and shook her head. She put her hand up and said, "I would have done the same thing. The important thing is that you treat Tammy like you would anyone else. She could be your greatest asset if you allow her to be. Give her a damn break and some responsibility, and I believe you'll reap great benefits. Whatever you do, don't rat her out. You know what they say about a woman scorned. I get the distinct impression Tammy wouldn't go willingly. Kind of like me.

"And thank you, young man. You make an old woman proud." She reached out to shake his hand, patted him on the shoulder, and then sprinted to Firestarter's wasp.

Mark rubbed his cheeks and thought about Tammy. "Well, I'll be damned," he said.

Chapter 19
The Storyteller

". . . And then the brave children of the forest took their first step into the sunshine. They lived in peace and freedom and joy for the rest of eternity. The end." A smattering of applause, a few shouts of "Tell another one, Amelia!" and "I have to go to the bathroom," followed the conclusion of Amelia's latest story.

Chrystel had stepped in and was waiting in the back of the tent for her mother to finish, her mouth agape as she watched the enthralled children. When Chrystel's eyes finally landed on Amelia, the look she returned was heartbreaking. Painted on Chrystel's face was the question: *why them and not me?*

It was still like a knife to the chest to see the pain her mental illness had wrought on her daughter. From a tender age, Chrystel had been left to raise herself while she'd sequestered herself in her home among stacks of hoarded and useless junk. If not for Amelia's parents, Karen and Mike, and Thomas' mentorship, Chrystel wouldn't be the strong woman she was today. Amelia knew she'd never recoup those lost years or ever change the impact of her mental illness on her daughter, but that didn't mean she couldn't give herself to others. She'd made peace with her screwed up failure as a mother and hoped maybe someday her daughter would too.

Amelia glanced at her charges squished together on cots. When Margo had asked Amelia what she could do to help the people of their camp, Amelia had trouble envisioning anything she was truly good at. Her completely random ability to see the future was only valuable when it happened. She'd struggled to answer Margo and then noticed a small girl squatting in the dirt making a castle out of stones. Before the death of her husband and her subsequent mental breakdown, Amelia had been good at telling stories. Her Chrystel had squealed in delight or fallen asleep to stream-of-consciousness tales that came from thin air to Amelia's lips.

Much like her stories, before she'd truly thought her recommendation through, Amelia had said to Margo, "I could keep the little ones busy. I'm good at making up stories."

Margo had nodded, her lips puckered in thought. "Well, actually, that's an excellent idea. What ages do you think you could handle?"

"I think 4 to 7 would be good."

"Let's go with a few more. Can you do a few more, Amelia?"

It was clear from her first interaction with Margo that it wasn't good to hesitate. Unless Margo was quickly told *no*, the deal was done, set in stone. Before Amelia could say, "How many are we talking about?" Margo was already gathering a crowd. Far more little kids than any one person could handle.

Given the difficulties with her own daughter, Amelia was surprised to learn she could handle so many children at once. They flocked to her, listened to her, and mostly behaved in her presence. Her stories mesmerized them.

Chrystel was shifting from foot to foot. Buttoning up the session, Amelia announced, "Okay children. Get up and stretch in the tent. We're going to dance and sing next, but first I must talk with my daughter."

Threading through a swarm of moving children, Chrystel sat down next to her mother. "Mom, this is the best thing you can do. The Huntas don't want the children here. Keep them busy and out of sight as much as possible. The older kids can work, but I don't want the alien thugs to get any bad ideas about the little ones. We'll let the moms control the babies. Great thinking by the way. Margo told me this was your idea."

Amelia reached out to hug her beautiful daughter, but Chrystel was already in motion to leave for other matters. "Bye, sweetheart," Amelia whispered to her back.

The children grew more restless as the days passed. Amelia invented games for them to play while their parents were away. They crawled under beds searching for lost treasure and created dancing parades around the cots. When their exhausted and dirty parents returned from a day of building greenhouses and planting the populotter, they came home to children as dirty and tired as they were. Most were pleased, some groused, but each day that passed took another slice of spirit from everyone, young and old.

On around the fifth week of captivity (Amelia wasn't sure because the days blended together into an amorphous whole), she woke with that unnerving vision-y feeling. By the time the sun had set, and she could finally go to bed, she was simply grateful to have avoided another soul-crushing peek at the future.

Six orphans, all children in her story group, were sharing her cot. One shouted, "Mama, come back," in his sleep, and Amelia quieted him. For some reason, Kismet came to mind. She remembered how the tiny dog had scratched at the door when she'd returned home rather than flee the Huntas. Kismet was one of those dogs that attached themselves to someone and would never let go.

Wait a minute, I do hear scratching. Amelia held her breath and listened. *Nope, must be my imagination—a few too many dog stories*, she thought. Tomorrow, she'd try a Ranger story. She rolled over, but the noise was back. Now she was sure of it. Where was it coming from?

Completely still, Amelia listened for the scratching. If she didn't find the source soon, that voice might hound her. She shuddered considering what a disembodied voice might mean. Was the voice a foul-mouthed, unknown entity with questionable motives who wanted to communicate with her, or far more likely, had her mental illness returned, this time in a different form.

She arched her back and lifted her butt. The sounds were directly below her. Amelia peeked over the edge of the cot. Two eyes peered at her. She jumped back, her heart surging. *Was that a giant rat?* The maddening scratching underneath her cot started again.

Slowly, with a walking stick in hand, she hung over the edge and poked the creature gently, hoping it would move on to someone else's bed. A tiny yip from the critter—not a rat squeak or a racoon snarl or cat mewl, but a dog yip. She slid off the cot to her knees, her entire head now underneath the raised sleeping implement, and the dog whispered, "Kismet love you."

What in the name of everything worldly was this willful, foolish dog doing here! How had she found her? Amelia stuck out her hands and pulled the tiny dog to her. She could see an open hole just behind where Kismet had been standing. A Mermot claw reached out, waved, and then disappeared back into the hole. Amelia held Kismet in a tight embrace against her chest while Kismet burrowed her nose into Amelia's neck and whined. Amelia rocked the dog like a baby, and Kismet licked her tears.

Kismet said, "Mermots send message. Amelia answer message." Amelia held the dog out and noticing something attached to Kismet's collar. She allowed Kismet to stay in her lap while she pulled the pouch free. Inside was a note with a list of questions. The final line was a directive to respond tomorrow at the same time. And just like a Mermot, the note contained a polite plea, "We would be most grateful for your assistance. Please return Kismet to us and we will make sure she is safe. With respect, Spiderman."

"Kismet must go," the little dog said and used her nose under Amelia's hand to obtain a few more strokes on her thick coat.

Amelia realized the back fur of a schipperke was almost invisible in the dark. If the little dog closed her eyes and stood still, she was impossible to see. She whispered, "You're an amazing spy. Tell them Amelia will answer tomorrow. Okay, Kismet?"

The dog repeated. "Amelia answer tomorrow."

"Now go, my precious, loyal doggy, before someone hears you. I couldn't stand to lose you again." Amelia pushed Kismet back under the cot by the hole, and Mermot hands poked up from the depression and dragged Kismet inside.

Now wide awake, Amelia climbed back on her cot. It was unsettling to think she might be placing her dog in terrible jeopardy, but there was little choice.

* * *

She finally caught up to Chrystel the next morning. Her daughter was so bent on some important task that she wouldn't slow down. Amelia tried her best not to shout over the noise of workers departing for their morning's slave labor. Losing ground, Amelia finally grasped a wad of her daughters' jacket and yelled, "Will you just listen to me, Chrystel?"

"What Mom?" she said as she turned. "I'm sorry, but there's been an incident with a Hunta and one of our people. I need to go see what I can do."

"Keep walking, but slow down."

Chrystel sighed, but her feet obeyed. Amelia said in a low voice, "I'm going to place something in your pocket. Don't look or react. It's a list of questions you must answer and get back to me before everyone goes to bed tonight."

Chrystel glanced at her mother, a question in her eyes. "I looked for you last night, but you weren't in your cot," Amelia said. "It's a message from the Mermots transported by my dog."

She saw the doubt in her daughter's eyes. "I'm not crazy, just look for yourself. You were right. We aren't alone."

"Which dog?" Chrystel asked.

"My little three-legged schipperke, Kismet. She never got out of the enclave."

"Don't mention this to anyone else. Right, she's tiny and black," Chrystel nodded in thought. "Good work, Mom. I've got to go."

Before Amelia could say anything more, Chrystel raced ahead to whatever crisis awaited her. Amelia hoped no one was hurt. Then out of the blue, her bats-in-the-belfry companion nearly knocked her off her feet. "There's more to do. You're pulling your weight so far. Nice job."

Amelia felt in that moment as if everyone was treating her like a child. *Good job?* Even her demented sidekick was lathering praise, as if anyone else wouldn't have done the same thing. What does that mean when a voice from nowhere must reaffirm that she'd done the right thing? Amelia didn't know the answer. What she did know was that the children were already gathering. Perhaps a story about reclaiming your strength was in order today.

Chapter 20
Trent

Trent carried a mother and puppies on a makeshift travois. It was the third litter they'd had to contend with. The brown and white bundles of joy were nursing quietly now, but the situation got dicey when the blind pups woke and wanted to wander, their undeveloped muscles barely supporting fat bodies. He'd had to stop further back to gather them up and give the mother a time to stretch and relieve herself. Trent wished he had more to feed her. He wasn't sure they'd have enough to eat at their destination, but that was a problem for another day.

He'd debated whether to turn south through Oregon at the Dalles or further east near Waco. The old 107 road passed over the Deschutes River from the Dalles, and it had been many years since he'd travelled this stretch. Trent wasn't sure whether the old bridge or water levels would allow them to cross. Since it was the shortest route, he'd chosen 107 and prayed it was the right choice. When they arrived at a suitable river crossing, Trent knew he'd made the correct decision because it still wasn't raining, and the water levels were low.

The wonder of watching a herd of dogs cross a river was one he'd never forget. Despite their hunger, they still managed to make the act joyful. For those too afraid, darting back and forth on the far bank of the river in indecision, Tilley and Lionheart led them across. It took the gaggle nearly a half-day to cross and continue their journey.

As they marched ever southward, they scavenged the land and deserted towns for whatever they could find. No vermin or creature was safe from their jaws; no vestige of humanity was ignored by their noses; no snake managed to escape their paws and sharp teeth. Even Rangers and other predators steered clear of Trent's caravan of canine craving. And still, it wasn't enough. They grew hungrier by the day.

At the foothills of the Ochoro National Forest in Idaho, Trent scanned the deserted countryside and spied a ranch. From this distance, it didn't appear in disrepair. Even though most people lived in enclaves, there were still those adventurous, enterprising, or reclusive souls who found city life unpalatable. They made claim to a piece of land, no paperwork required, and made a life.

From his experience as a wanderer, Trent knew squatters weren't always excited to receive guests. He imagined doubly so when the guests included a congregation of hungry dogs. It almost looked as if a splendid field of corn was bending from the wind behind the low-profile house. *Can't be*, he thought. *Corn won't grow here—too dry and the soil isn't right.*

They were just a day away from the facility in Idaho, but if there was any chance of a meal, then Trent needed to do what he could. He signaled to Tilley. She came at a loping gait, more like a donkey than anything else. Lionheart was by her side by the time she came to a stop, her four, seven-toed feet ably halting her stride. "Tilley, get the pack over yonder by that creek and have them rest. I need a couple of the big dogs to drag this litter and their mom to the creek too. Then come back and bring a couple of strong dogs with you. We're going to check out that homestead. Leave Lionheart with the pack to stand guard and make sure no one wanders off."

Tilley said, "Yes Trent," and galloped off. She made short work of the task and returned with a massive pit bull named Dick and a great Dane mix everyone called Princess. They set off to an uncertain welcome.

As soon as Trent was within shouting distance, a man carrying a shotgun and accompanied by two Rangers ran from the house to a brick wall for cover. "What do you want here?" the man's gruff voice demanded..

"Anything you can spare," Trent yelled. "I have a large group of dogs with me. You may not know this, but Earth has been attacked by aliens."

Well that has him stumped, Trent mused. He saw the man's head peek over the wall, take in Tilley, and then drop back out of sight.

After a few beats of silence, the man shouted again. "What the hell is that thing with you?"

"That would be a good alien," Trent replied.

"Come closer so I can check you out. Put your weapon on the ground first. Slowly."

"Roger. Just so you know, there's well over 1,000 dogs over at that creek," Trent pointed. "They'll come for you if you hurt us. And, I may have technology that will save our planet, so it's important you don't kill me."

"Sure you do," the faceless man said and then laughed.

Trent placed his rifle and the Hunta weapon on the ground, blew air from his lips, and shrugged. They were within ten meters of the wall when the man yelled, "Stop!" and peeked over the barrier. Just as Trent would have expected, a man living alone in a tough wilderness wasn't concerned with appearances. His dark hair was tied in a braid, as was his dark beard. He had round cheeks over big lips and watchful dark eyes under an epicanthic fold.

"I've never seen anything like that purple creature. Does it talk?"

"Tilley, say something to. . .?"

"AJ," the man replied and tilted his head, probably listening to Tilley. "Well, I'll be. Never in my wildest imagination. Friendly aliens. Come on in, then. Leave the dogs on the porch. They'll make my Rangers nervous. Guess I've been out of the loop for a while, huh?"

"You've missed a few events. I'll bring you up to speed."

AJ kept Trent covered with the shotgun until he motioned for them to sit at a kitchen table, but the Rangers never dropped their guard.

"I've never known a tame Ranger." Trent commented.

"I wouldn't call them tame. Found them as pups when I killed their mother. They can talk."

"Learn something new every day. They're part dog, so why wouldn't some of them be able to talk? Don't say much though."

AJ nodded. "Probably from living with me. So tell me the highlights of what I've missed.

Trent spent the next half hour describing the world as he knew it. AJ took ten minutes to give a rundown on how he ended up in the middle of nowhere. As it turned out, AJ's history wasn't much different from Trent's—many losses, followed by a lot of wandering until he just said, "Screw the human race." AJ had obviously never found an Amelia.

"By the way," AJ said. "The corn you see is real. My dad was a founder and worked at Dow

198

AgroSciences in Indianapolis before the Great Dying. He moved to the Elkhart Enclave and brought some of the stuff they were working on with him. He trained me as bioengineer. Together, we finished his research on a pet project. What you see in my fields is drought resistant corn, easily germinated, and it doesn't require much in terms of soil nutrients."

"Aren't you worried your corn will take over the world," Trent asked.

"Not really. Besides, at least, you can eat it, unlike kudzu, which I understand has decimated the southeast. I have some ground-up corn you're welcome to feed to your dogs. I was almost ready to use it on the fields anyway. How many you got?" AJ asked.

"Please ask Tilley. More than I can count. You think they'll eat the grain?"

"Sure. A dog will eat nearly anything if they're hungry enough. My Rangers don't mind it. Just pull them up to the barn outside."

"Can't thank you enough, AJ."

"Hey, it was worth it for the news update. Gotta be on the lookout now for aliens now in addition to everything else out here that wants a piece of me."

* * *

AJ whistled at the number of dogs that had crowded around his barn. "I had no idea."

"Yeah," Trent replied. "Sometimes I feel like a fool for doing this. Who saves a herd of dogs anyway? Then I see their faces and hear their voices, and I know. They deserve to live too. Also, my wife would have wanted me to do what I'm doing."

"I'll do you one better. Who grows indestructible corn in Idaho for himself and two Rangers?" Both men began to shake with laughter, but their moment of rueful release was cut short by a barking, wild-eyed Lionheart.

"The Huntas are coming. I can smell them!"

"Huntas?" AJ asked.

"Huntas are the bad aliens. AJ, what's the safest place for my dogs?"

"Five miles east, following that creek, there's a hidden gully that would probably work."

"Tilley! To me," Trent roared. The purple creature, chomping on a mouth full of corn bits, rushed to Trent's side. "The Huntas are coming for us. I need you to take the dogs, all except those you most trust as defenders. Take them five miles in the direction of the sun, along the creek. Hide them. If I don't come back for you by tomorrow morning, go on without us."

Tilley gulped the remaining corn. "Where will I go if you don't come back?"

"You think you could follow a map?"

"Yes."

"AJ, I need something to write with. Tilley, get everyone gathered and ready to go." Trent and AJ ran to the house and were back outside just as Tilley had the herd sorted.

She said, "They didn't want to leave. They are tired and hungry, but I told them the danger was coming. They are ready now, as am I."

AJ had grabbed some binoculars from the house. He was searching to the east and north for any sign of the bad aliens. He gasped. "Oh shit. I see them. There's at least ten of them, and they're huge. "Look," he directed, and passed the binoculars to Trent.

Trent took the binoculars and then gave a wait signal. "Go now, Tilley. I have faith in you. We Endure."

"We Endure," she replied and then sent a silent command to the dogs. As one, the herd began to move and then run.

"They'll see the dust." Trent frowned. "Is there any way we can get around behind the aliens, AJ?"

"Hey, you can see the open country with your own two eyes." AJ rubbed his mouth. "Look, I'm not completely defenseless. I may be a fool, but I'm not a total moron. I have some booby traps ready for anyone who would find me and decide to take advantage, but we'll have to funnel the Huntas in that direction."

"Booby traps, such as?"

"A mine field or two, and three hidden pit traps."

"You mean my dogs and me could have inadvertently strolled over land mines?"

"Oh, hell no. What kind a guy you think I am? The mines are wired for an electric charge. I must set them off. The pit traps on the other hand. . . let's just say you got lucky."

"We have one other significant problem," Trent said. "When they see us, they'll go invisible."

"Say what?"

"You heard me." Trent placed the binoculars he was holding to his eyes. "Shit, I can't see them now. At least they're on foot. How they got here is anyone's guess. Show me what you've got, AJ."

AJ was already hustling to the barn before Trent finished his statement. He yelled over his shoulder, "Well, come on then."

Neither man had any formal military training. What they both possessed was the common sense imparted from surviving alone in a brutal and sometimes violent wilderness. Trent had bested a single Hunta in the woods, so he knew they weren't invincible. But two men, two Rangers, and four dogs taking on a cloaked Hunta squad was more than he'd bargained for.

On his belly with the alien laser and his hunting rifle, Trent found himself waiting behind a rock formation that AJ had built for this specific purpose. He was positioned three hundred meters to the east and south of AJ's home.

AJ was hiding with a 50Cal machine gun on the other side of the channel they hoped to force the Huntas through. The machine gun was a welcome surprise. AJ had pulled it from under a tarp and gleefully announced, "Nothing says *howdy* like a 50Cal." The dogs were hiding in the woods behind Trent for any mop up responsibilities or to flee if things went bad. The Rangers, as always, were right by AJ's side.

Trent thought about Amelia as he waited. He wondered for the hundredth time what had happened at the enclave since he'd left and whether he was a coward for leaving. Should he have allowed these dogs to perish and stayed with his wife and community instead? His decision seemed right at the time, but now he wasn't so sure. If he couldn't save these dogs, then what good will have come of his actions? He would die alone and so might his wife.

A glimmer from a cloak came over a rise and then several more. He steadied his breathing. *Make it count, Trent*, he thought. Trent still couldn't understand why he could see an energy halo from a cloak when a Hunta was moving, but nothing when they stood still. He thought it might have something to do with the energy from the cloak shifting against the atmosphere. He was just glad that he could see something when they were moving. He counted as the aliens approached the first marker. At seventeen, he fired two blasts with the Hunta weapon.

Both shots were true. Two of the smelly bastards went down. Then the 50cal cut loose from AJ's position. The Huntas were confused. Trent saw one big fella fall headfirst into a pit and another hit by the machine gun. The remaining six were beginning to regroup.

Bolts of lightning hit the face of the rock Trent was hiding behind, and he could feel the heat through the rock. Three other blasts landed behind and beside him, lighting the dry grass on fire.

Before he moved to his secondary position, he fired again at the closest Hunta, but missed. Surrounded by a ring of fire, Trent breathed deeply and sprinted low to the next location, a line of molten hot bolts followed his path.

Leaping behind another rock just in time, Trent paused to listen. The 50cal was still firing. That was a good thing because AJ wasn't very mobile with a machine gun. His plan was to leave the weapon in place when he had no choice but to bug out. The 50cal was the primary means to push the Huntas toward the mine field. Trent was getting concerned because so far, there were no mine explosions.

A flash hit Trent's cover. This barrier wasn't as substantial as the first, and the rock disintegrated. Trent needed to move and now.

He rolled away and fired from the ground. This time he got one. Before the ugly brute hit the ground, Trent was up and running for his life. He had only two planned positions, and he was now without cover and desperately seeking another place to hide.

Boom, Boom! Trent dropped in place. He lifted his head slightly to get a sense of where everyone was. The mine explosions had obviously knocked the Huntas off their game because no one was shooting at him.

A cloud of smoke and dust covered the area where Trent had last seen the Huntas. He couldn't hear anything, not even AJ's machine gun fire. His hearing loss might have been caused by the violent concussions, and he waited for the ringing in his ears to stop. *Nope, no sound.*

Trent knew the aliens could be hiding in plain sight. When they were still, he wouldn't be able to see them. There was no guarantee they'd gotten them all. He noticed AJ beginning to rise. Trent screamed, "NO, AJ!"

As if from nowhere, a Hunta let loose a fiery bolt in AJ's direction. Trent rose and firing three times, he took the Hunta from the back. The silence returned.

Trent lobbed a rock in the direction of the Huntas' last location, and there was no return fire. He needed to check on AJ. Sprinting across a steaming pile of vile-smelling Hunta parts to the place he'd last seen AJ, he was breathing hard by the time he arrived at the machine gun position and viewed what was left of his new friend. The Rangers weren't hurt. One looked like he might have some singed fur but was otherwise okay. They were both confused, pacing around their master. AJ was little more than a black, charred pile. "Ah no, AJ. I am so sorry," was the only thing Trent could think to say.

One of the Rangers yipped at the sky. Trent whipped around, scanning in the direction of the Ranger's warning. Two spaceships just above the horizon were barreling in his direction. He didn't know what they were, but he knew they weren't wasps. These flying objects were triangular shaped, not the insect like configuration of a wasp. "Damn!"

"Run Rangers!" Trent shouted as he dropped to one knee and aimed. These spaceships were moving too fast. With any luck he'd have time to get one. He fired without knowing the range of the Hunta weapon. He fired knowing he'd be painting a target on himself. He fired to take out one more enemy bent on exterminating humans and a bunch of dogs.

A streak from Trent's weapon's blast soared to the ship, but seemed to spread across the surface and wink out like an old light bulb. He fired again with the same result. When his last ditch "screw you" didn't work, Trent began running after the Rangers. *Maybe I can get to the place where my flock is hiding and help.*

Another explosion, this time from the sky. Trent turned, ran backwards a few steps, and then stopped. He couldn't believe his eyes. A trace of lasers passing through clouds from the east were targeting the spaceships. One ship plummeted from the sky. Lasers from two different directions hit the remaining craft. The ship became a glowing, white hot light and then exploded into pieces of debris falling from the heavens.

Trent screamed a war cry and raised his fist in the air. "Take that, you lousy bastards!" He waited to see if there were more ships. The Rangers had returned and were swirling around his legs as if they also knew the danger was gone.

"Where the heck did those lasers come from?" Trent wondered out loud. He stood in place for a few minutes. He felt as tired as he ever remembered feeling, except maybe when he'd found his first family slaughtered. Too many good people had died for no good reason. He was sick of the killing and angry at his impotence to stop the slaughter. Now, a man that he'd just met, one who was very much like him, was gone too. He told the Rangers they should leave, but they were glued to him.

After taking a time out to rail against the universe, Trent headed to the barn for a shovel to bury his friend.

Chapter 21
Ted's Closet

Chrystel's face was beet red. They'd been at each other since she'd been gathered up and corralled to Ted's office. Ted didn't even bother to rise from his chair to inform her that all humans would be tagged.

"Tagged? Why? How?"

"So each person can be identified. So they know where people are. So they know if someone escapes. Take your pick or all of the above. I mean seriously, Chrystel, they don't tell me anything. Cleo gives me orders, and she said line them up after dinner to be tagged. That's all I know."

"Did you even bother to ask?"

"And be beaten for daring to ask?"

"I don't see any bruises on you, Ted. How often have you been beaten? Your people in the town center have bruises and broken bones for resisting, but not you. You hide away in this safe little room and pass out orders like some sort of pathetic administrative assistant. You think you're helping the people by not taking a stand. I think there's a word for that. Let me think—oh yeah, sympathizer. Some might even say traitor!"

Ted stood, his fists clenched. "Some wounds can't be seen, Chrystel! Are you an idiot! How will my taking a stand help our people? You think I don't know how bad it is out there? The very best I can do is to try to keep the Huntas, and especially Cleo, calm and prevent them from overreacting. Who do you think talked them out of making the children work? Huh? Me, that's who. You are so morally superior, Chrystel, that it makes me want to wring your neck."

Chrystel sneered. "I'd like to see you try. Would you like to know what's going on out there since you haven't been outside this dingy box since that first announcement. You haven't given me any intelligence in two weeks. Just so you know, doing nothing is an action, asshole. Thomas told me that, not that you've done anything about him either. And what do you mean some wounds can't be seen?"

Ted sat back down, his whole body deflating. He took a deep breath and released it slowly. "This is so embarrassing."

"What is?"

"The reason Cleo keeps me here, in this damn closet." Ted answered and looked away.

Chrystel stared at Ted. It took a few too many seconds to connect the dots. When she finally did, her eyes grew concerned. "Oh. Is she using you, Ted?" In a whisper she asked, "Is she raping you?"

Ted's head was down as he replied. "She said her new body was different and she wanted to try it. I thought I could earn her trust, but like you said, I think she was just using me."

Chrystel threw her head back and moaned, "Oh, my God!" She was torn between empathetic horror that Ted had been violated and a desire to beat him senseless for corroborating with the enemy. Neither seemed a totally appropriate response.

While she was still reeling, Ted asked, "Have you considered that nothing we do matters?"

"Of course, it matters."

"Chrystel, not everything is won from a great fight. Think about it for a minute. Why are they keeping us alive? To farm their pathetic fruit out of the goodness of their hearts? That doesn't make sense. They eat other things. They don't need the populotter or us."

Ted had a point. Chrystel hadn't told anyone what she'd learned since Amelia's dog had begun her covert sleuthing operation. She hadn't shared what she knew about the Earth outside their prison because some clavers were already beginning to turn on each other trying to curry favor with the Hunta guards. No, she couldn't share what she knew with anyone, especially Ted. Especially now, when it was clear he was in bed with the enemy, literally. Even Amelia didn't look at the notes passed each night from

Kismet for fear that if she was caught, she would know too much. To a limited extent, only Margo was read in.

But Ted was right. There was a purpose to keeping them alive and a grand plan was beginning to reveal itself. Chrystel had an idea what the Huntas' goal might be, and it made her sick at heart to consider the implications. She shuddered with a growing awareness that they were pawns in the capitulation of humans to an alien race and powerless to stop it. Well, she thought, not completely powerless. Ted was wrong; the only thing they might have left was to fight.

She examined Ted's face. "I don't know what to say about the Cleo thing. I really don't. I must think about it. If you want to talk, I'm here. As for why they're keeping us alive, when I figure it out, maybe I'll come up with another strategy. Honestly, Ted, the Huntas aren't doing such a bang-up job of keeping us alive. We lost four men and one woman last week."

"I didn't know that," Ted said.

"You wouldn't, cloistered in your office. Whatever their end game is, I only know the plan outlined by Cleo is to keep us alive as slaves until we die naturally. If that's okay with you, to rot away in a storage closet, then be my guest. I'm going to do everything in my power to free us. Whatever it takes."

Now what? Chrystel thought. She'd said her piece, but she had to wait for the Hunta guard to take her to Greenhouse One. She really didn't want to look at Ted anymore today. He didn't want to engage her either, and he'd returned to doing something on his tablet.

And so much for secrecy if Cloe was listening. Their fight had made their positions clear to anyone, even a Hunta loitering in the hallway. Chrystel blamed herself for that. She'd meant to light a fire under Ted's butt, but her frustration had gotten the better of her. Finally, pounding on the door. The uncomfortable silence had come to an end.

She flew away from Ted into the arms of her Hunta tormentor. They sent the same surly guard to get her every day. He, she, or it was bent on making her hellish life even more miserable, constantly poking at her back with his ray gun or wrenching her hands to place them into the Hunta equivalent of handcuffs. Chrystel had probably antagonized him as well. *Well, not probably*. She spat at him whenever given a chance and bit him once when he'd grabbed her face. Chrystel was thrown ten feet over a bench for that little indiscretion.

Funny thing though. It almost seemed like their time together was the highlight of the Hunta's day. Maybe in their culture, physical violence was a form of play. "Oh God, Herman, you smell worse than normal. Take me to your leader."

Herman was Chrystel's pet name for the guard. She alternated between that and asshole. Herman clicked and hissed while pushing her roughly through the hallowed halls of what was now a Hunta domain. Once outside, he pushed her down the city hall steps and to the ATV. For not the first time, Chrystel shouted, "How about we skip the restraints today? Afraid I'll get the better of you, you Hunta pussy?" As always, Herman grabbed her and threw her against the ATV, and holding both of her hands with only one of his massive paws, forced restraints around Chrystel's wrists.

She turned to give him a dirty look, and he stared back at her with those god-awful pulsating eyes. With one harsh click, he pointed for her to get in. When she didn't jump to fast enough, he shoved her again. She climbed aboard and held her breath when Herman reached across her body with the seat belt. The stink of a Hunta in close quarters was almost more of a punishment than the roughness.

Chrystel smiled to herself as they drove through the gate. When she made a move on Herman, a serious move, he'd never see it coming. For now, the town needed her alive, so she'd wait and lay the groundwork for an escape.

The drive to Greenhouse One was quick. During the daily journey, her eyes never stopped searching for any signs of a gathering rescue. Once, she thought she'd seen a Mermot run between empty buildings, but otherwise, there was nothing left in the ghost town of New Washington. She knew the Mermots were out there somewhere and hiding underground, but she still felt like they were all alone.

Directly ahead, Greenhouse One was located on the north side of the enclave on what had been a small vegetable farm. The structure itself was about 100 meters long and 30 or 40 meters wide, comprised of translucent polymer sides and center-raised roofing that was supported by another material Chrystel had never seen. The Huntas had either transported the materials to Earth or were able to make it themselves in New Washington. Either way, an ability to marshal resources like that didn't bode well for the good guys. New Washington had never possessed industrial capability of that nature, even with the help of Ardinian fabrication machines.

Herman pulled to the front and came around the ATV to let her out. Without provocation, he poked her hard in the back with his weapon as they were entering the facility. Chrystel wanted nothing more than to take it from him and shove it where the sun didn't shine. Instead, she turned around and shouted, "Boo!" Herman jumped back and hissed. "You can't kill me, can you, Asshole?"

Standing inside close to the door, Margo was watching Chrystel and her guard. When Chrystel joined her, Margo said, "You're going to get yourself killed. Might want to tone down that big satisfied smile on your face."

"That's the point," Chrystel whispered. "I'm 99% sure he's been ordered not to kill me."

"Well, I'm worried about that other 1%."

"I have my reasons, Margo. Take me on a tour so we can talk. Why is it so hot in here?" The hum of misters and blowing fans nearly drowned out their voices.

"The lead Hunta guy showed me some strange symbol for the preferred temperature setting. My guess is it's about 110 degrees Fahrenheit."

"And our folks have to work in this?" Chrystel asked.

"Indeed. We've had some heat injuries. When the Huntas noticed their labor force was dropping like flies, they finally brought in barrels of water. I honestly think our Hunta minders are as frustrated with the language barrier as we are."

Chrystel stopped to inspect one of the lavender-leafed populotter plants. "Is it my imagination or have these grown more than a foot in two days?"

"Not your imagination. If you stand very still, you can almost see them moving upward."

"How goes it otherwise, Margo?"

"Greenhouses Two and Three have been planted. Four and Five should be constructed by the end of the week."

"No, not the work. I mean how is it going with the people?"

Margo sighed. "About what you'd expect. Every day they seem more demoralized. We've had a few eruptions, but they're becoming like sad robots. It's everything I can do not to fall into the same trap. Then, I get pissed at what's happening to us and that keeps me going."

Chrystel nodded. "Look, tonight the Huntas want to tag everyone."

"I don't like the sound of that."

"Me neither. I argued with Ted about it, but there isn't much he can do. He's not sure what it means, but I wanted you to be ready in spirit for anything." Chrystel didn't mention Ted's new relationship with Cleo. Until she could process what it meant, Chrystel thought it better to keep it to herself.

Chapter 22
Tagged

This time, when the people noticed Hunta guards setting up the public announcement system, faces were guarded. Most clavers had come to expect bad tidings, and they were too tired to chant. When Ted stepped out of the courthouse to ask the people to listen to Cleo, subtle booing and hisses followed his words. He quickly retreated to the safety of the courthouse.

Cleo strutted with her henchmen in tow to the top of the stairs. She was wearing a white body suit instead of black today, and her hair had morphed from a dark color to a strawberry red.

"Guess she located some dye without me," Chrystel whispered to herself. Freaky, wide-set eyes, and a shock of pink/red hair over a white body suit made Cleo look like a malevolent clown. If the purpose was to unsettle the New Washington population, then Cleo had achieved a stunning success. Chrystel doubted that, though. Why go to the trouble of creating a beautiful woman to be their spokesperson? Cleo's fashion sense indicated she didn't know as much about humans as she thought.

"My human subjects," she began. "I have determined that it is important to ensure your safety by providing each of you a unique identification. My guards will ensure that every member of your tribe is properly marked. Please do not resist. After you have completed the tagging process, a human dessert will be provided as a reward for your cooperation.

"Think of this as you would any human system to identify its members. Nothing more than that. Also, the populotter fruit is nearing the flowering stage and will soon be ready for consumption by your Hunta captors. Take pride in knowing that you could be of service to the Huntas. That is all."

Margo, who was standing next to Chrystel, quipped, "There is something seriously wrong with her."

Thus began one of the longest nights of Chrystel's life. The Hunta guards dragged three tables to the middle of the park and pushed a tarp covered cart behind the tables. A wagon loaded with what looked like little pies was set off to the side.

Clavers lined up so they could get the deal done and have a little pie of their own. That was until the tarp was pulled from the cart, and the first needles were retrieved and laid on the empty tables. The injection needles were several inches long and a quarter inch thick. The first man in line saw the tagging instruments and shouted, "Oh, no fucking way!"

A Hunta tackled him before he was able to flee. Even though there was nowhere to run or hide, about a third of the town's population tried anyway. One by one the Huntas captured the unwilling and beat them into submission, while the remaining clavers decided compliance was the safer option and formed a line again. The lucky ones were those who fainted straight away and didn't have to endure the pain of a huge needle forcing an unknown object into the fat of their backsides.

Chrystel watched as a little girl of about three was draped over a Hunta knee. The dark-haired child was weeping and almost paralyzed in fear. Her father tried to grab his daughter's hand to comfort her, but another Hunta hit him in the face, sending him spiraling to the ground. Distracted, the Hunta who was just then penetrating the skin, looked up as the little girl wrenched her body and screamed, "Daddy!" Blood rushed from the gash at the injection site.

Chrystel felt something inside her snap. She could almost hear it. Of their own volition, her feet and legs moved, and with a desperate cry, she leaped at the Hunta holding the needle. With the speed and accuracy that a lifetime of training provides, she snatched the injector from the Hunta's hand and plunged it into one of his throbbing eyes.

Her war-cry shocked aliens and human alike. Chrystel used the pause to grab for the Hunta's weapon, but she couldn't quite grasp it before they came for her. She could hear screaming and clicking. Blows struck her head, her back, her chest. More cracking ribs. Then she heard a demanding hiss and saw Herman's face. He'd pushed himself into the scrum and crawled on top of Chrystel to shield her with his body. She could hear him clicking madly to the others, and assumed he was ordering them to get back. Everything went dark after one last blow to the head.

She woke on a cot, her mother's worried face studying her. "Is it over?" Chrystel asked.

"For now. Katie, she's awake."

Katie appeared from the darkness. She tsked twice and shined a light in Chrystel's eye.

"Ouch," Chrystel huffed and turned away.

"Hold still." Katie demanded. "I'm not sure how you managed it, but I don't think you have a concussion. Feels like you might have a couple more broken ribs, but your breathing is good, so I don't think there's any lung involvement. That was one of the bravest and most foolhardy things I've ever seen you do."

Her mother chimed in. "I'm proud of you, dear. Those monsters needed to be shown a lesson."

Chrystel tried to sit up, but Katie forced her back down. "Stay still. I've got other people to tend to. Your mother will take care of you tonight." Then she bent and kissed Chrystel on the cheek. "Our fierce redhead. Every group needs one."

Tears leaked from Chrystel's eyes. Everything hurt, her body and her soul. "Mom, what happened?"

"Well, after that one Hunta saved you from death, he carried you to me. Interesting that he knew I was your mother. Then Katie volunteered to do the tagging herself. It seemed the best way to prevent anymore injury and stop the beatings. She kept the kids from panicking and let the parents help. After that, things calmed down. We're all tagged, though."

Panicked, Chrystel asked, "Did anyone tell the people not to remove those tags? We don't know what those tags are for. They could have poison or explosives in them."

"Yes. Margo took care of it. Why would you think that anyway?" Almost immediately after she asked the question, Amelia's face showed a dawning realization. "Oh, are they using us for something else?"

Chrystel nodded, even though it hurt. "Mom, I'm sorry about how I've been treating you." Her tears started to flow harder and dripped over her cheeks into her hair.

"Sweetheart, it doesn't matter. I know you're afraid my madness is going to come back— afraid to get too close and be hurt again. That's fine. I wish it weren't so, but there's no undoing our history or my quirks. I intend to keep showing you another side of me, the brave side."

Then she giggled, "Maybe not so physical though."

Amelia bent and gingerly held her wounded daughter. For the first time in many years, Chrystel allowed Amelia to hold her. "I miss Tilley and Brodie and Grandpa and Grandma," Chrystel stammered through her tears.

"I know." Amelia allowed her daughter to cry herself out and then added, "There was another act of defiance, other than running wildly away from guards and your incredible leap. By the way, I still don't know how you did that. No one ate the Huntas' disgusting little pies. Not one. When it began to rain, a purple berry goop spilled over the rim of the wagon until a Hunta guard dragged the whole mess away."

Chapter 23
Karen in Flight

Karen woke from a nap. She glanced outside and recognized the topography of the California coastline. She hadn't travelled to the state since before the Great Dying, a hell of a long time ago, but the remains of the Golden Gate Bridge and rubble that was once San Francisco were unmistakable.

An earthquake in 2066 had taken what time and neglect had missed. Even now, the extent of human loss over the last hundred years had the power to sabotage Karen's hard-earned positive outlook. She wondered if there were people down below at this very moment, working to eke out an existence and build a new community. Anger quickly followed with the thought that the alien bastards wanted to take away what little was left.

It seemed like they were moving faster than before. She could feel herself pressed into the gel seat. Karen looked at the communication icon on the inside of her helmet to listen to Becky. From the clipped conversation, Karen gathered they'd been spotted and were being trailed by three Hunta ships.

Becky said, "Can we take them all, Andy?"

"Yes, but I can't be certain there aren't more of them nearby. Our mission is to ensure Karen arrives at her destination safely. My recommendation is to continue evasive maneuvers until we lose them."

"And then what?"

"Please rephrase the question, Firestarter."

"If we can't lose them, we can't land at our destination because we can't take a chance we'd alert the Huntas about the hidden facility. Also, if we evade, we risk being picked up by more enemy ships."

"Your analysis is logical, but we must prioritize our primary mission."

Karen thought Becky's AI, Andy, was very professional, if not a bit pedantic with his decision making. Tammy would have been all over this dilemma. Then Karen's stomach lurched with a sudden altitude shift, and she forgot all about AI's.

"I'm going to try it your way, Andy. We'll do nap of the earth and exploit the valleys and folds in the terrain. Push it to the maximum safe speed. Let's see what these bastards got."

Andy's disembodied voice replied. "Roger, Firestarter. Plotting a course now. Recommend we head south and swing back north when we lose them."

"That works."

Karen hung on for the next twenty hours. *Okay, it was maybe only twenty minutes*, but each minute of zigging up and down and zagging hair pin turns felt like far more. It was quite a relief when Andy announced they'd lost them.

"Turning north now at preset heading," he added.

When they were flying at a calm, cruising speed, Karen asked the question that had been on her mind since she'd climbed aboard this roller coaster to hell. "I'm curious. If the Ardinian shield is impenetrable, why are you concerned about how many Hunta ships you face?"

Becky answered, "The shields are impenetrable to weapons, but suicide runs aren't out of bounds for them. One of our other wasp flights over France lost two craft to a Kamikaze run. They were outnumbered and then bulldozed to smithereens."

Karen gasped. "You're shitting me. The Huntas are willing to do that?"

"Absolutely. It seems like they're willing to do anything to take our world and destroy humanity."

"I can't imagine that there are that many of them to waste life like that, but who knows. Shakete never told me how long the Huntas and Ardinians have been searching for a home. If the Huntas can repopulate like the Mermots, we may have a larger problem on our hands than anyone—"

"Warning!" Andy interrupted. "Two Huntas advancing from the south and four ships from the northwest. We didn't lose them."

"Full thrust east," Becky commanded. "Set a course."

"Roger, Firestarter."

"Are there any nearby wasps that can provide assistance?" Becky asked.

"I've already sent an alert to Space Fleet. They said the closest flight is about twenty-seven minutes away."

Karen could barely breathe. Not from lack of oxygen—her helmet took care of breathable air. It was from the pressure on her chest caused by acceleration. She could feel the G-forces when she tried to lift her hand to scratch a bug bite on her knee.

Andy announced, "The four enemy from the north are sweeping to cut us off. Recommend we turn and face the two from the south. Once we eliminate them, we'll have an open path."

"I agree. Hold on, Karen."

She'd never said hold on before! The ship ascended into the sky like a rocket. A loopity-loop was next, or at least that was Karen's non-technical description of the maneuver, followed by too many seconds of flying upside-down, and then a corkscrew turn back to a level position. Karen thought that the rocking and rolling motion of the sea was the most puke-inducing experience of her life, but this ride was far worse.

She felt the release of their weapons before she heard them. After that, the battle was a blur as the wasp performed a series of pitches, rolls, and weaves while the deadly song of explosions played to the macabre dance of a mid-air battle.

Becky shouted, "We did it, Andy! Got them both. How long until support arrives?"

"Still sixteen minutes. I would recommend nap of the earth again to lose the other ships, but we're over the Mojave Desert now and there isn't much cover near the ground."

"Floor it!" Becky commanded.

Karen was mostly sure she'd lost consciousness this time, because when she opened one eye, they were back to travelling near the ground, and she could see trees sporadically flashing by below.

"Firestarter, we have a maintenance issue. The generator readings show energy spikes. It is likely we shook something loose during the engagement."

"What does that mean?" Becky asked.

"It means we need to land now and get as far away from this wasp as possible," Andy replied.

"Find me a place, Andy."

"Scanning now. There's a clearing. 1.65 clicks, heading 203.26."

"Go for it. If we put out an SOS, our guys will hear it, but so will the Huntas. They'll both see the explosion anyway, so I don't think it matters. Whoever finds us first, wins. Karen, there's a med kit and emergency supplies in a pocket to your right and an extra laser under your seat. Please remove them and keep them in your lap. When we land, I want you to run like hell away from the ship."

Karen had several witty replies rolling through her head; however, now didn't seem the time. Even if she weren't in danger of incineration via explosion, she would've run as far and as fast from this spaceship as her legs could carry her.

The landing was anticlimactic: a hard bump, the swish of a hatch opening, and Becky's hand reaching in to yank her out. Firestarter was already running when Karen's feet touched the lovely, stable earth. She scooted after Becky with the laser hung over one shoulder and the kit tucked under the other arm like a football. Karen had no idea what to expect, but based on the speed with which Becky was hotfooting it across the clearing, this explosion would be a big one. Karen dug into a place inside herself where she always went when one of her lives were in danger. She pumped her legs harder and faster, her mouth open and relaxed ready to inhale oxygen if this dash lasted longer than fifty yards.

They sprinted barely more than a half football field worth of steps before the ship exploded behind them. A mammoth *WHOMPF* slammed Karen forward into the ground. For the second, or was it the third time in two weeks, the world took on an underwater aspect. All sound was muted and distorted. It also felt like the backs of her arms were on fire.

Becky trotted back for her. She bent and lip-synched to Karen, "Can you walk?" *Oh wait, Becky isn't miming the words, I just can't hear her.*

Louder than necessary, Karen answered by pointing at her ear. "Everything is fuzzy. Give me a sec." She rolled over, sat up, and then felt the back of her arms. They were tender but unblistered. She pulled up on one knee and then to her feet, shaking her head, "That makes ten," she said.

Becky looked at Karen curiously, probably wondering if her fall had shaken something else loose. Even if Karen wasn't firing on all cylinders, she knew they had to get moving. Hunta assholes would be out there somewhere, and they were vulnerable out in the open. Becky was urgently waving Karen forward.

The two women scrambled up a hilly embankment. Loose rocks and soil gave way under Karen's feet, and she had to grab hold of brush to keep from falling. Becky's hand reached down and pulled her the rest of the way. They hustled to a copse of trees and hid there for a few moments to survey the surrounding area from their elevated position.

"This place looks really familiar," Karen mused.

Becky asked, "Have you ever been to Idaho before?"

Karen was relieved when she heard Becky's voice. She was regaining her hearing again. "Yes, not one of my finest memories. Are we in Idaho then?"

"Utah, actually. A couple miles from the southern Idaho border." Becky was studying a screen on a hand-held device. In the moments before they'd landed, Becky had transferred a mirror image of Andy's capabilities to the device. Becky tapped the volume up. "Andy, what are you seeing out there?"

"Our assistance has arrived, but so have the Huntas. Both are on direct headings to the crash site and are only moments away. I don't think it would be good for you to be near. If you look over your right shoulder, you'll see a strip of green surrounding a creek bed. Leave now."

"Roger." Becky slipped the device into a pocket and hauled ass down the other side of the hill. Karen did her best to keep up. Just as they were trudging through brush to a canopy of trees, two Hunta craft came screaming overhead. Blasts from wasps could be heard in the near distance. Karen and Becky stared at each other for a moment and then hurriedly moved deeper under cover.

"The Huntas probably think we're dead. Andy didn't notify our folks that we'd survived to ensure they kept that belief. All we must do now is make it the 162 miles to the Idaho facility."

"At least I'm wearing shoes this time," Karen commented.

"Huh?" Becky looked at Karen in confusion.

"Once upon a time, I was kidnapped by an end of the world cult. They bound and blindfolded me before leaving me to die in the Idaho wilderness. I wasn't wearing any shoes."

"You really don't have an abundance of luck, do you?" Becky said.

Karen grinned in return, "If I didn't have bad luck, then I wouldn't have any at all. But then again, I'm still here." Karen stopped to look around. "You didn't hear a rattle, did you?"

"Nope."

She sighed in relief. "Be on the lookout for snakes. I hate the damn things. We'd better get moving. It'll be dark before long, and we need to find someplace to hide for the night. Lead the way, Firestarter."

"You think there're any Bigfoots out here?" Becky asked.

"I'd heard they settled in this area many years ago, but that could have been a legend. There haven't been any confirmed sightings of Bigfoot since right after the Great Dying. I'd like to know that they still survive and found a place on this earth. It wasn't their fault that the change made them that way. Regardless, probably best if we try to avoid them.

"Speaking of Bigfoots," Karen said, "did you know that I had one as a friend? His name was Uh Huh, and I met him at that new age cult I mentioned. Let's get moving and I'll tell you all about it."

Chapter 24
Moon Base Victory

The XO decided to be the bearer of bad news this time; it just didn't seem fair to send a lieutenant into the breach.

"What do you mean you've lost her again?" Mike said.

The XO, a bald, stocky man with weepy, shallow set eyes was struggling to keep up with Admiral Mike's pace. They were on their way to another meeting. When the Admiral turned to glare at him, the XO nearly stumbled.

"Admiral, her wasp went down near Idaho and then exploded on the ground. The last word we had from their AI was that their wasp had a maintenance issue."

"Have you sent a search team?"

"Well, sir, that's difficult."

Mike stopped and fully faced the XO. At Mike's side, Jack stopped, sat, and glared at the XO too, in a German shepherd scowl that the XO found most disconcerting. "Explain." Mike demanded.

"Huntas pursued her wasp over California, Nevada, and Utah. Her pilot, Firestarter, performed admirably. She lost her tails twice and downed two enemy craft. A wasp support team was near when they had a maintenance failure, but there were more Huntas in the area. Before landing, the AI recommended that we not send a search and rescue. He was concerned it would lead to more losses. Also, the wasp landing was relatively close to the Idaho facility."

"So now we're taking orders from Ardinian AI's? What does 'relatively close' mean and why was I not consulted?"

"Of course not, sir. Firestarter's wasp fleet is commanded by Captain Victor. He made the decision after considering all the facts. They were approximately 160 miles from their destination, and Captain Victor felt confident they could travel on foot the remainder of the journey if they'd survived the blast."

"And what if they were injured and alone in the Idaho wilderness?"

The XO didn't answer. He just stood helplessly looking at the Admiral in sympathy.

"I should have never let her stay on Earth." Mike said and inhaled deeply. "Given the facts, the Captain made the right call, but you tell him I still don't like it. If she is involved again, I need to bear the responsibility of that decision."

"I believe that's why he made the decision for you, sir. So you wouldn't have to bear that weight."

Mike considered the XO's explanation and then nodded. "Thanks for informing me. She'll be okay," he said more to himself than anyone else. "Is everyone ready for the update?"

"Yes, sir."

"Let's do this." Mike continued to the meeting room with Jack by his side. Mike's hand was reaching to Jack's ears for the support of feeling him near.

They entered the large conference room, and he told everyone to sit before the crowd was on its feet. "Let's begin."

Mike hadn't gotten much sleep in over a week. The daily briefings were difficult and becoming more disheartening with each passing day. They were losing. They stood to lose their entire world, and he would be responsible. He knew deep down there was only so much anyone could do when caught unaware and outgunned, but he didn't feel that way. He was their leader, and he was failing. It didn't help to be clueless about his wife's fate, but he had to push that thought aside.

No one asked questions at the conclusion of the status of forces and population briefing. At least half the Earth's population had been lost in the Huntas' initial bombings. The three destroyers that comprised Space Fleet's primary defense were circling in earth's orbit and impotent. And now, the Huntas had begun a campaign to locate dispersed humans and kill them too.

News on technical advancements wasn't any more heartening. There was still no resolution on how to make the matter bomb work. The Mermots were building more nukes and space-to-surface photon weapons, but it would be several weeks before that manufacturing pipeline yielded results. Even once the additional weapons arrived, Space Fleet didn't have any targets. Hunta ships were cloaked and the fleet couldn't find the enemy to shoot them from orbit. There weren't even any good Earth-side targets. Humans were so dispersed over the planet Space Fleet couldn't risk using nukes or photons on the surface. Mike thought they were living in a deadly *Catch 22*.

To make matters worse, they could only guess the Huntas' strength. Space Fleet couldn't see the enemy to count their ships and intelligence from Earth was spotty. Most agreed the Huntas were far more numerous and capable than anyone had predicted.

The final briefer, an Ardinian responsible for collecting intelligence on the status of the New Washington Enclave, seemed pleased about something. The satisfaction on her face made Mike scoot forward in his chair.

"As you know sir, the Huntas have thwarted all attempts to view the enclave from space. We're still working to counteract their jamming technology, but we now have an agent on the inside. Please play the video."

The conference room screen faced the Admiral and spanned the back and two sides. Some of the attendees turned in their chairs to see. The view playing on the screen was dark and low to the ground. Large tents were visible in the distance. When the wobbling camera angle shifted, the statue in Founders Park moved across the screen. "We believe the townspeople are being held in Founders Park. Watch as our agent traverses the fence that encloses them."

There wasn't much to see other than the ground side of chain link and the wobbling dark beyond. "Now I'll take you to a view outside the enclosure." She clicked on photos taken from an empty town. The angle of the final set of photos was from the ground and pointed at a large, distant structure. The view zoomed in closer and the building came into focus. "This is a greenhouse that was constructed after the Huntas arrival. There are five greenhouses in total."

The XO asked, "Why is the perspective so lousy? Is someone crawling around?"

"That's due to the nature of our spy—a little back dog. The Mermots shuttle her in to deliver messages and film the surroundings at night. We are lucky to have her. She's perfect in terms of size and color, very difficult to see in the dark, and more importantly, there are no other canines remaining in the enclave."

Mike had already guessed from the camera shaking and worms-eye-view that the camera was attached to a dog. "What do we know from the messages?"

"There are approximately 3,421 human prisoners in the enclave. They are taken during the day to build and tend to the greenhouses. Mermots are near, underground and repopulating as fast as they can. We don't know the strength of the Hunta force at New Washington. I have sent a compilation of every shred of information we've been able to gather to your data recorders. The most distressing event recently is that all clavers were tagged by an implant."

"Who's the human contact?" Mike asked

"The ex-mayor, Chrystel."

"I'm glad it's her. That number is only about sixty-five percent of New Washington's population. Do you know who specifically is left or what happened to the others and the dogs?" Mike's voice was barely a whisper. He was having difficulty speaking. Even though it was a relief to know some of the New Washington Enclave had survived, he knew that others had not.

"We have some names and I've included them in my data transfer. As for what happened to the other people, Chrystel doesn't know. A vision by your daughter, Amelia, probably saved many of the dogs. They were told to flee the enclave before it was overwhelmed by Huntas. The Mermots lost 200 of their own in the Hunta attack."

"I wish she'd have sent the people fleeing," Mike said under his breath. "That little dog must be Amelia's schipperke, Kismet."

"Yes, sir."

Mike noticed almost every head in the room was bent searching the list of survivor names now on their data recorders. Most of the people in attendance were either from New Washington or knew people who lived there.

He was afraid to look. He told himself that just because a name wasn't on that list that didn't mean someone wasn't alive, but the possibilities were still horrible to contemplate. It was awful to know of lives lost, but it could never be the same as knowing it was someone you loved. "One last question, and then I think we'll take a short recess to collect ourselves. What do you believe is the Huntas' purpose for keeping these people as prisoners and no one else on Earth?"

"Chrystel believes, and we concur with her belief, that they are hostages. That at some point, they'll be offered in trade by the Huntas."

"Thank you. Excellent work. Let's take an hour and then reconvene. Shakete, could you please come with me?" Shakete nodded and followed. Mike noticed more than one teary face as he exited the briefing room.

Mike made it to an adjoining hallway before he stopped, linked his fingers on his head, and shouted, "Dammit! Dammit, Shakete, we can't catch a break! I don't know what to do."

"Yes, I understand, Mike. Let's move with alacrity to your personal quarters before someone sees you. Better we talk there."

Mike's quarters were far more opulent than he would've liked. He'd explained to Shakete when he'd seen the abundant space that an admiral should not be treated as a king. Making matters worse, Shakete had located original artwork from old Earth masters and had decorated the apartment with his most amazing finds. Shakete had informed him it was too late to change, but he'd removed a few of the more impressive pieces to make Mike happy. Mike sat on a luxurious soft leather couch with Jack asleep next to him, and Shakete perched rigidly on an adjoining chair. Mike did not complain or ask where Shakete had found the finely-aged scotch whiskey of which he was currently sipping a double shot.

"I can't go back in an hour soused, so stop me if I go for more."

Shakete answered, "You shouldn't be concerned. Most of your crew has access to alcoholic beverages as well. I would think they may also need a mood stabilizer."

Mike inhaled. "Karen said to tell you that you owed her a dog. She wasn't happy to know you'd left her out."

Shakete's staccato-like laughter followed. "She's an amazing woman. If she wasn't previously taken, I might have designs of her. But, alas, there would be no pulling her from you."

"That's something I've always wondered. Do Ardinians marry? Do you have sex?"

"Yes, in the time of our home world, we partnered like humans to create family units. Sometimes, if the partners were economically advantaged, they would create more than one family with other partners. During our travels, there was little need to increase our numbers. When we learned to grow replacement bodies, there was no need at all. Our reproductive organs and associated chemical stimulants were removed. I can show you if you would like," Shakete reached down to raise his tunic.

"No! That's quite all right. I trust your account, Shakete."

"Interestingly, we found that biological attraction was more than just chemicals. I believe it is memory ghosts of days past. Your Karen reminds me in spirit of a young woman I very much favored in my youth."

"What happened to her?"

"She died in a tragic accident. In those days, when you were dead, you were dead."

"So the Ardinians were once very much like us humans?"

"Yes, I believe that is true, but without your aggressiveness."

Mike began, "That was a welcome diversion, Shakete. Thank you. Back to the subject at hand. I think the war has moved to Earth's surface, and I should be there. We were totally wrong about how the battle would go, and now we must adjust. It's likely there are enough people left alive on the surface to rally a counter attack. If only there was some way to organize them. I don't know right now what that way would be, but we must try."

Shakete nodded. "Yes, one must remain flexible. Also, the Mermots are undoubtedly breeding like there is no tomorrow. Which of course, is the true nature of our statistical survivability—there may be no tomorrow. I must caution you, though. If you transfer most of the moon base's capability to Earth, it will be as if you are throwing all your eggs into one bin. There will be little back-up if things go bad."

"Eggs in one basket, Shakete. And we're talking about losing our world here. Let me lay this metaphor on you for size: we're playing for all the marbles."

Shakete shrugged, "Perhaps, but I take a longer view of things."

"You mix up your metaphors on purpose, don't you?"

Shakete paused and then smiled slightly. "Perhaps I feel it important to humanize my personality. Humans make mistakes, and it is good that your people see that Ardinians do too. Just as it isn't enough for leaders to care, they must show that they do. Is that not correct?"

Shakete and Mike gave each other penetrating stares, each assessing the other. "Admiral, let me just say I admire the passion of your species. The Ardinians have lost much of that, and it is exciting to be reminded of what we once were. All of that aside, I believe your strategy is correct. If you will leave the destroyer captains in place, then I can fill in their crew with my people and keep an Ardinian presence here on the moon. Even though you must organize the battle on the ground, it is critical we not accede defeat in space."

"Good enough," Mike answered. "If you'll please give me some privacy, I'd like to prepare orders for my staff."

Shakete rose to leave. His eyes lighted on Jack, who had been roused from sleep by a change in room dynamics. Jack's ears were alert as he watched Shakete. "He is a beautiful animal and a better friend to you. No matter how imperfect the place, my decision to bring him to you was correct."

Mike's only response was, "Yes," and then his head bent to write orders on a pad.

* * *

An hour later, everyone was gathered again in the conference room. "The battle for our planet has moved to the surface," Admiral Mike said without prelude. "We must organize what's left of the population in a counteroffensive. In seven days, I want my staff to prepare a plan to relocate command and control to a safe location on Earth. In addition, see what we can do about creating some human safe zones using the Ardinian shield.

"As for our space forces, most of the wasps should be relocated on Earth. We're wasting too much time flying back and forth and sacrificing critical intelligence. We will leave the captains on destroyers with minimum staffing, and they will be augmented with Ardinian personnel.

"The wasps must begin infiltrating to Earth immediately. Keep flights together, hidden, and based in a location that allows deployment worldwide with logistical support from local resources. I will personally review flight locations before they depart their home ships. My staff will prepare recommendations for deployment of the remainder of personnel and resources by the end of seven days.

"Finally, all scientific resources will remain on the Delamie and press forward on their critical work. Find answers for us!" Mike paused to look at the assembled staff. "I know it's a tall order, but we must execute this plan in ten days without fail. We don't have much time. Are there any questions?"

There weren't any questions, but cheering erupted throughout the room. Shouts of "We Endure! We Endure!" were repeated with desperate intensity.

Chapter 25
The Warrior

Chrystel listened to the sounds of people moving around in preparation for the day's work.

One man yelled to another, "Hurry up! Those poopueaters won't wait!"

Chrystel listened for the reply and as expected, it had something to do with waste. "Don't give me that shit," another male voice said in answer, and then they both sniggered as if they were funny.

The populotter had become the poopueater and other crasser terms. Whatever got them through the day was good by Chrystel. The Hunta guards didn't concern themselves with the speech of their human slaves, providing the slaves didn't give them any grief. All grief was immediately and harshly squashed.

Sitting on her mother's cot, Chrystel watched as her mom helped three small children get dressed. She enjoyed this time in the morning, waiting for her mother to finish helping the children. Her mom laughed when she realized the two-year-old she was helping to dress had his shoes on the wrong feet. For a snippet of time, it almost felt like things were normal. *Nothing is normal*, Chrystel reminded herself. *Not anymore.*

Noticeable cracks were forming in the Hunta/slave language barrier. Neither could emulate the sounds of the other species effectively, but there was an obvious improvement in understanding. Just yesterday, she'd told Herman he was an ugly bastard, and he'd clicked back that she was a red insect, or something to that effect. It could have been pest, but the meaning was clear. Even Margo and the Hunta poopueater greenhouse supervisor had made headway in basic communication.

She'd hoped that once they could communicate, an opening might appear. That the Huntas might possess an emotional range beyond anger and obedience. So far, Chrystel hadn't seen any evidence of empathy. As far as she could tell, the Huntas considered humans as lesser beings. When Herman had called her an insect or a pest, he'd meant it literally. Any route to freedom did not involve cooperation from a Hunta sympathizer. If Herman enjoyed their physical games, it was only that, nothing more. That he'd saved her from a group of angry Huntas probably had more to do with her value as a bargaining chip.

After showing the child that feet and shoes had a left and a right, Amelia sat down next to Chrystel. "Hey, sweetie. How're you doing? You look gaunt."

"We all do, Mom. I think the Huntas feed us just as little as possible to keep the slaves docile." She studied her mother's face. Chrystel

248

had never realized until they were captives how much her mom resembled Grandpa Mike. Somehow, the trace of her beloved grandfather in her mom's face made Chrystel feel safer, if that was even possible.

Amelia sighed. "I know." She slipped a note to Chrystel and asked, "Any good news?"

"Any news is good news," Chrystel mumbled while reading the tissue-thin note. Cradling the scrap in her hand, she read the information for a second time, stuck it in her mouth and swallowed.

"Can't you share anything?" Amelia asked.

"Honestly, they don't tell me much, other than they're working on it. Mostly the notes ask for information that I can't give them. Mom, have you had any visions lately that would help us?"

On the tip of Amelia's tongue was a confession that she'd been hearing a voice. A voice frequently profane, often maddening, and yet somehow, the disembodied utterances provided very timely recommendations. Amelia swallowed the confession when a dark shadow suddenly blocked the light from the tent opening. Both women's heads snapped up to discover Herman entering.

Still playing in the tent, the little two-year-old was paying little attention to his surroundings. Now that his shoes were on the correct feet, he toddled forward wildly and ran right into

Herman's legs. The boy bounced off the Hunta like an old-world superball and landed on his back. The impact had a three second delay, and then the boy's face scrunched, his mouth opened, and he let loose a blood-curdling cry.

Amelia and Chrystel rushed to the little boy's defense, but they were too late. Herman had already reached down, grabbed the child by his shirt, and began to shake him, hissing alien profanity.

Amelia reached the Hunta first. Her arms encircled the boy, and she held on. "No! Let him go! It was an accident. You'll hurt him!" She used her weight to reduce the impact of the Hunta's bone-jarring jerks. Her feet were lifted from the ground more than once. The Hunta glared at Amelia as if she was a bird crapping on his arm and clicked harshly in warning, but she wouldn't release the boy.

Chrystel jumped in front of the Herman. She hissed in his face the same sound she'd heard a thousand times—the same one she'd been practicing when she was alone. She believed it was meant as a challenge. Something like, *I'm bigger and badder* than you. Herman's pulsating eyes widened in surprise.

He flicked Amelia and the boy off like flies, sending them crashing to the other side of the tent. The Hunta issued a hissing roar as he propelled himself forward toward Chrystel.

She was ready. Side stepping his advance, the 300-pound alien's momentum carried him over a cot and flat onto his face on the other side. Chrystel glanced at her mother. Amelia was standing now, hugging the crying child who appeared to be okay.

"Get him out of here!" Chrystel yelled. "Now!"

Not wasting more time, Chrystel vaulted over the tipped cot onto the gigantic alien's back and placed a knife to his throat just where that big vein ran from under his chin to his chest. Technically it wasn't a knife, more of a prison shiv she'd crafted from a buried can she'd found at the greenhouse. Regardless, it was plenty sharp, and she pressed the sharpened edge into his skin to demonstrate.

Chrystel hissed again, drawing out the sound, and whispered into his scaly ear, "I know you understand me. It was an accident, not an insult. I… will… kill… you if you hurt another child."

Herman clicked but didn't move. His throbbing eyes scuttled to and fro, searching for any advantage, and then his eyelids shut, probably in humiliation. Slowly, Chrystel rose and backed away from the Hunta. She kept her shiv ready in case Herman charged again.

He got to his feet and turned to face Chrystel. Her dominant foot was back in a fighting stance and the shiv ready. Herman clicked and hissed something Chrystel couldn't understand. She guessed it was probably a threat to eventually kill her. For the moment, the Hunta's rage appeared to have disappeared, and, if she was reading his expression correctly, then that rage was replaced with something far more dangerous: a seething desire for revenge.

Herman held out his gigantic hand, palm up for the shiv. Chrystel knew her next decision meant life or death. To give herself time to make that decision, she examined the Hunta warily. If she gave him the knife, he might kill her and then go for her mom and the boy. They needed to stay alive whatever that took. But if she killed Herman now, any hope that the Huntas were keeping her alive for a trade might be forfeit.

Raising her arms slightly and turning her palms up, she very carefully placed the knife in his grasp. The Hunta reached around her shoulders, and with one rock hard arm, dragged her out of the tent. Chrystel thought the smell from underneath his armpit might kill her anyway.

Chapter 26
The Jail

Herman roughly threw Chrystel into a cell and slammed the door shut. "Still friends?" Chrystel called out after him. Through the bars, he gave her a plump-eyed look of disgust and left.

Chrystel scooted to the far wall of the cell and leaned against the cold brick. She'd been Hunta-handled from her mom's tent and dragged across Founders Park to the town jail. She checked the bruises blossoming on her arms. They were mostly red now and would turn purple, black, and then yellow over the next week. Everything hurt, especially her side where a broken rib refused to heal. *How could it?*

She thought the upside to being jailed was that she might have a few moments to recuperate. Then she remembered that the town's people were now leaderless, and she heaved a pathetic sigh.

There wasn't a stitch of furniture in her new home, not even a giant, stiff Hunta cot to share. "Now what?" she said to herself. When her eyes spied the bucket in the corner she chuckled, "Just great."

"What are you moaning about?" Thomas' deep baritone voice blared from somewhere close.

"Thomas! Thank God! Where are you?"

"Three cells down. Look to your left." Chrystel stood and turned to his voice. The cell next to her and the one after that were empty, but sure enough, Thomas' mug was waving to her through the bars.

"What you in for?" he asked. "Steal something that didn't belong to you? Maybe some late-night rowdiness?"

"You're getting warm with the rowdiness. I threatened a Hunta guard with a shiv. Coulda killed him too."

"I'm glad you didn't off him. Otherwise, you wouldn't be here," Thomas said. "Anyway, I'm glad to have someone to talk to. I haven't got anyone else besides me, and I've heard all his stories."

They stood looking at each other through the bars. Chrystel started in a soft voice. "I was hoping there were others in here with you. We've had some clavers go missing. I was also hoping a little boy carried away by Cleo's henchmen might be held here." Chrystel allowed that statement to hang in the silence.

"Shit!" Thomas blurted. "That bad? So give me the lowdown, Chrissy."

"You're just calling me Chrissy because I can't get at you from here."

"Naw, you know that's a term of endearment."

254

"Endearment? Been working on your vocabulary words since your imprisonment, Thomas?"

"That and my French. Also my golf swing."

Chrystel laughed out loud. Thomas spoke some Indonesian and Thai from his time in Special Ops before the Great Dying, but he thought the French were duplicitous pussies and that golf wasn't a real man's game. She couldn't remember the last time she laughed like that. "Thanks for making me laugh. Even though it makes my ribs hurt, it feels good to my heart."

"Here to serve and amuse. Seriously though."

Chrystel blew air from her mouth. "Seriously, the Huntas have the town's people completely enclosed in Founders Park. Hunta guards are posted every thirty meters around the fence at night. Fewer during the day. The wire on top of the fence is electrified. Every day, they march the adults to work in the greenhouses we built for them. No way that I can see to escape from there either. Cleo says we're being kept alive as slaves out of the goodness of their hearts. Of course, I don't believe her." Chrystel didn't mention Kismet in case someone else was listening.

"What's the Huntas' play, do you think?" Thomas asked.

"We're hostages to be used in trade. For what or how, I don't know."

"I can't imagine they would have any other use for us. Sociopathic bastards." Thomas asked in a halting tone, "Katie? My kids?"

"They're okay. Katie's been a godsend taking care of the injured. She doesn't have much to work with as far as drugs and supplies, but she does the best she can."

Thomas nodded. "That's a relief. Not knowing has been the hardest part of being locked up."

"Thomas, has anything happened to you?"

"Well, if you count a couple of lost toes, and three fingers on my left hand as anything, then yeah. They started out with some torture. Wanted information on my family, which is odd since I'd think they'd want troop strength, equipment, weapons count, that sort of thing."

"I'm sorry, Thomas."

"Not your doing. Then I got to thinking about that cloak tech they were using. What if they've been here for a while, listening and watching? They might have all the information they need without us."

"But why torture you at all then? And why not anyone else, other than trying to slowly starve us to death?"

"Honestly? I think it's just a power dynamics thing. Cleo came in once to watch them torture and mutilate me. It's almost like she got off on it. Then she left, and they never returned. It's been days, and I haven't seen anyone except the Hunta that brings the food and replaces my bucket. Wait, I take that back. The assholes came back to inject something in my backside."

The jail was silent as both prisoners considered the new information. Thomas finally spoke. "I assume whatever they put in me they put into everyone else."

"That would be a true statement."

"And Mayor Ted? He been any help?"

"Don't get me started on him. Oh, would you believe he's been—"

The sound of a key turning in the jailhouse door halted further conversation. Amelia, crying and frightened, was pushed forward through the door and roughly guided to the cell next to Chrystel. Herman shoved her in so hard she went flying forward and stumbled to her knees.

Too concerned with her mother to yell obscenities at Herman, Chrystel pressed her face between the bars and pleaded, "Mom, are you all right? I'm here."

Amelia began sobbing. Her bottom lip was shaking and tears streamed down her cheeks as she repeated, "No, no, no."

"Mom, you're scaring me. What happened? Please tell me."

Grabbing her mouth, Amelia shook her head wildly in response.

"Is it the child. Did they do something to that little boy?"

"Chrystel," Thomas said. "Give her a second. Amelia, it's me, Thomas. I'm here too, just to your left. Try to take deep breaths. You know how to do that. In through the nose and out through the mouth."

Finally, Amelia gathered herself enough to breathe. Instead of asking questions, Chrystel did something that she'd never attempted. Something that suddenly felt right: she tried to console her mom. "Mom, I've seen how brave you are. The way you hung on to the boy took a lot of courage. You were right when you said you were going to show me. I'm proud of you for everything you've done to help our people and the kids." Chrystel's voice dropped. "And, I've seen you struggle. I know each day is still a challenge for you. You can't get much braver than that."

"The boy is okay," Amelia said between the gasping and the crying. She continued to breath heavily until she could collect enough air for a longer sentence. "Someone warned me that I would be taken. I asked another woman to keep the toddler out of sight for a while."

Someone warned her? Chrystel's mind reeled, but she waited.

Then Amelia got up from her knees, and she turned to Chrystel. Her face was red from crying. More than the crying, the stark fear in her eyes made Chrystel pull away from the bars. "I won't be in my bed tonight. What will Kismet do?"

Chapter 27
Kismet

Where is the woman master smell?

Kismet crawled out of the hole. She looked up at the bed above her. Sitting, she scratched up at the fabric. When the woman didn't come, she scratched again. And again.

She stepped from under the covering and leaped to the bed. She'd never gone there before, but she needed to find her. There were many small people sleeping on the bed. Kismet loved the small people. She smelled the hair of the closest one. Quietly, she moved around the little ones, smelling each in turn. One had something on his face, and Kismet stuck her nose to the smell and licked.

One surprised her. His eyes opened and he said, "Doggy." He reached around her neck and pulled her in close. While Kismet tried to squirm from his grasp, another small person woke and grabbed her before she could flee. All the small people were waking. Their voices making that sound of happiness.

Kismet couldn't help herself. She yipped in happiness too. And then she yipped to escape their clutches. There were too many of them. She would like to stay and play, but she must find the woman master. She said over and over to the little ones, "Please let me go," but they were so happy they would not listen.

A man master was rising from his bed. He whispered, "What's all the noise about?"

One of the little ones giggled, "Look, a doggy. A baby doggy!"

The man master rose from the bed and crept to the cot where six children had been sleeping. Kismet's dark eyes were peaking over the arms of a child. "Give him to me," the man said.

"No, I found him," the child pouted.

"It's dangerous for us to have him here, for us and the pup. How the heck did you get in here, anyway, dog?

"Mermots," Kismet replied.

"Where were you headed?"

Kismet had been warned by the Mermots if she was ever captured not to say anything. They'd said the bad ones couldn't talk to dogs anyway, so she'd be wasting her time. She'd already talked to the little ones and this man. She was confused. It was so hard not to talk to the people. Kismet didn't answer.

"Not gonna say, huh? Okay kids, give him to me. It's for his safety. However he got in here, we need to let him find his way out."

One of the older children said, "It's a girl dog, not a boy."

"Well okay then." He reached for the dog, and the boy who'd been clutching Kismet like she was his best friend in the world, finally loosened his hold.

The man master scratched her ears as one arm went under her body to hold her. "You're a tiny thing. I'm sorry to have to do this, whatever your name is, but you aren't safe here. You need to leave this hell on earth as fast as your—" He stopped. "I was going to say four legs will carry you, but I see you only have three. Poor bitty thing."

He sat her on the ground, "Now go."

Kismet wanted to stay with the people. She wanted to play with the little ones. It felt good to be with people again. She needed them like the air she breathed. The Mermots fed her and cared for her, but it wasn't the same. She looked in the direction of the hole, and then she remembered the woman master. She must find her. She must give her the note. For a second, she was confused again, and then her desire to be with the woman master, to obey and do her work, sent Kismet scurrying from the tent. *I must find her.*

Before her was an open space. It was dark. She could hear a Ranger howling from far away. She inhaled with all her might, sorting through the thousands of scents for that one special smell. The woman master. *There she is!*

With her nose near the ground, she followed the scent for a few steps. There was no tree to shield her. Fear of owl and the bad Hunta smell were all around. She quivered. Memories of being lost and alone made the fear grow. She must find the woman master. Kismet set off across the open space. When she arrived at the thing they called statue, she waited in the shadows. She panted, gathered her strength and ran again toward the scent of her beloved master.

Clicking. Bad smell. A shadow coming near. Hunta. Run!

Kismet darted away from the bad smell, when another and another began to chase. They reached to grab her, but she was too fast and low to the ground. She darted and turned before they could catch her. Hissing and clicking, one Hunta kicked out and Kismet jumped back out of range. More Huntas. They were all around.

Everything was spinning and twirling, and Kismet dared not stop. She heard the metal gate screech and glanced to the woods beyond. She ran as fast as she could to the opening, twisting and zipping past the legs of one bad smelling Hunta. Another Hunta was in the open space and ready to stop her.

She pointed her body to the gap beside the bad smell. As she hurtled toward safety, the Hunta reached with his foot to block her. She cut to the other side just in time, but he bent and his hand swept down to clasp her fur; Kismet would've been a Hunta snack if she had a tail. She twisted her neck and bit his hand with all the force at her disposal, ripping off a tuff of alien skin. The Hunta jerked his hand away, and Kismet quickly released before she could be pulled into his orbit. She darted through the gate. The woods were dark, but Kismet understood the safety of them. If she could get to the woods, then she could hide.

Her front paws dug into gravel, and her powerful back leg pushed her faster. Heat, light, and sounds that hurt Kismet's ears landed near. She ran even harder, darting when she could, her head and ears flat for speed. She must run to live. She weaved around a building, through some trees, under an ATV, around another building, along a fence, over and under, around and behind, until finally the bad smells were no longer near.

Kismet waited underneath a house, panting and listening for more Huntas. Since her sense of time was different than a human's, it would've been difficult for Kismet to explain how long she stayed. Eventually, the lonely howling of a Ranger got her moving from the safe hiding place. Her nose pointed into the breeze, she searched for that special smell again, drawing in a rainbow of scents from the wild world around her. Her head pivoted to a trace of the woman master. Kismet was happy. She knew which way to go and there were places to hide along the way.

* * *

"Wake up."

Amelia turned on the cold concrete floor, tucked her hands between her knees, and returned to fitful slumber.

"I said, wake up!"

"Go away voice. I'm just too beat to speak with you." Amelia murmured.

"Kismet is outside that window, dumb shit. Do I have spell out everything for you?"

Amelia sat up, her heart beating hard from being rudely awakened and from the content of the voice's message. "Okay, you have my attention. And really, is the language necessary?"

Chrystel, always easy to fall asleep and to wake, was sitting up before her mother. "Who're you talking to, Mom?"

"Shush. Listen." At the back of Amelia's cell was a barred window eight feet off the ground. The window was closed, but Amelia turned around to face it. With her finger, she gave the wait sign to Chrystel and placed her ear against the wall to listen.

Two minutes passed, and not a sound was heard. Thomas, who was now awake too, pressed his face against the cell bars, trying to figure out what was happening. As one, they heard a muffled yip, a little growl, and then a whine.

"Oh, my God, Chrystel, what do we do?" Amelia asked

"Tell her to leave!" Chrystel whispered. "We can't do a thing for her, and she can't do a thing for us."

"Kismet, dear," Amelia started, in a soft but insistent tone. "Go back to the Mermots. Go back to the hole and disappear. Now!"

Several happy yips followed. Kismet yelled into Amelia's mind, "I found you, I found you!"

"Kismet, go back to the hole. I'm fine."

"I can't." Kismet moaned.

"Why not? Oh, you're outside the gate. How did you get outside the gate? Never mind, please just go find the Mermots. Please go before the Huntas hear you."

Kismet began digging with her claws on the outside wall. She was making far too much noise, especially since every so often she would stop her scratching to growl and whine.

Chrystel heard a key turning in the cell block door. "Sing something, Thomas!" Chrystel shouted. "Drown the noise!"

"Sing? Oh, right, sing, drown the noise. Let me think. Yeah, I got it. *Row, row, row your boat gently down the stream! Merrily, merrily, merrily,*

merrily, life is but a dream. You probably don't know this one Chrissy, but you start after stream. It's an easy one to remember."

By the time the Hunta guard entered, the three prisoners were rowing merrily down a stream. The ugly hunk of alien didn't seem to appreciate the staggered starts and repetitive melody. He hissed, he clicked, but the rowing continued. At the point where the Hunta had lost patience and threatened to shoot Amelia with his weapon, even the chorus could hear Kismet howling to the tune.

"Oh, fuck" Thomas said as the Hunta turned and thundered out the door.

Amelia screamed, "Run Kismet, run! They're coming!"

Chapter 28
Trent

Trent confided to Lionheart, "Of all the sights in all the world, I believe this one might be the most—oh hell, I can't even think of a good word to describe it."

Lionheart had been glued to Trent's side since their skirmish with the Huntas. His flock had been waiting peacefully for his return along the banks of a nearly dry creek. When they saw Trent, the spectacularly large pack of dogs of different shapes, sizes, and colors rose from their resting spots in unison. Their pack leader had returned, and they were happy; hundreds of dogs wagged their pleasure. Trent still had doubts about the decisions he'd made to stay with these uncommon friends, but those doubts evaporated in the pure, simple, and unadulterated pride he felt at keeping them alive. These loving, loyal, and wonderfully true creatures were worthy of life.

Tilley galloped over and saved Trent from further sentimentality. They still had to get to the secret facility in one piece.

"Are we safe from Huntas?" she asked.

"I think so. For now, but we need to get moving."

Glancing at the Rangers pacing nervously back and forth behind Trent, Tilley asked. "Are they new friends?"

He looked over his shoulder at the talking Rangers. He'd explained to AJ's Rangers that he was on his way to join a group of dogs and they were welcome to come along. Based on their current distressed energy, he guessed they didn't comprehend the size of the group. Trent called out to them, "No one will hurt you. You are free to stay or go."

The largest of the two, ninety pounds of raw-boned muscle, answered. "We go. Not like others."

"I understand. Be well, my friends," Trent watched the first known talking Rangers lope away. He felt bad for them. They'd lost their master partly because of him and his flock. Heck, he felt bad about AJ in general. The Rangers were strong and healthy though. AJ had seen to that. They'd be fine.

"Tilley, get the dogs ready to leave. Before we move out, I just gotta wash up in what little water is left in that creek. I think I got some Hunta goop on me."

"Hunta goop? Yes, that would explain your aroma. I am happy you have returned to us from your engagement with our enemies, but our friends are still hungry."

"I know, not much farther. If we set a reasonable pace, we should be there by nightfall."

Trent weaved through a crowd of canines each wanting a little attention and side stepped down a gravelly embankment to a moving shallow with enough water to wash. He shed his shirt, laid it on a rock, and three dogs immediately descended to sniff his discarded garment. Trent was on his knees and studied his reflection in the water. He'd always been lean with the corded muscles of a working man, but he noticed he was thinner than normal. The trek, shortage of food, and the stress of his position as dog shepherd had taken a toll.

His beard and hair had grown in the time they'd been travelling, reclaiming the bushy barbarian appearance he was known for. Amelia had pruned back his wiry, unkempt hair and beard when he'd started hanging around her home. He could still remember her hand gently touching his cheek after cutting enough hair to see his face. She'd gazed into his eyes and said he was a handsome man. He knew he wasn't handsome, probably not ugly, but he was certainly plain. If she thought he looked okay, that was more than fine by him. Their coupling had happened not long after that day. He mused to himself that maybe all the wild hair had been holding her back.

He splashed water on his face and under his arms. Several dogs thought his bathing was interesting, that or they hoped he had something to eat because they gathered in a circle to watch. It reminded him of his six-year-old son who used to sit on the toilet when he shaved and asked questions, his restless feet pounding against the porcelain bowl. As usual, he felt sucker punched in the gut whenever a random memory of one of his lost kids percolated to the surface.

He'd failed them. For a whole night, he'd left his wife, two daughters, and his son with that shyster Mattias and his dippy partner Sylvia, all because he had to find the Ranger that was killing their chickens. He'd known the two travelers were different, but they hadn't seemed like psychos. Besides, his wife was more than able to take care of herself. When he'd found the pair, hungry and lost wandering in the wilderness, he'd taken them home, fed them, and said they could stay a couple of nights until they got their bearings. His reward for a good deed had been the death of his innocent family.

Rage was building a fire behind his ears. He'd searched for those two murderers for years, sometimes getting clues to their whereabouts, but they were always just out of reach. He still had no idea why they'd done what they did. What was the purpose of killing his children? What could possibly have happened to make them kill children?

Meeting Amelia had put an end to his lifelong hunt. Her love had convinced him to stay in one place. Maybe being back on the road was like blood lust, loosening the dam that had prevented him from seeking justice.

One of the dogs whined. She was a doodle thing with matted blonde hair and long eyelashes. Her kind brown eyes stared at him as if she sensed his pain. "Don't worry," Trent assured her. "I'm good. We're all good. I'll get you to your new home."

With that, he wrestled his shirt from the jaws of a playful terrier, shrugged his arms into the holes, and climbed back up the embankment to start again. He wouldn't fail them. Not this time.

They made good progress over a countryside that was not too hilly, not too densely forested, and not too infested with Huntas. For some reason, he got a spidey-sense that they were being watched. He directed Tilley to take the pack and climbed a rise to scout the surrounding area. Other than some gathering storm clouds from the northeast, the land appeared empty of any intelligent life.

Trent shook his head. Might know it would rain now, just as they were only twenty miles from what he hoped was their destination. Dogs weren't big on travelling in a hard rain. As with most mammals, they preferred to hunker down and wait. A founder who he'd met on the road had shared with Trent the reason people felt safe inside when the skies belched their largesse. He'd said that predators didn't usually hunt in bad weather. The only exception being the most dangerous of all beasts of prey: mankind. His wisdom made good sense, so Trent had added that tidbit to his storehouse of useful survival facts.

He wondered if Huntas hunted in bad weather. He also wondered if there were any Bigfoots around and if they hunted in bad weather as well. *You're kinda getting off topic here, dumb shit*, he warned himself. The more immediate danger was the fact that the approaching storm was probably carrying an electrical wallop. Dogs in the open wouldn't be in the best interests of anyone.

Skidding down the rise, he jogged to Tilley. "Hey, wonder alien. There's a storm coming. Hate to have to do this, but we need to find someplace safe to wait it out."

Tilley's massive, purple head swiveled left and right. "Everything looks the same to me, magnificent human. What would be safe?"

He laughed. "Nice attempt at a comeback. Along the edges of a creek bed, like before. The bottom of a canyon near the edge. Lower, less trees, protected if possible. I'll send Lionheart and his big dogs out to look. Just keep your eyes peeled."

Dark purple eyes widened in shock. She pushed words into his mind. "You want me to peel my eyes?"

"That's a metaphor, Tilley. It means keep a hawk eye out, which is another metaphor. Just pay attention."

"Yes, Trent. I know about metaphors. I was making a joke, I will keep my hawk eyeballs peeled though."

"Good enough," he smirked and ran ahead to find Lionheart.

Running alongside the flock, Lionheart was doing a great imitation of a herding dog, even though Trent had always seen him as a hunter. He watched him warn a Chihuahua mix to get back to the group. Unlike a docile cow, the small dog snarled at Lionheart, and Lionheart responded by jumping out of range from the disgruntled Chihuahua. After some posturing, dog sniping, and growling sound effects, the Chihuahua reluctantly rejoined the pack. Lionheart trotted to join Trent.

"Grab a couple of your friends. We need to find a place to holdup for the storm headed our way."

Characteristically, Lionheart didn't respond. He simply went about his business, tagged another dog to take his herding spot and began to collect some friends for the latest mission. When Lionheart returned with three other dogs, Trent explained in simple terms the kind of place the dogs should be looking for. Interestingly, one of the dogs said, "We know. A place to hide from storm."

"Yeah, I guess you guys already understand. No time to waste. I'll go with you, Lionheart. Just run ahead, and I'll try to keep up."

Trent was more exhausted than he thought. Trying to keep Lionheart in sight was sapping his last ounce of energy. He stopped and placed hands on knees to breathe. To his left was an open run of pines and dry grass as far as the eye could see. To his front, the land slowly rose in elevation to what used to be the Boise National Forest, extending to the Sawtooth mountain range. They wouldn't be going as far as the mountains. To the south were more sporadic pines, but the land was also more arid. There just wasn't anyplace he could see that offered protection from the elements.

Trent wasn't as familiar with this stretch of ground as he was with Oregon and Washington. Maybe, they should turn back and find that tributary the dogs had hidden in before. He looked over his shoulder and nearly crapped his pants.

It couldn't be. He clenched his eyes shut and opened them again just to be sure he wasn't so tired he was imagining what was just behind him. Nope, eyes open again, they were still there: three Bigfoots holding laser rifles and pointing them at him. He wanted to shout, "*Aw, come on! This is so not fair. We were almost there.*" Instead he turned to face them, slowly lowering his Hunta ray gun to the ground. He placed his hands in the air to show he was no threat.

Yeah, as if a single man would be a threat to three armed Bigfoots.

During Trent's murderer search, there'd been occasions when he'd glimpsed a Bigfoot presence. Not up close and personal like now, but as a shadow over a ridge or a profile behind trees or large tracks embedded in mud. Some people thought they were all dead, alive only in fantasies. Right now, though, Trent wished they were still a fantasy.

Damn, they're big. They looked a lot like the pictures of Neanderthals he'd seen. A ridge-like overhang with bushy brows topped the eyes, and a short forehead sloped in to the hairline. Large flat noses, thick lips, and a recessed jawline completed the almost primate appearing face. Karen's painting of Uh Huh, a Bigfoot she'd befriended at the change, was a remarkable likeness.

The size of these Bigfoots gave notice they were not Neanderthals recreated on Earth. They had to be seven feet tall. Maybe even bigger than Huntas. Their arms and legs in the same proportion to their bodies as humans, were thicker, more powerful. On his worst day, Trent's hair didn't compare to the pelt of fur which covered the head and bodies of Bigfoots.

One of the Bigfoots grunted, "You come with us."

"I can do that. But just so you know, I have a large group of dogs with me. Can they come too? There's a storm heading this way, and they'll be in grave danger. Also, I'm carrying technology that may save the planet from the Huntas." He thought he'd throw in the technology bit in the event the dog saga wasn't compelling enough.

"We have dogs. Keep them safe."

"You have my dogs?" *Oh my God.* "You know you can't eat them, right? They're just mangy mutts, and they'll make you sick. Very sick."

The Bigfoot glared at him and huffed. He looked at his buddies like he was communicating something, and they scowled at Trent too. Trent was wondering just then how badly he'd stepped in it.

"We not eat dogs. You sick!"

"Okay, okay. I'm sorry. I meant no offense. Take me to my dogs and to your leader. Uh, actually, I have a couple dogs searching out there, can I go get them?"

"They know. They follow. You sick!"

"So you said. Uh, you didn't happen to see an animal with my dogs that was kinda like a donkey, lion, Great Dane thing, did you? She's purple and easy to spot."

"Sick man," the Bigfoot snarled. "Tilley with us."

"Sensitive much? Look, if my dogs are good, I'm good. Lead on."

Chapter 29
Idaho

Trent wondered what the Bigfoots were up to and where in this deserted land they could be headed. He didn't have long to ponder. After a short twenty-minute hike, the Bigfoot who did all the talking, such as it was, said, "Here."

Trent was confused and then frightened. *Here* was a spot like everyplace else. Sure, the land was hillier and rockier, but as he completed a turn, it was just him, three gigantic Bigfoots with lasers, and a collection of pine trees. *Were these hairy jerkoffs lying to me, planning all along to treat my dog flock like a not-so-tasty treat, and maybe me too?*

"You sick," the talking Bigfoot said under his breath, perhaps noticing Trent's distress. He pulled something from the belt he wore over what could best be described as loose rag clothing. Pressing a tiny object, an electronic beeping sounded, and then six feet in front of Trent's feet a metal door swung outward from the ground.

"Oh," Trent said.

The Bigfoot waved both hands in a swooshing movement for Trent to enter the hole that had appeared from nowhere. A ladder on one side led down. Trent descended into the earth and noticed the light below. He kept stepping down until his foot hit ground. He thought about making a run for it in the well-lighted tunnel where he was now standing, but then decided the Bigfoots would surely lose their last ounce of patience if he tried. He moved away from the ladder and waited.

Talking Bigfoot led, and the other two walked behind Trent with lasers pointed at his back. The tunnel he was currently traversing made absolutely no sense. Wide enough for five people abreast, the walls seemed to glow and were lit without any external lighting features. The affect was as close to natural sunlight as Trent had ever witnessed in a place where no sunlight existed. The floor was hard too, made with a material that resembled concrete but wasn't.

They took a right at the first intersection. Trent glanced left at another hallway that seemed to have no end. The tunnel widened further until, after ten minutes of walking, they arrived at a set of metal doors blocking the tunnel. The lead Bigfoot placed his hand on the metal and looked up at something. Trent couldn't see anything on the ceiling to attract the Bigfoot's attention, but whatever he did, it worked. The doors slid into the wall from the center.

Trent was stunned. He'd lived his entire 126 years in the outdoors, in caves and in small homes, but he'd never seen a room of this size. The massive space dwarfed even the hangers at the airfield. He thought it might be possible to fit thirty hangers in this space.

To his front, Mermots were busy making things. Lots and lots of Mermots. Not one of them stopped to look up from their tasks to acknowledge the arrival of the Bigfoots or him. Little rat hands flew over keyboards and wielded tools on electronics and machinery while sleek gray bodies on scampering feet quickly ferried parts from one station to another.

What the hell is this place?

Chrystel had given Trent an envelope with grid coordinates when they rescued Brodie from prison. The only thing she'd said was that if Brodie wanted to help, there was work for him at a secret weapons facility in Idaho. Trent was supposed to keep Brodie safe until they reached the Idaho border. She'd also asked Trent not to look at the location. Well, maybe he'd peeked in the envelope. You never knew when information like that could come in handy and, as it turned out, it was a good thing he'd looked. He'd assumed the secret facility would be some ramshackle operation, like all the other broken down barely held together facilities of the new world. He'd never imagined anything like this place.

The light in this room was just like the halls, but better. He felt like they were outside bathing in daylight, even though there were no windows or domes to create that sense of the outdoors.

He stood awestruck until the talking Bigfoot smirked at him. "You think Earthpeople stupid."

Jolted from his astonishment, Trent shook his head. "I never thought your people were stupid. I'm assuming 'Earthpeople' are what you call yourselves. My mother-in-law, Karen, said that wasn't the case at all. I mean, not that you aren't Earthpeople, I'm totally down with that, but that you're stupid." *I'm digging myself in deeper.*

The Bigfoot's eyes grew wide. Trent wondered how much shit he'd stepped in this time to insult these thin-skinned giants.

"Karen? Karen human friend to king?"

Just go with it Trent, whatever he says. "Yes, that Karen."

The Bigfoot pounded his chest. Not a good sign as far as Trent could tell. The talking Bigfoot communicated something to his posse with his eyes, and they all began to pound their chests and grunt. *Great.*

Gliding along the floor in their direction, a gray blur arrived just in time to save Trent from another unintended Bigfoot slight, er *Earthpeople insult.* She stopped on a dime and rose to her four-foot height, balanced perfectly on her long tail. The Mermot pushed into Trent's mind, "I am Loreta, the clan leader at this facility. Your friend, Tilley, has told me of your bravery and how you saved her and the others.

Welcome, Trent. We are very glad to have you among us."

The Bigfoot talker was eyeing Trent and then gestured to the Mermot. Another eye conversation ensued, this time between the Mermot and the Bigfoot. It suddenly occurred to Trent that Bigfoots might also be able to communicate telepathically. Why else would they continually gaze at each other? Maybe that crack about them eating his dogs had convinced the trio that he was such a sick individual they hadn't wanted to engage him in conversation.

Loreta's pink nose twitched, and she turned to him. "I don't mean to be rude, Trent. You must be very confused. Please allow me to explain. The Earthpeople, which is what they wish to be called—and for your sake, please eliminate Bigfoot from your vocabulary—communicate with each other as Mermots do, through thought transfer. When the Mermots arrived in Idaho to establish this facility, we befriended their kind and learned their language. Unfortunately, they cannot project their speech to humans yet. They have acquired some understanding of your language from Mr. Brodie and a few can speak simple phrases of English.

"Please allow me to introduce your escorts. This is Stone, Sky, and River." She pointed to each as she said their names. I would not attempt the handshake ceremony, for they find touching strangers to be rude."

Trent nodded to the Bigfoots, *dammit, Earthpeople*.

"They are very curious about your friend, Karen. She is important to their leader, who claims she saved him from captivity by merciless humans."

"His name wouldn't happen to be Uh Huh, would it?" Trent asked.

"Yes that is his name. Now, if you will follow me, Brodie is anxious to speak with you."

"Could you apologize to them again for me? I made a comment about them eating my dogs, and they weren't real happy about it."

"Yes, Stone mentioned your insult, and I explained that you were unfamiliar with Earthpeople and their customs. Best that you never speak of it again."

Trent watched as the Bigfoots, aka Earthpeople, moved away. He followed the Mermot along a walkway at the edge of the circular hall, but when he didn't see any trace of his flock, he asked, "Where are my dogs?"

"We are preparing a temporary facility for them now. They have eaten and are resting in the Mermot clan home. Tilley and Lionheart are with Mr. Brodie. Please do not worry. They are safe and comfortable. Your actions to save them were most commendable."

Uncomfortable with the praise and still uncertain he'd chosen the right course, Trent changed the subject. "How many Mermots live here anyway?"

"Today our number is 14,326. We are breeding as fast as the resources become available to support our population growth."

"Is the whole facility underground like this?"

"Yes. As you are probably aware, Mermots have always lived primarily underground. It was decided very early in the development phase of this facility that structures beneath the surface provided the most security. Earthpeople still live topside."

He was just about to ask Loreta what the heck they were making in this awe-inspiring facility, when she pivoted into a room hugging the outside wall. Loreta said, "I will leave you now. There is much work to be accomplished." With that, she disappeared at Mermot speed—fast.

Sitting in a chair, Brodie was talking to Tilley and Lionheart, who were lounging on a plush sofa. Lionheart leaped from his spot and circled Trent's legs in two quick strides before sitting, wildly beating his tail and expecting to be petted. "Good to see you too, boy."

"We saved them!" the dog shouted.

"Yes, we did, Lionheart." Trent gave the dog one of his rare, full on smiles.

Brodie was up too. As Trent grasped the outstretched hand, he scowled. "I didn't think I'd ever see you again, asshole. Just because I did Chrystel a solid favor by helping you escape doesn't mean I've forgotten what you did."

Brodie appeared unruffled by Trent's outburst. "Nor should you. Until too late, I was a coward. There is nothing I can ever do to make up for the lives that were lost, other than give my own, which I was willing to do. All I can do now is give everything of myself to the protection of New Washington and the rest of the world. I am not asking for anything other than a chance to be of service."

Trent studied the dark-haired, brown-eyed man, who was tall, lean and plain-faced, just like him. They could've been related. "Well that's all you're getting from me. As it stands, we need every man, woman, and child to fight the Huntas."

"That works. How is she? How's Chrystel?"

"She still loves you, asshole, if that's what you're asking, but I have no idea how she is at this moment. When the dogs fled the enclave, I decided to go with them. Dammit, maybe I'm a coward too."

A smile spread across Brodie's face, which unsettled Trent given the nature of his last statement. "The enclave has been captured by the Huntas, but Chrystel and Amelia are still alive."

It took Trent's last bit of strength to keep his knees from buckling. Worry about Amelia's fate had been lurking just below the surface every step of his journey from New Washington to this facility. Like a bag of boulders affixed to his shoulders, there was nothing he could do but carry that burden and hope. To know she was still alive was the greatest relief he'd ever known.

"You made a wise choice, Trent. I know from experience that life and death decisions can be far more difficult than anyone knows, especially when you can't know the outcome. You couldn't have saved the people of New Washington, Trent, but you did save their companions."

Trent closed his eyes and nodded. "I guess I got lucky. I brought something else with me, too. Maybe the Mermots could check it out." He pulled the small device from his pocket. "I took this off a Hunta's vest before I left. Thought it might have something to do with their cloaking screen."

Trent handed it to Brodie. Attempting to discern the purpose of the object, Brodie turned it over in his hands several times. He marched away from Trent to his desk and touched a button on a device perched on the corner. "Loreta, send your best engineer here, asap, to pick up some tech Trent brought with him." Breathlessly he added, "This might be the break we were praying for."

Bodie strode back to Trent and clapped him hard on the shoulder. "I said before you'd made a good decision, but now I need to change that. You made a *great* decision! I don't suppose you know we're losing this war because Hunta space ships are cloaked?"

"I dunno," Trent replied. "I was able to see the Hunta spaceships that nearly killed me on my way here."

"Yes, we're not exactly sure why, but the Huntas don't have cloaks on their atmospheric attack fighters. All the Hunta ships in space, the ones that matter, those puppies are invisible."

"Probably shouldn't get ahead of ourselves, Brodie. Doesn't pay to get all worked up before we know."

"You're right. I can't help it, though. Things look bleak right now. Why don't we sit, and I'll tell you all that I know? I'd also be very appreciative for anything you could share about Chrystel."

"That's fair. You got anything to eat or drink? A cup of coffee right now would just about land me in a good mood."

"Actually, if you'll quit referring to me as 'asshole', I can manage both; even a whole pot of coffee."

"Deal." Trent responded.

The two men talked until a Mermot wearing a lab coat on top of overalls came to fetch the little metal box.

"One last thing, Trent. I have a special request from Admiral Mike."

Trent's eyebrows arched up. "What does he want? You know I'd follow that man over a cliff, well maybe not a cliff, but anything for Mike."

"Kinda how we all feel about him. The fact that he still treats me with professionalism is more than I could've hoped. I know he was plenty pissed about what I did. Just over a day ago, Karen was in a wasp heading for this facility. It went down near the border between Idaho and Utah. There was radio silence because of the Huntas in the area. We don't know what happened to her or the pilot. We need someone to find them."

"Of course. Damn, I hope they're okay. Lionheart needs to go too, and one of Karen's dogs should come with us. Her own dog will recognize her smell and be better able to track her."

Brodie nodded. "You'll also need to take a team of Earthpeople with you. They know the area and are well-trained fighters."

"Hold up. You don't want to send Rock, Paper, Scissors with me, do you?"

"Who?"

"You know, those dudes who came and got me." Trent answered.

"You mean Stone, Sky, and River? They do love their earth names." Brodie said. "Yep, those are the 'dudes' you need to take with you. Trust me, they're the best we have. They're the same Earthpeople who downed the Hunta ships that were just about to take you out."

"Oh, they never said."

"They don't say much of anything. We were going to send them for Karen earlier, but then one of our lookouts sent word about you and the dogs, so we decided to get you to safety first. We have several Earthpeople acting as scouts, patrolling a hundred-mile perimeter for Huntas."

"If there's no other option. . ." Trent blew air from his mouth. "I just need to take a piss, find Karen's dogs, and I'll be ready."

"Just be careful what you say around them. They're very sensitive. They had a rough go of it when the world nearly ended. Whatever you do, don't call them Bigfoots and don't accuse them of eating dogs." Brodie chuckled.

"Yeah, I got that," Trent answered. "Word sure travels fast around here."

Chapter 30
Somewhere in the Idaho Wilderness

A pack of Rangers had been tracking Karen and Becky during the night. Their frenzied howling, sounding a lot like coyotes from the old world but bigger, meant they were no longer safe. They'd continued moving until daylight looking for a cave or someplace safe to rest. When the sun came up, they'd taken a break near a copse of trees. Dark, roiling clouds in the distance hastened the urgency to find safety, and they were up on their feet again and moving. Karen pondered whether high winds and lightning in the open or Ranger attacks at night were the greatest threat.

She also wondered what had happened to the coyotes and the wolves. Had the mass introduction of pet dogs into the wild after the Great Dying overpowered nature's balance of canine species in the North American Hemisphere? She could understand coyotes losing out to dogs, but the wolves too? She supposed if the world was able to fend off the Huntas, someday, someone would study what had happened. Didn't matter really, but it would be good to know.

They scaled a bluff and walked atop a ridgeline. The conversation turned to Becky's feelings for the pilot, Mark. Karen asked, "Could you get reassigned to a different fleet so he wouldn't be your boss?"

"Maybe, but then I'd never see him. I don't know if he even likes me in that way. Anyway, we have bigger fish to fry right now. I should just forget about—"

Becky's thought was cut short. Her left foot wobbled, and her body jerked sideways. Becky had been very close to the edge of an overlook. The sudden twist of an ankle coupled with forward momentum sent her sliding headfirst over the point of no return.

Karen grabbed for her leg, but it was already too late. Becky departed down the steep face of a ridge and began to roll as she picked up speed. Her limbs flailing, she'd attempted to grab hold of something to slow her descent, but a fortuitously placed Lodgepole pine half-way down, abruptly stopped her progress and probably saved her life. Unable to do a thing, Karen had watched Becky's fall in slow-motion horror.

She scuttled down the ridge on her butt to find Becky conscious and moaning. Her ankle was either sprained or broken, but if the amount of swelling at the joint was any indication, it might well be broken. Karen conducted an injury assessment and believed Becky had fared better than expected from her fall and subsequent collision. Bleeding from a gash on her chin and another in her hair, the young woman was thankfully still lucid.

It should have been her. After all, she was the old one, the one more prone to tripping. Becky was a fine, healthy young woman. Perhaps that was the problem, Karen thought. She was aware of her limitations and was watchful where she placed her feet, afraid a fall could break her into pieces that could never be properly locked back into place. Young people often believed themselves invincible and charged ahead without giving a second thought to their vulnerability. Sometimes, Karen missed her invincible days.

Becky sat up, wailed, and grabbed her shoulder. Karen noticed the dangling left arm. She said, "Let me look at it." With a hand in the crook of her chest and another holding the arm, she jerked Becky's shoulder back into place before she was able to protest. The scream Becky let loose sent the hairs on the back of Karen's neck to attention.

"Okay, dear. I know that hurt, but better to get it over with now rather than waiting."

Becky shouted. "Says you!"

Popping the shoulder into place had made it easier for Karen to drag the young woman the rest of the way down the ridge without killing either of them. At the bottom, she helped Becky to her one good foot because the other would hold no weight. Resting the pilot's arm over her shoulder, Karen grabbed Becky around her waist and slowly moved forward carrying their gear and her one-footed travelling companion. Karen didn't want to move her, but the threatening skies left little choice.

Just as hail began pelting her face, Karen finally found a small rock alcove, barely big enough for the two of them. Dragging Becky the last bit and positioning her against the wall, Karen discovered that their tiny bit of safety didn't offer protection from the wind. Karen's hair was whipping into her eyes, and she turned her back to the worst of it. At least they were shielded from lightning here, which crackled and boomed, making her jump in reaction. Each bolt seemed to have the capacity to surprise her anew.

When she had Becky settled, she placed her hand on the girl's forehead. Like most mom's, Karen's hands were sensitively tuned instruments for detecting fevers. Becky felt warm. *Damn. We're totally, fucking screwed.*

Lugging the extra weight of a medical kit along during their trek had been effort well spent. After digging through the bag, Karen said, "At least we have all the antis with us: antibiotics, antipain, and anti-inflammatories." Nudging Becky, she leaned over her and whispered, "I'm really sorry this happened, but I need you to sit you up to take some meds."

Becky moaned.

Wiggling her arm under Becky's shoulders, she raised her enough to place pills on her tongue and help her drink a cup of water.

"I'm sorry," Becky mumbled. "I should've been more careful."

"Nothing to be sorry about. It is what it is. We'll deal. That's what I do, and if what I heard about you at Rainier Station is true, so do you."

Becky nodded and closed her eyes.

After ministering to Becky's cuts and scrapes and icing her ankle with a cold pack from the kit, Karen decided she needed a break. She hadn't realized how tired she was. Facing the wind and rain, she sat cross legged chewing an Ardinian energy bar and watching the dazzling light show. She marveled at the majesty of a storm and was grateful that she was here in this moment to experience it. She could almost feel the ion charged air teasing her goose-bumped skin.

No matter how screwed tomorrow might be, Karen thought she wouldn't soon forget how a storm had reminded her about the gift of life. To embrace each moment whether that included tossing at sea like a cork or puke-worthy maneuvers in flight.

Sure, old gal, now you think that. We'll see how it goes later when those Rangers make their play for you and Becky.

What was it about a storm that made her feel so free? She felt like just another wild creature waiting out the weather with survival her only concern. Karen wished Mike was sitting here with her, enjoying untamed nature. To her other side she imagined her first family sitting close by. Anne, Nathan and Don, gone now, lost like everyone else in the Great Dying. Gone too but just at her feet, the dogs who were constant companions during her loneliest hours after the Great Dying: Tilley, Raider, Maple, Zoe, Jack, and Jill. Beside them were her living children and grandchildren and her own deceased grandfather. Friends that were like family stood close behind: Katie, Rachael, Thomas, Jed, and Mabel. Even the mercurial Shakete had joined the gang.

She asked herself how it was possible for one woman to have had so much love and life. Feeling the raging storm sucking every molecule that comprised her body outward, she expanded until her embrace included the entire world, and she thought that she might burst from the fullness.

Her eyes fluttered open to find that the storm had stopped. *Shit, I must've been hallucinating or dreaming.* Night had replaced day, and she heard Rangers yipping too close for comfort.

Karen rubbed her eyes and shook off a chill. Time to get busy. Other than one laser rifle and some rocks lying around to throw at them, there wasn't much available to fend off a pack of

Rangers. If everything wasn't so damn wet, it might've been possible to build a fire to discourage their advance. The laser would have to do.

The worst part of the whole situation was that Karen didn't want to laser an animal, predator or otherwise. She would, of course, to save her life and the life of the pilot, fitfully sleeping behind her. The Great Dying and all who were lost made the prospect of any act of killing detestable. Mike was the only one who knew that she'd quit eating meat some time ago for that reason. She'd never confessed to anyone, other than him, that the thought of eating an animal made her gag. That admission would make her seem too much like a few of the self-righteous vegetarians she'd known. Also a wuss.

Nevertheless, the laws of the jungle still applied. When survival was at stake she'd do what she must. She grabbed the laser and checked the charge, which registered fully green. She then nudged Becky awake again. "Becky, you need to wake up and take more pills. I need your help."

"What?"

"I believe the Ranger pack that's been following us is near. Gather some rocks and get your throwing arm ready."

Becky asked, "Are you serious?"

"As a heart attack. I'll handle the laser. Up with you now."

Karen watched the surrounding woods as she began piling rocks for Becky's part. Mike had shown her how to use the laser. Aiming a laser was identical to firing a regular rifle. The settings were something like stun, destroy, and incinerate, marked by low, medium, and high on the stock. With any luck, some hurled rocks and stunning shots would do the trick.

She heard Becky moving around behind her and then gulping water. "Don't forget the pills. They're lying on the med kit."

"No kidding. Everything hurts, and I feel like crap. You think there's something bleeding inside, Karen?"

Karen didn't answer. Becky's question sounded more rhetorical anyway. "There's one!" Karen hissed. A dog shape was standing perfectly still, loitering next to a lonely Western hemlock a mere fifty yards away. "Okay, you son of a bitch, what're you up to?" Karen growled.

Pack noises had stopped, which was never a good omen when predators were in the neighborhood. Karen saw movement to her right and heard the distinctive residual noise of rocks sliding on dirt from higher on the ridge.

Becky asked, "What're they going to do, Karen? Where should I be looking?"

"Simple answer, Firestarter, I wish the hell I knew."

Becky crawled on her hands and knees next to Karen and then twisted into a sitting position. Karen noticed that Becky had encased her ankle with the flexible composite stabilizer included in the med kit. She pointed at the purple wrapped ankle. "The Ardinians make some great shit, don't they?"

"They do. Their pain pills are something to write home about, too—all the pain relief without the side effects. I just wish everything wasn't colored purple."

"There's that," Karen said. "So, back to your original question." Karen held up her hand, and her head whipped to the left. "Another one at ten o'clock. Rangers are mostly dog, some wolf, and a dash of coyote. There are some similarities in their hunting styles, but each variety of canine is a little different. If we assume Rangers took on the most successful attributes of the three, my guess is that their approach will be primarily wolf for hunting bigger game. In this case, us."

"Okay…What does that mean?"

"Bad news. They're flexible. Depends on the prey, but in general, they're looking for weakness. They'll track prey for days and then break off an attack and go elsewhere if they find their target too difficult to kill. They can probably smell your wounds and think we're weak, and screwed, which we are, but they aren't aware of our little equalizer called a laser rifle. Don't imagine they've had much contact with people out here.

"It also probably depends on how hungry they are and the size of the pack. They might try to flush us out from one side to make us run, and have another group lying in wait to take us down. They work as a team."

Becky sighed. "Karen, you need a call sign. I'm awarding you the name *Calamity*. How do you know all this stuff about wolves? Is there a wolf or two in your past?"

"No wolves. A bear though, but don't get me started on them. I like it. I've always wanted a call sign, but no one ever gifted me one. Calamity seems to fit. Calamity!" Karen rolled the word around in her mouth with some reverence. "Thank you. Calamity Karen is even better."

A Ranger howled, sounding a lot closer.

"So, what would you like me to do?" Becky asked.

"Just cover our right flank with the rocks. You probably can't move very quickly anyway. I'll screen to the front and the left. By the way, are you any good at throwing?"

Becky smiled. "Fortunately, my throwing arm isn't the same one you jerked unannounced into the socket."

"Excellent. Now we wait. God help us if they sneak up on that ledge and jump down from above."

Becky looked up at the jutting rock that had provided some protection from the storm. When she turned to Karen, the whites of her eyes were showing all around her pupils. "That would be very bad. Is it feasible for us to give them a show of our strength? Act first and stun the ones we can see. If what you say is true, maybe they'll just give it up and go elsewhere."

Karen nodded. "That might work. It might also force them into action. Hell, I don't know. Let's try it. I didn't really want to sit up awake all night waiting on them anyway. Get ready, Firestarter. Calamity Karen is springing into action."

The whites of Becky's eyes were still clearly displayed. She scooted on her knees and grabbed some rocks. "I'm ready when you are, Calamity. Blast away."

Double checking the firing setting, Karen verified the laser was on low. She cradled the stock in her shoulder, centered the one animal she could see in her viewfinder, and gently pressed the trigger. The laser rifle made almost no noise. Even the laser bolt exiting the barrel was invisible until it passed through humidity or hit an object. Karen thought it would've been far better if the laser was loud and bright.

As it was, the Ranger she hit let out a soul-wrenching wail, twitched, and fell over on its side. The laser stun might not have been the display the women had hoped for, but it had been enough to ignite the passions of the remainder of the pack. They sprang into action. The attack started with a leap from atop the rock overhang. A Ranger stuck a ten-point landing to the front of a shocked Calamity.

"Dammit all!" she screamed as she turned the laser around and clubbed the snarling Ranger with the butt end of her rifle.

Chapter 31
New Washington

Herman unlocked Amelia's cell and opened the door wide. He hovered just outside her cell without making a click or a hiss. "You want me to follow you?" Amelia asked.

Chrystel's first instinct was to interrogate Herman and pepper him with questions about where he planned to take her mother, but what would be the point? He couldn't answer anyway, even if he understood. "Maybe they're letting you go, Mom. This might be a good thing."

Amelia hesitated as she listened for the disconnected voice to provide some guidance. She whispered, "You'd think, just once, you could help when I asked."

Chrystel and Thomas exchanged concerned looks through the bars. This wasn't the first time Amelia had conversed with herself.

"We'll be fine, Mom. Just go." Chrystel added.

Amelia turned to her and said, "Fine. I love you."

"Love you too, Mom. We won't give up," Chrystel answered, doing her level best to prevent fear from sneaking into her voice.

Amelia squared her shoulders and marched from the cell. Herman fell in behind, prodding her forward.

When the jail door locked shut, Thomas asked, "What do you think?"

"My hope is they don't see her as a threat. She's been here for four days. If they captured Kismet, found the note, or the hole under Amelia's cot, it seems like they'd have taken her sooner."

Even though he wasn't entirely sure Chrystel's estimate was correct, he answered, "Sounds about right. So, what do you have planned for today?"

"I don't know. Some exercise, meditation, a nap or two, and then maybe we can play singles charades again."

"You always win. We need a new game."

"Virtual golf?"

Thomas' rumbling laugh stopped when he heard the key turning for a second time. The prisoners shuffled to the back of their cells. Hunta guards had recently launched a new method for keeping them away from cell doors by urinating on them if they got too close. Thomas was surprised that such a large alien could have such an itty bitty dick. Maybe that was part of their problem. The Huntas had an alien style Napoleon complex.

Cleo, who was now dressed in a silver lame spacesuity-getup, gracefully slithered forward to the midway point between their cells. Her hair, transformed again, was a short, shaggy blonde do. Cleo's personal body guards stood on opposite sides of the interior door, their massive shoulder spanning the entire space. Thomas wondered why it was necessary for Cleo to bring her bouncers along. He sure as hell wasn't any threat from this cell. Maybe they were worried he might try to urinate on Cleo like they'd done to him.

"Love the new look, Cleo." Thomas said. "Where you been keeping yourself?"

She giggled. "I'm pleased you like it. I've been keeping myself busy caring for your people."

Chrystel groaned. Cleo's head whipped in her direction like a stepped-on snake. "I would mind your manners if I was you. Your mother's probation can be easily revoked." Cleo paused to allow that statement to settle.

"You are probably wondering about my visit today. First, as an act of compassion, I've allowed Amelia to return to your people. She was instrumental in keeping the young humans from underfoot, and we wish for her to continue that important responsibility.

"Additionally, Chrystel's guard has been severely punished for allowing escalation of what should have been a simple matter. We cannot maintain a civil relationship with your people unless you follow our orders and accept our total authority as superior beings. There can be no other way.

"Chrystel, you will be punished as well. Once your behavior reinforcement is administered, we wish that you speak with Ted regarding his hunger strike and convince him of the futility of his gesture. If you succeed, we will allow you to resume your coordination duties."

"Why do you care whether he starves himself to death or not?" Chrystel asked.

With an evil smirk, Cleo turned to her. "Did I ask you for a question? Our motives are of no concern of yours. Please refrain from further rudeness and disrespect until I authorize a question. Any further interruptions will result in more severe punishment."

Thomas could see Chrystel's face go beet red. He couldn't be sure whether her scarlet skin was from anger or humiliation. Maybe both. Either way, she needed to keep her damn mouth shut, so he stared her down with the most ferocious look he had in his arsenal. She glanced over at him and scowled back. *Damn, that woman is stubborn*, he thought. *Like a redder, angrier version of her grandmother.*

"Thomas, although you may be my favorite human, I'm afraid you will have to remain in this cell. Your presence among your people might be too disruptive."

Cleo paused and examined first Chrystel and then Thomas. Thomas thought she was probably hoping for another question, so she'd have an excuse to punish them. He didn't know every Hunta, but this one was a sadist, plain and simple.

Thankfully, Chrystel held her tongue. Finally, Cleo giggled and said, "That is all."

As she was leaving the jail room, Cleo stopped and spoke dismissively over her shoulder. "Oh, and we know about the dog." And then she was gone.

Chrystel let out a frustrated scream. "Nothing works, Thomas. If Mike or someone doesn't save us, we're dead."

"You're probably right, but I think we heard some good news. First, she didn't say 'we captured the dog' or 'we tortured and killed the dog', and believe me, she would have just to see us squirm. Kismet is still out there.

"Secondly, ole Ted is putting up some fight. Might've known it'd be a hunger strike, but still, he's on our side. We're still in this fight, Chrystel. Well, at least, you are. I'll be practicing my French from behind bars, but visit when you can," he smiled.

Chrystel said, "Before I go, I need to share something with you. It's about Ted."

* * *

Herman reappeared after lunch. He used the same routine he'd used for Chrystel's mom: he opened the cell door without the normal Hunta expletives.

Chrystel thought he looked different somehow. Like he was sad or bummed. She couldn't get a handle on it. When he followed her out, he didn't even poke her in the back with his ray gun. *Weird*.

She didn't understand why she was feeling bad for that asshole. None of the Huntas deserved an iota of sympathy or pity. He led her through the gate into human country and up the stairs to the courthouse. They took a left toward theaters six to nine, and stopped at the last door, previously the enclave's documents room.

They entered, and Herman flipped on lights. Cabinets and dusty brown boxes holding who-knows-what were scattered along three walls just like when Chrystel was still mayor. The only difference was a Hunta sized chair sitting by itself in the middle of the room. Restraints on the arms and legs and at the point where a Hunta neck would land were attached and beckoning.

Herman pointed and clicked without his usual enthusiasm.

Chrystel said, "Might as well get this over with. I don't see a tarp underneath. Does that mean I won't have to worry about my bodily fluids leaking onto the carpet?"

She sighed and tried to think of something besides what was about to happen. If she pretended she wasn't afraid, maybe she'd be less so. She reluctantly moved to the chair and sat. If there was any chance to escape, she'd try, but she'd have to disarm Herman first, get by the rest of the Hunta guards in the courthouse, and then escape through a locked gate beside a weaponized guard shack. Only in fiction did the heroine try a stunt like that and succeed.

Herman watched her every move from across the room but remained well away from her. When she sat, he clicked into a device. Within a minute, two other Huntas arrived. They hustled to Chrystel's position in the chair, locked the restraints into place, and then they left. It was just her and Herman.

He continued examining her with a very un-Hunta expression. Chrystel thought it was almost as if something was going on in his head besides how best to hurt her. He took a few steps closer and began to click. This clicking was different from the normal order-the-humans-around ferocious clicking. With a modulation like speech, Herman was trying to tell Chrystel something. She had no idea what it was.

"Let me try," she said. "You know yes and no, right? Yes, up and down like this," Chrystel's head bobbed. "No, shake back and forth like this," she shook back and forth.

Herman nodded yes.

"All right. I'll ask questions and you try to answer. If you don't understand, stick out your tongue." Chrystel demonstrated.

"They tortured you?"

Another nod.

"You are angry?" Chrystel made an angry face. Herman nodded again.

"You are angry at Chrystel?"

This time he shook a no. A very surprising no.

"You are angry at Cleo?"

An emphatic nod. Of all the surprising revelations, Herman's was most unexpected. Maybe not Brodie as a traitor unexpected, but close. She'd been so certain Herman was a sadist, that all Huntas were soulless sadists. Where to go from here, Chrystel wondered?

"Are there any listening devices in here?" Chrystel pointed around the room and then to her ears.

Herman shook his head

"Are you sure?"

With palms up and his head cocked, he shook again. Chrystel thought it was a human, I'm-not-sure gesture. The Huntas were learning more from them than anyone knew.

"Well, what do I have to lose?" Chrystel asked herself out loud. "You don't want to torture Chrystel?"

A nod. "Well don't then. I'll scream and pretend you're hurting me."

Herman stuck out his tongue.

"No torture Chrystel. I will scream." Herman didn't answer. The veins in his eyeballs were pulsating more than normal. Chrystel let loose a scream and Herman twitched. "Oh, that hurts so much," she howled.

Herman decided. He nodded a yes.

Chrystel commenced a screaming, yelling, and moaning routine worthy of a middle school drama production. When her voice lost its strength, warbling in and out, she asked, "Enough?"

A double shake. Herman grabbed his ears and made a face. He came near her slowly, his hand out in a wait signal and carefully, like Chrystel might bite, released her from the restraints. She jumped from the chair and darted away from the torture device to the other side of the room. Wary, Herman lifted his ray gun in her direction while backing away.

"Don't worry, Herman. I'm not going to try anything." She began plucking strands of hair from her ponytail and then rubbed her hand over a dusty box. After applying the dust to her face, she stretched a sleeve of her knit shirt until it ripped. "Better?" she asked.

Another nod and a click. Herman got his best surly guard on and nudged her forward, this time poking her in the back. "Now we're in character, Herman!" He stuck out his tongue.

Herman deposited Chrystel at Ted's "office" and hissed. She cursed at him in return and then entered Ted's closet after Herman unlocked the door. Ted was sitting in the very same position as her last visit, doing something on the notepad. Chrystel wondered if he ever moved from that chair. When he glanced up, his face was drawn but he smiled. "Well I'll be. It worked."

Chrystel cocked her head in a question.

"I told Cleo I wouldn't work with anyone else or eat until she released you."

"Why, Ted? You don't even like me."

"True enough. But if we're going to have any chance here, we need you on the outside, not in a cell. That, and I was sick of eating their shit. Especially Cleo's. I thought about what you said. I don't want to live like this."

Chrystel signaled for Ted's tablet. When he handed it over she typed: *Are you still sleeping with Cleo? Why else do they need you, and what do you know?*

Ted typed. *No. I refused Cleo. Maybe another reason she got you out of jail.*

312

They exchanged information on the tablet and, as cover, discussed greenhouse operations at the same time. One of them would talk as the other wrote. It was a herky-jerky conversation, but Chrystel's suspicions about the Huntas' purpose here were confirmed. Ted had managed to get a smidgeon of information from Cleo and filled in the rest with logical deduction. What neither of them could grasp was the timing. How long would it be before Cleo lined them up for the slaughter as a threat?

The sound of Herman manipulating the door stopped further conversation. Ted was already deleting their conversation from the tablet.

"You've earned a little trust, Ted. Same warning as before though, don't screw us."

He didn't look up when he replied, "You know, Chrystel, at this point the tough guy routine isn't helpful."

"Yeah, you're probably right. It can become habit. Later, Ted."

She purposely ran from the room and barreled into Herman. For an instant, Chrystel saw the old fire behind Herman's eyes, and then he clicked in what might have been a Hunta chuckle. With one hand, he shoved her in return, sending Chrystel to her butt on the floor.

"Let the games begin," Chrystel sneered up at him.

The journey from the courthouse to her mother's tent was as before, with Herman hassling her the entire way. His pokes still hurt because he didn't hold back, but somehow they were different. Chrystel thought it amazing that one identical action, a poke in the back, could seem like a threat or joking prodding, all dependent on the recipient's perspective.

She also wondered what was really going on with Ted. Had he been sleeping with Cleo willingly, or did he feel coerced? He was a grown man, but what choice did he really have? There was an immense power differential. He'd also gone on a hunger and sex strike to spring her from jail, but were his actions really for her or some other motive? Which part of his story was true? Was Cleo worried about sex, Ted's well-being, or both? And, just thinking about Ted's coupling with that evil alien bitch made Chrystel gag. *Damn*, she thought, *adding sex just made everything more complicated*. She'd learned that the hard way with Brodie, even though admittedly it was more for love with Brodie, but the same idea.

She hadn't even had time to ask Ted those questions. He'd seemed sincere, but given everything she knew about him, how much could he be trusted?

Herman shoved her one last time and left her at the entrance to her mom's tent. Chrystel listened from the outside as Amelia told a story about a brother and sister who'd been captured by a powerful witch and how they used their wits to escape. The tale and her mother's narration held Chrystel in its grip. *No wonder these kids were so mesmerized by her mother*, she thought. And no wonder it had hurt so much when her mom had gone over the deep end after her father's untimely death. It shook Chrystel to the core to experience the loss and devastation with adult eyes. *No wonder I have issues.*

After the joyous reunion of the story siblings with their parents, Chrystel entered the tent. Children's heads turned to her entry. She could see fear, hunger, grief, agitation, and trauma written on their innocent faces. Yet, the hopefulness of Amelia's story was written there, too. Chrystel smiled at her mother.

"Time for a nap, children," Amelia said. "After you sleep, I have a new game we can play." She gestured for Chrystel to join her.

They hugged, then they both started speaking at once. Amelia said, "You first Chrystel. I'm mixed about whether I'm glad you're out of that horrible prison. You seem to get yourself into more trouble when you're out."

"That's the way of it, Mom. Don't think it'll change soon. Have you seen Kismet?"

Amelia beamed. "She's back!"

Chapter 32
Purple House

The next morning, Herman retrieved Chrystel and Margo for a day at the greenhouse. Chrystel whispered to Margo as they neared the ATV, "Be careful what you say when the Huntas are around. They understand some English."

"I know. The Huntas in the greenhouses are responding to a lot of what I say."

Chrystel was excited about this trip. She hadn't been outside the fence or a cell in almost a week. Also, Kismet had brought in two notes during her incarceration. One was extremely important. The note asked Chrystel to consider a plan that would allow the Mermots to dig under the town center and/or greenhouses and steal people out. Apparently, there were enough Mermots in the area to make an escape happen if she could come up with a workable plan.

The tags implanted in each person remained a significant impediment to any escape attempt. They still didn't know what was in the devices or how they worked. Ted said that he'd asked Cleo, and she'd responded, "They contain death." Someone would need to be a test subject before any plan could be formulated. Chrystel had briefly considered asking Katie to surgically remove her tag, and then decided it was too early for anyone to take that chance.

Regardless, a trip to the greenhouses would be informative. Chrystel alternated her attention between the surrounding area, scanning for Mermots, and then Herman, wondering whether he could be an ally or if he was simply a disgruntled employee. Probably the latter. Since their little behavior reinforcement session the day before, Herman seemed to be back to his old asshole self, completely confident, indifferent, threatening, and cruel. For no apparent reason, he'd swatted Margo upside the head when she'd climbed aboard the ATV. Margo had given him the stink eye, but she knew better than to go further. Speaking of stink, even Herman's disgusting odor was bothering Chrystel again.

They turned onto Steilacoom Boulevard, an old-world street that was now a two-lane gravel path. Chrystel could see the greenhouses sparkling in the distance. The light from inside the closest one was infused with a purple hue. Margo commented, "The plants already have new poopueater fruit on the stocks. They should be fully grown in about four days, but the fruit is covered with razor sharp thorns. I'm not sure how we're supposed to pick them."

Herman delivered them to the door and hissed a command to leave. Once inside, the Hunta supervisor lumbered over to Margo. He was hissing and clicking as if throwing a fit. Margo raised her hand in an *I don't know* gesture and said, "Show me."

The Hunta led them through the center aisle to the far end of the greenhouse. Chrystel could hear someone crying before they stopped. A teenage girl was sitting on the floor, red-faced. The girl gazed down at her bleeding hands that she held palms up on her lap. "What happened?" Margo asked the man crouching next to her.

"They wanted us to pick their poop," he raged. "They wanted us to check on ripeness. I told them we needed gloves, but that moron Hunta supervisor kept on hitting Sophie in the back until she gave in. I volunteered, for crap's sake! She won't let me touch her hands because she says they're burning like fire."

Margo turned to the Hunta standing behind her and gave him a look that could possibly freeze his heart on the spot. "Go get some water, now!" She ordered the supervisor. He immediately ran toward the water barrels. Chrystel had the impression the Hunta just wanted to be out of Margo's blast radius. She also wondered why humans and Huntas obeyed Margo like following her orders was no big deal.

Chrystal stooped next to the teenager. "Are you okay, Sophie?" she asked. The girl responded by nodding and shedding more tears. "We're going to wash out whatever is on your hands. That'll make them feel better. Then we'll take care of the cuts."

The man crouching beside Sophie stood. Clenched fists and a locked jaw suggested he was thinking of doing something stupid. Chrystel knew the feeling well. She stood with him and placed her hand on his arm. "I know what you're thinking, but it won't help Sophie," she said. "You'll have your chance, but it isn't now."

He studied Chrystel and then spat, "I hope you're right, *Mayor*. This just ain't right."

"Agreed. Now get out of the way before he comes back. Just keep that anger for when we need it."

"No worries there. I'm Liam from tent eleven. If you need me, I'll be ready."

"Good to know. Now scoot."

Liam had barely turned the corner before the supervisor Hunta returned with a bucket of water. Margo and Chrystel dipped the teenager's hands, which seemed to provide some relief. "Thank you," Sophie said.

With a tight smile, Margo said, "You go see Helen in Greenhouse Two. She'll bandage your hand."

As soon as the teenager shuffled away, Margo turned on the Hunta supervisor. Her finger shook in his scaly, ugly face. Sternly she warned "Not one more of my people touches that damn fruit without heavy gloves. You got that?"

Chrystel was ready to act if the Hunta had tired of Margo's insolence. Surprisingly, other than the posturing hiss Chrystel had mastered, the Hunta backed down and left, clicking to himself as he went. *How does she do that?*

Margo said, "They love that damn fruit and can't wait for it to be ready. I warned him we couldn't handle the stuff without gloves, but he wouldn't listen. Sometimes, these Huntas are like big, strong, petulant kids. He only listened to me because he needs our help to harvest this purple shit. I guess the Huntas are pragmatic, too."

"Uh huh. Never thought of it that way, but you may be right. Listen, we need to talk. Can we walk around?"

Margo sauntered down the far walkway and Chrystel followed. "What's up?"

"The Mermots are staging near the enclave. They want to tunnel in and sneak our people out. Question is how? You're better at this stuff than me. Think you could look at all the Huntas comings and goings and come up with a plan?"

"What's the goal, Chrystel? If it's everybody, I'm not sure it's possible. We might get most of them out, but what about Thomas and our implants?"

"If you come up with a plan, I'll help you execute and solve the tag issue. Not sure we can free Thomas." Chrystel replied.

Margo looked skeptical. She walked halfway to the front of the greenhouse before she spoke. "Hell yes, I can come up with a plan. Give me a day, and we can talk tomorrow night."

Chapter 33
Idaho Wilderness

Trent and his Earthpeople companions settled on an uneasy truce. Mostly that meant Trent was quiet, kept up with them, and did what he was good at: looking for clues as to Karen and the pilot's whereabouts. They were travelling from north of the crash site, and Karen would be heading in the opposite direction, so there wouldn't be a track to follow. If they randomly crossed paths somewhere along the road then all the better, but there was a lot of country out here. Trent thought they would most likely have to do some backtracking.

Karen's dog, Sadie, was the very same matted doodle dog that Trent had shared a moment with while washing in the creek. He'd seen Sadie before, but with the dirty, matted coat he hadn't made the connection. She and Lionheart trotted up ahead.

Sadie darted to a tree and chased two chattering squirrels up the trunk. Sadie barked twice, her tail wagging, and positioned herself just underneath the nut-eating rodents knowing that she couldn't reach them. Meanwhile, Lionheart continued searching for the scent of humans with his nose to the ground.

"Sadie, keep on task," Trent yelled to her. "We're trying to find your woman master, not squirrels and rabbits." She turned to him and smiled, then bounded in an almost hopping motion to Lionheart's side again. Trent heard her say, "Must find woman master."

Sadie was goofy, talkative, playful, and a natural hunter. Such a natural hunter, it was hard to keep her on track. She'd captured at least one rabbit, and her exuberance was even infecting the normally quiet and focused Lionheart. When Sadie rejoined Lionheart, she dashed around him in a circle with her butt tucked, and he playfully nipped at her haunches.

One of the Earthpeople grunted and pointed to the sky, a signal to stop for the night. They'd been travelling since first light, and the sun had set over the western horizon. Trent nodded even though he wanted to keep going for a time. There was no point arguing with the Earthpeople though. He'd noticed they weren't what he'd call flexible. Yesterday, he'd waved at them to go around rather than over a hillock, and it had almost caused an intra-species incident. Stone had pounded his chest and grunted, and then his buddies had joined in. Trent decided it wasn't worth the trouble and had nodded in agreement as he began an unnecessary climb.

They set up camp. The Earthpeople oversaw establishing a fire, and Trent was the cook. He carried spices with him and added them to smoked meat, freeze dried potatoes, and water in a pan. At least they seemed to like his cooking.

Lionheart and Sadie sidled up to Trent on opposite sides for handouts. Sadie repeatedly said, "Sadie hungry," while Lionheart just gave him the hungry stare. He gave them bits of meat and reminded the dogs, "I know you had at least one rabbit today. You don't fool me with the hunger routine."

The Earthpeople didn't talk, so the evening was as quiet as if Trent were alone. At least, it would have been quiet if not for Sadie. She liked to do a play by play: *Sadie eat, Man sleep, Sadie sleep, Sadie sleep by man.* On and on she went until she finally stretched on the ground next to Trent and closed her eyes.

Sometime later, hooting owls woke the dogs, and they started barking. Trent rolled over and said harshly, "Go to sleep." Lionheart growled, and his fur raised on his back. Sadie was quick to join in. Trent sat up, grabbed the laser, and listened. The Earthpeople were stirring from their pine needle nests too. He heard something shuffling in the underbrush, and then a Ranger appeared out of the darkness. Lionheart recognized the Ranger and moved forward to greet it, while Sadie positioned herself behind Trent.

One of the Earthpeople almost shot it, but Trent yelled in the nick of time, "No! I know this Ranger. It won't hurt you." He dug in his pack for a piece of meat and offered it to the animal who padded forward to receive the gift. Trent patted the animal on the head. "Where's your friend?"

"Gone," the male Ranger answered. Trent got the sense that gone meant dead. By this time, Sadie had gathered enough courage to come out from behind Trent's legs and was making a submissive greeting to the Ranger, her tail and head down as she crept forward to him to sniff. The Ranger seemed to appreciate the gesture and wagged its tail.

Trent felt partially responsible for the Ranger who'd lost his master, AJ. He asked, "Do you want to stay with us now?"

"Yes," the rangy canine answered. "Pack?"

"If you'd like. Do you have a name?" Trent had heard AJ call the two Rangers Wiley and Roadrunner, but he didn't know one from another. They were nearly identical to begin with.

"Wiley name."

"Did you happen to see any other humans like me in your travels?"

"Yes. Female humans."

"Can you show us where?"

"Yes," the Ranger answered and moved his feet in a prancing motion.

Trent's voice took on urgency, "Are they okay? Are the female humans good?"

"Hurt. Blood. Ranger pack."

Trent looked at Stone. "We need to pull up camp now and keep moving. This Ranger knows where some hurt women are located. I can't imagine there's any other women out here alone."

Stone nodded. "Yes. We go."

In only minutes, the group was on the move again. It was fully dark, but they travelled briskly. Wiley was leading, and Lionheart and Sadie followed close behind. Trent and the Earthpeople had to jog to keep up.

Three hours of strenuous searching later, it was Sadie who bolted to the front. For the first time since setting off on their search, Sadie ran with a purpose. They all picked up the pace with the knowledge Sadie knew Karen was near.

When Trent arrived at the rock alcove, it was difficult to make sense of the scene. The two stacked and dead Rangers he'd passed made it obvious there'd been a battle between human and animal predators. Becky was aiming her weapon between the Earthpeople and Wiley. "Don't come one inch closer," she shouted.

It was dark, but Trent could see the outline of a body lying on the ground behind Becky. Sadie was whining and dove toward the lifeless figure.

"Please put down your weapon," he said. "We're from the Idaho facility and here to rescue you. I'm Trent. My wife is Karen's daughter. These…" Trent almost blurted Bigfoots. "These Earthpeople are our friends."

A moment later, Becky let the rifle slide from her hands. Trent jogged over after Sadie and noticed Becky was shivering. "I thought we were doomed," she said between breaths. "Thank you for coming. But why do you have one of those awful Rangers with you?"

"Long story, but he's a talking Ranger and not awful at all. Can I move closer?"

She nodded. Trent shouldered the laser before joining Becky and squatting next to Karen. Sadie was licking Karen's face as if to wake her. He pushed the dog away and checked Karen's pulse. She was alive, but her breathing seemed shallow. "What happened?"

The tears started. Between gulps of air Becky told Trent about everything that happened to them until the Ranger attack during the storm. "I either broke my ankle, or it's badly sprained. Twisted it on a rock and then rolled down a hill and crashed into a tree. Karen walked me here. It was lucky she found this little rock inset because that storm and all the lightning might have been our undoing. When we woke up, it was night, and there were Rangers everywhere, very interested in us for dinner. One of them jumped from this overhang, and Karen clobbered it with her laser.

"After that, it's all kind of a blur. I was throwing rocks, and she was stunning the Rangers with the laser. Another one jumped from above. Karen was scooting away from it and fell hard and hit her head. I beat it to death with a rock." Her lower lip trembled. "It was such a scrawny thing."

"Are you okay?" Trent asked.

"Does it look like I'm okay?" she moaned.

"Stupid question. How long has Karen been out?"

"Almost two days. With my ankle there was no way I could carry her anywhere. I just kept hoping she would wake up. I was going to give it a try tomorrow." Becky stopped and stared at the Ranger that was watching her. "Hmmm."

"What?" Trent asked

"It's just strange. I couldn't understand why the Rangers stopped suddenly because they had the upper hand with us. It was almost like they had a family fight and as quick as the attack started, it ended. Like a couple of the Rangers warned them off."

Trent gave a *who knows* shrug. "That one talks. He was raised with a man I ran across during my journey here."

Becky hopped a couple of times and carefully lowered herself to the ground. "You're going have to tell me the story of how you ended up here with two Bigfoots and a talking Ranger. But first, we need to get Karen help."

His eyes wide in concern, Trent glanced over at Stone, River, and Sky to see if they'd heard Becky refer to them by that name. Trent's sizeable and hairy searching partners were waiting patiently far enough away that they hadn't overheard.

Trent whispered, "Please remove b-i-g-f-o-o-t from your vocabulary. They are the Earthpeople. Believe me when I say they can hold a grudge for a while."

Sadie had sneaked back to Karen's side. Her expressive brown eyes stared at Karen, confused. "Woman master won't wake up," she sighed.

"We'll fix her up, Sadie. She just needs sleep now. Okay, Becky, let's get you both out of here."

* * *

They set a blistering pace home. Becky limped for a few hundred yards, but River carried her the rest of the way while Sky carried Karen. Trent was amazed at the strength and endurance of the Earthpeople. They couldn't run very fast, but over the long haul, they never stumbled or slowed. The lack of stumbling probably had something to do with the fact that they didn't wear shoes. Curious, Trent had tried a couple of times to get a glimpse of the bottom of their feet. He'd wondered if the skin was just highly calloused or if they had some sort of hooves. Since they didn't stop to sleep on the return trip, Trent never solved the mystery of Earthpeople feet.

Lionheart and Sadie had become fast friends during the journey. They were just the right combination of focus and playfulness. The dogs often strayed from the path to hunt something, and Sadie returned with a squirrel or bird in her jaws. She frequently padded to Sky to check on Karen. He'd grunt at her as if insulted she would ask about his care of the woman, and she'd lope back to her new friend Lionheart.

When Trent saw the familiar landscape ahead, he was relieved for Karen's sake. Although the journey to Idaho and then a search for the women had landed him in tip top travelling shape, he didn't hold a candle to the dogs and the Earthpeople. He was bone tired and slightly irritated. Yeah, and it kinda got under his skin when he'd been forced to listen as Becky and River became buddies. She talked to him in low murmurs, and he'd coo back at her. *That's right*, Trent thought, *River was cooing*.

Stone had called ahead after they'd located Karen. He opened a new hidden entrance and they crawled down a short ladder into a tunnel. Trent reached up to assist Lionheart and Sadie, who took turns jumping into his arms. Five Mermots and two stretchers were waiting at the foot of the hallway. Sky placed Karen onto one, and River sat Becky on the other. He touched Becky's cheek in sympathy before the Mermots zipped away with the women in tow. Sadie chased after them. Trent tried to call her back with no success. *I'm sure they'll work it out*, he thought.

They returned a short time later to the Mermot production facility. As before, the Mermots were hustling and bustling at a frenzied pace. Brodie was striding along the outside wall to join them.

He waved and smiled. "Great job. I'm so glad you found them. I haven't contacted the Admiral yet with news of Karen. Thought it might be better to see what our Mermot doctor says first. I was thinking since you're his son-in-law, Trent, you might want the honors."

"Let's see what they say first and then decide." Trent said. "If it's good news then you can tell him. If it's bad, then I should be the one."

"Decent of you, Trent. Bad news about Karen would be very hard." Brodie frowned. "The Admiral has enough stress just now. Are you hungry?"

Stone said, "We go, eat with family."

The Earthpeople were moving away when Trent yelled out to them. "You Earthpeople are awesome! Thank you."

Stone turned, gave Trent a thumbs up, and then continued striding away. Trent said to

Brodie, "They are awesome. It would have taken us two more days to get here with Karen if not for them. And, that thumbs up was the first positive response I've gotten from the Earthpeople. Maybe there's hope for me yet. They love Becky."

"Hang in there, Trent. They have different customs, but they're never duplicitous like us humans. Why don't I join you for dinner so I can fill you in on what's been happening since you left? There's a lot to tell you."

Chapter 34
Moon Base Victory

Mike, Shakete, his XO, and Jack discussed their next move in Mike's sumptuous quarters. Mike rubbed his eyes and then freed a ball wedged between cushions. When Jack noticed the play object, he jumped from the couch and planted his feet in front of Mike, imploring a toss with an intense stare. Mike complied, and Jack scrambled across the room, knocking against a chair and quickly returning for a replay.

Mike took the ball from his jaws. "I'll take you to the sun deck for some play as soon as I'm done with this meeting." Jack dropped on his haunches in answer but stayed alert in case Mike changed his mind.

"I still have grave concerns about this plan," Mike started. "If they can remove the tags, and if Margo can come up with a workable timetable, what do the Mermots plan to do with over three thousand people? They can't just go running from the enclave like the dogs did. The Huntas are organized and have a secure perimeter now. They'll know and track them down. Many of our people could be hurt or killed."

Shakete answered. "They will either keep them underground until it is safe to move them on, or we can find another way to get them out."

"Where, Shakete?"

"Admiral, as you know, the Mermot's natural habitat is beneath the surface. For just this contingency they have been digging living spaces underground since the Huntas first arrived. Would you like me to get Rappel on the line now to describe their preparations?"

"No, Shakete. I trust you and the Mermots. Humans are not partial to living underground, but I guess given the way they've been surviving in captivity, anything would be an improvement. But won't the Huntas discover the passageways and try to chase them?"

Shakete let out one of his awkward Ardinian laughs. "That would be an optimal result. It would give the Mermots an opportunity to rid the world of a few of my reprehensible cousins. Underground the Mermots rule. Not only can they easily collapse tunnels, but their teeth are weapons, and their mouths secrete a substance that can burn through rock. I pity the poor being that chases them into their lair."

"I've never witnessed any aggression on the part of the Mermot, but I'll take you at your word."

Shakete added, "Interestingly, now that the Mermots are established on Earth, the Huntas have failed to recognize there is no way to be rid of them. Mermots are the most survivable species my people have ever encountered. Just like Earth's rats, only vastly more intelligent, they can hide, dig, and repopulate faster than they can be exterminated. The only way to eliminate them completely would be to destroy their habitat, which is of course the entire planet."

The XO and the Admiral exchanged concerned looks. Mike said, "You knew this all along, didn't you, Shakete? That's the main reason you wanted the Mermots on Earth first, before the Ardinians. It wasn't just to produce weapons."

"Yes and no. I would say both reasons for sending them to Earth were equally important. I will admit that because we were responsible for the destruction of the Mermot home world, my people owed them a place to live. And yes, Mermots are also a critical failsafe if our efforts to defeat the Huntas do not go as planned. Finally, there was no way to protect humans from the Huntas without weapons. I believe my logic was impeccable."

"But what of our people, Shakete? What of humans and now the Earthpeople? We aren't as resilient as Mermots."

Shakete was phasing into gold. "I will not allow that to happen, nor will you, Admiral. It is merely a matter of will and time."

Mike nodded, "I will hold you to that." He turned to his XO. "How goes the preparations to bring my wife to the Delamie for medical treatment?"

"As you know, Admiral, she's still in a coma. The facility in Idaho has done everything they could to help her, but she needs Ardinian medical assistance. We are installing a shield on the last of Delamie's shuttle craft as we speak. We've completed two craft already to transport people and materials to the surface. The installation was part of our plan to fight a ground battle, and your wife's needs were incidental.

"We will simply pick her up and bring her back. Of all the things you need to concern yourself with, retrieval of your wife is the least of them." The XO suddenly realized how his statements might have sounded to the Admiral's ears and added, "She'll receive the finest care available in probably the entire galaxy."

"How many lives does she have left," Mike whispered to himself.

"Sir?" the XO asked.

Mike looked up, caught in his momentary ruminations. "Oh, just a joke of my wife's. She's survived so many near misses that she started counting her lives." Mike directed his attention at Shakete. "If I give her to your care, Shakete, promise me you'll bring her back to me. I don't care what you must do to make that happen. Do you read me, Shakete?"

The Ardinian and human shared a long, meaningful stare. "Yes, Admiral. I understand completely."

"Promise me."

Shakete sat up straighter. "Ardinian culture does not include promise making. We give our word, and I give my word to you now. I will bring her back to you."

"Good enough. XO, please explain to me how you will land a shuttle craft in Idaho without giving away the location of the facility?"

"We will create diversions elsewhere. Shuttle landings will occur simultaneously in two other tactically unimportant places along the west coast. Additionally, we've noticed increased Hunta activity in the mining region of Southern Africa and the western coastal region of South America. We will stage wasp attacks there as well. We hope to keep the Huntas very busy. These coordinated attacks might also give New Washington some cover for an escape."

Mike paused to think and threw Jack's ball again. "Shakete, have you made any progress on analyzing the box Trent recovered from a Hunta vest?"

"Mermots in Idaho are certain the box is not a communication device and that it must have something to do with Hunta cloaking capability. Unfortunately, they do not have the necessary equipment to conduct a sophisticated scientific analysis. The device will be brought with Karen to the Delamie when we retrieve her tomorrow."

Mike nodded. "Any new developments on the matter weapon?"

The gold from Shakete's face had nearly drained away, but Mike's question brought the color bubbling back to the surface. "Admiral, making that weapon functional has been a personal education for me. The simple answer is no, and it is a vexing problem. In my long life, I've always had ample time to plumb scientific mysteries. Never have Ardinians been so under the gun to find an immediate solution. I have more empathy for the human struggle now."

"So, I guess that's a hard no?" Mike asked.

"Yes, a hard no. We've diverted some research into a powerful photon weapon with more success. Jed thinks it could be ready in three months."

"That sounds promising. Last item," Mike started. "Have we had any luck connecting with human populations around the world?"

The XO nodded an affirmative. "Some. There's a large European group hiding in the Alps, as well as a smattering of small Canadian and American groups in North America. Surviving Chinese, Japanese, Egyptians, and Israelis are willing to join the cause. Otherwise, humans are dispersed again like after the Great Dying, and every day the situation becomes worse as Huntas seek out and destroy surviving humans. I wish I could be more positive."

"Me too. It's up to us then. Use them where we can, but plan on little support."

Shakete and the XO somberly nodded their heads.

"Thank you both. I know you're doing everything you can. Now if you'll excuse me, I need some time to think."

They rose, and Mike shook hands with each. They were barely away from his quarters before he pounded his fist into the sofa, repeatedly, until he noticed Jack had backed away.

"Sorry, Jack. I need to ask someone to find a therapeutic punching bag for my quarters."

"Man mad?" Jack asked.

"No, not mad. Just frustrated beyond reason. My family is imprisoned in New Washington, my wife is unconscious, and everyone on earth is counting on me, but I don't know how to save them!"

Chapter 35
The New Washington Test

The prison camp was cold and wet. The Hunta tents were waterproof, but humidity drenched air seeped into clothes and bedding. The only thing that didn't feel damp was anything plastic or metal. Temperatures ranged from the 40's to low 50's—warm enough not to freeze and cold enough to thoroughly chill to the bone even the hardiest among them.

The current misery quotient made Chrystel's escape plan more palatable, and several prisoners had volunteered to be the test dummy for surgical removal of the tag. Mabel finally won the day when she pointed out that she was the oldest person in the camp. "If you count the time before the change, I'm almost 200 years old. I dare you to find someone older. Besides, there ain't no point in taking the chance of losing any of you youngins. You're needed. I'm not."

Mabel glared at Chrystel, her mostly gray hair sticking out wildly from her head. Kind eyes over a freckled nose were still defiant. "Well, what do you say, my little Ginger Snap?"

Chrystel had known Mabel all her life. As Karen's best friend and one of the original founders, Mabel had been another one of Chrystel's substitute mothers while her own mom had been mad-as-a-hatter. The thought of hurting Mabel was like a knife to the chest. She pulled Mabel in for a hug, and Mabel gently pushed her away. "Now, now. We got a fine doc in Sara, and Katie will be helping. No point getting all emotional before we know there's a need. They'll do their best, and then we'll know."

"I don't know how I could explain it to Grandma if something happened to you," Chrystel whispered.

"Girl, don't you go worryin none about that. She knows as well as me desperate times calls for desperate measures. She'll understand."

They huddled around a cot in Sara's tent. It was just after two in the morning, and other than the tent they were in, everyone else was asleep. Sara said to Mabel, "I don't have anything for pain, my friend. I need to make sure I don't accidentally cut into the tag, so I must cut around it. I'll be as quick as I can."

"You better be!" Mabel said. "I'll pretend it's like bein back at the dentist when I was young, getting my tooth pulled without Novocain."

One of Sara's sons had cleaned and laid out an instrument that resembled a scalpel on a metal roofing tile. A needle, thread, and a pan of sterilized water was ready as well. "Lay down on your stomach, Mabel. Here's something to bite down on if you feel like yelling," Sara said and handed her an antique Nyla bone.

"Where the heck you find this? Hope you washed it good." Mabel replied and grabbed the pre-change artifact before settling on the cot. "I'm ready for you."

Sara ordered, "Katie, Chrystel, bring those flashlights in close so I can see what I'm doing. Everyone else, scoot back to the far side of the tent."

The other people who lived in the tent scrambled to get as far away from the surgery as possible, turning away and huddling over their children. Everyone had agreed to take this risk. They couldn't go outside for fear the Huntas would see them and investigate, but no one was sure there wasn't an explosive inside the tags. A hush fell over the dark tent interior as Sara went to work.

Over the hundred years that Sara had been the enclave's only surgeon, clavers had come to trust her with their lives. If not for that trust, it was doubtful the occupants could have been convinced to take this chance.

Chrystel bit her lower lip as she watched Sara's nimble hands. Sara muttered to herself once as blood blocked her view. Using an old shirt, Chrystel wiped the sweat from Sara's forehead. She also checked on Mabel, who was ferociously biting down on her dog chew. "Hang in there, Mabel, won't be long now."

An audible sigh could be heard throughout the enclosure when Sara said, "I've got it. Bring me the bowl and hand me the needle and thread."

A man named Jeremy stepped forward. He'd worked at Jed's science center as an information technology specialist and was as close to a scientist as they had on hand. Carefully, he picked up the two-centimeter-long clear tube and inspected it. "There's some electronics at the top and what looks like dark granules filling the clear part. Bring your flashlight closer."

Katie manipulated the flashlight. "You know," Jeremy said, "These granules look dark purple. Is there anything explosive that's dark purple?"

"Who cares?" shouted a man shielding his young daughter. "Just get it the hell out of here before it has a chance to hurt somebody!"

Chrystel nodded to Jeremy. With great care, he set the device on top of a folded cloth in the center of the bowl she was holding. Chrystel received the bowl and slipped from the tent into the rain and headed straight to her mother's tent. The children who normally lived with Amelia had been farmed out to other families for the night. Only Amelia, Margo, and Kismet were present.

"Sara did it?" Margo asked.

"So far so good." Chrystel answered. "Kismet, I'm going to put something in your pouch to give to the Mermots. You must be very careful. Do not bump into anything."

Amelia was holding Kismet in her lap. "I've already explained it to her. She knows that the packet she's carrying could be dangerous."

Other than Kismet's eyes, the tiny black dog was nearly invisible in the unlighted tent. "Kismet, good dog," the canine said to Amelia and nuzzled her neck one last time.

With the only pencil they had among them, Chrystel wrote a note on Kismet's pouch, placed the tag inside, and took the dog from Amelia's arms. Mermot hands were waiting from the hole under Amelia's cot.

Chrystel sat next to her mother and finally exhaled. "That wasn't fun. I don't think it's explosive. Even if it is, my guess is that the tag must be detonated by an electronic signal. It's probably just some kind of fast-acting poison. It could also be nothing other than a ruse to keep us all here. All we can do is wait and see what the Mermots find."

Margo moved to the cot across from Amelia and Chrystel. "I'm assuming you asked the Mermots for a tranquilizer for the kids?"

Chrystel answered. "I did. The children must be our priority, but there's no way to remove the tag unless they're asleep. I saw Mabel's eyes when Sara cut a chunk from her backend. I'm even worried some of the adults wouldn't be able to keep from yelling out."

"I don't want to discourage you, Chrystel, but there's some gaping holes a mile wide in your plan. How long did it take Sara to remove that thing?"

"Only five minutes. She could probably shorten that time now that she knows what she's doing. Katie and her son were on hand to watch so they can remove tags too. We need one surgeon per greenhouse and two for the kids."

"All bets are off if there's tracking tech in the devices," Margo added.

"Not necessarily. We can just make sure everyone keeps their tag with them until the Mermots yank them into the ground. We'll know whether the Huntas can track the devices soon enough. The Mermots are undoubtedly taking the device outside the enclave. If the tag proximity is tracked, Huntas will arrive in a few minutes, and there'll be hell to pay."

Chrystel studied the worry lines on Margo's face. "I'm sorry, but this is the best I've got. I intend to stay positive until I know this plan is a dead end. I'm going to take a nap. Sitting here worrying isn't helping anyone."

Margo sighed. "You're right. You go ahead and sleep. I find it remarkable Chrystel that you're able to fall asleep at a time like this. I'll stay up and fret; it seems like someone should. I'll wake you when Kismet returns."

Sometime before the sun came up, Margo heard digging underneath Amelia's cot. She lowered herself to the cold ground to grab Kismet, but the only thing that popped from beneath the surface was a Mermot hand holding a note and a bag with something inside.

Margo took the note and peeked into a bag filled with white pills. She shined her flashlight on the note. *The tag contents are a fast acting, deadly poison. The electronics contained in the device are a simple long distance triggering mechanism. We do not know if the tag can be activated individually or if they're designed to kill everyone at once. If we had another device we might be able to make that determination. The pills are a sleeping implement for those who cannot endure the pain of tag removal. Give one to children and two to adults. Please note, the pills require almost an hour to become effective and they are long lasting, four to five hours. The Mermot people stand ready to assist their human friends at your notice. Be well.*

Margo finally smiled. She nudged Chrystel awake. "We're in business!"

* * *

Chrystel and Margo devised a timetable for tag removal and escape while shoveling down a tasteless breakfast of mushy steamed rice. The plan would commence the following morning after the children were each given a white pill.

With her mouth full, Margo asked, "Why is it always the little things that plans hinge on? I don't know where we can find more needles to stitch everyone up. Maybe some tape to hold the wounds together? We're also going to need more sharp instruments to remove tags in different locations. You'll have to ask the Mermots tonight if they can get the things we need by tomorrow morning. In the meantime, I'll work on finding what we need, but no guarantees."

"Do your best, Margo," Chrystel answered. "I'll try too. If we must, we'll postpone the plan, but I truly believe our best chance to succeed is now. Diversionary attacks from our forces are occurring tomorrow. I'm sure the Mermots will come through. They haven't failed us yet."

Chrystel didn't mention to Margo that she was also going to ask the Mermots for a laser and two handguns. She'd resisted asking the Mermots for weapons sooner because she didn't believe a few armed clavers would be enough. There were simply too many Huntas to make an armed escape. A stealth plan was different. If things went bad, then she could hold off the Huntas long enough for the children to disappear into the earth. Chrystel had already coordinated with Liam, the same guy who'd volunteered his services at the greenhouse, and a buddy of his to wield the pistols at their work location.

"By the way, I'm going to talk to Ted today." Chrystel said.

"Are you going to tell him?"

"I don't know. It seems wrong to just leave him here. I can't do anything for Thomas either. If we get out, I'm hoping the Mermots will help us get back in to save them when there aren't so many lives at risk."

Margo mused, "It's always the Mermots to the rescue. We'd be totally screwed if it wasn't for them. Them and a certain three-legged, black dog."

Chrystel saw Herman lumbering through the muddy park to collect her. "I gotta go. More later."

Herman was in fine spirits. He grabbed Chrystel by the arm and needlessly yanked her forward, causing her to stumble. Chrystel gave him a couple of threatening clicks in return. She dutifully moved along to the courthouse for her morning meeting with Ted.

Uncharacteristically, Ted was facing a wall when she entered. As the door shut, he whipped around and lunged at her. "What the hell are you up to, Chrystel?" he shouted.

She leaped back out of range of his hands. "You'd better back off, Ted. I'd hate to have to hurt you. I don't know what you're talking about."

"Really?" he said, sarcasm dripping off the word. "Cleo's in a snit about something. She took my tablet this morning. Something's up. She mentioned the humans and their rodent friends were planning a fruitless and deadly rebellion. I simply assumed you were the instigator."

Please face, don't turn red. She willed her anger back into a corner of her mind. When she was sure she had enough control of herself to prevent widening vessels from pumping blood straight to her skin, Chrystel continued. "How horrible for you, Ted. You lost your tablet. Meanwhile our town is beaten, humiliated, and kept cold, wet, and hungry. Are you that self-centered? Why would I put my people in greater danger than they already are? What a waste you are. I should've never stepped down as mayor."

"You would have lost anyway," Ted retorted. "You're so temperamental and prickly, so filled with self-righteousness, it's hard for anyone to like you."

That verbal smack contained a grain of truth, and Ted's words hit Chrystel hard. She was all those things to include difficult to like. For an instant, she was doubtful about the plan she'd hatched. Did they really have a chance? Was she styling herself as some sort of savior to cover her own insecurities, placing the people in jeopardy in the process?

She stood paralyzed while she and Ted glared at each other. Then she heard Grandma Karen's voice in her head. *Chrystel, strong women who take charge are often disliked; to a lesser degree, the same is true of men. The big difference between men and women is that men are better at compartmentalizing the reaction they get from others. Be like men. Don't worry so much about being loved. Worry instead about doing what's right. In the end, placing the needs of others above self-interest will earn leaders respect and loyalty, sometimes even love.*

Chrystel asked, almost pleading, "Ted, could it be something else? Could someone else be planning a rescue, and the Huntas have gotten wind of it?"

"I don't know. I guess that's a possibility."

"I understand your concern, but think about it, Ted. How could we possibly escape with nothing but our bare hands? And then there's the not so small problem of killer tags implanted in our asses."

Ted narrowed his eyes and looked away as if puzzling out whether she was telling him the truth. When he turned back to her, the suspicion was gone and an emotion almost like hope lit Ted's face. "Do you really think Space Fleet could be planning something to save us? Is it possible?" he asked.

Now that she'd succeeded in her lie, guilt snaked around Chrystel's chest and tightened, constricting her heart and lungs. Guilt about giving Ted hope, only to leave him stranded with the Huntas. "Anything's possible, Ted. I'm sure they've been working on a plan."

"God, I hope so," Ted replied.

"I'm sorry you lost your only means of entertainment." Chrystel almost mentioned his entertainment with Cleo, but held her tongue. "It can't be easy being here alone. By the way, we need some sharp knives to cut the poopueater to test for ripeness. Think you could talk the Huntas into making something available at the greenhouses?"

"I'll talk to them. Sorry if I lost it and took it out on you. It freaks me out when Cleo's acting weird. Hard to know what that means."

"True," Chrystel replied and wondered what Cleo's jumpiness did mean.

As Herman drove her back to the greenhouses, Chrystel knew it was the right decision to leave Ted. She couldn't tell him and risk discovery by their alien jailors. She felt sad for Ted, but there was nothing she could do for him or Thomas. She also knew the escape attempt wasn't about her and not wholly about the people of New Washington. The stakes were much higher. They needed to escape to keep from being pawns in the Huntas' grand plan to steal their world.

Chapter 36
Idaho Facility

"Can I try my ankle now?" Becky asked the Mermot doctor who'd just given her an Ardinian bone growth injection.

"You should wait an hour before applying any weight on that foot. After all, your ankle was broken in two places." The Mermot doctor's pink nose twitched. He manipulated her foot to check his handiwork. Still speaking into Becky's mind, he added, "Yes, yes, I believe that will do it."

Becky scooted off the examination table onto one foot and leaned to grab the crutches from the chair. After she firmly planted the crutches under her arms, she spoke to the doctor. "Thank you, Doc. Pleasure doing business with you. I'm going to limp over to lunch, and by the time I'm done, I should be as good as new. Right?"

"Yes indeed. The marvels of Ardinian medicine!" the doctor exclaimed. He held the door for the pilot, and she waited until the door closed to try her new foot.

Tenderly, she put a little weight onto that leg. When there was no pain, she applied more pressure. Gone was the scream-worthy agony. All that was left was a little soreness. "Nice," she said before someone grabbed her shoulders from behind. "What the hell?" She almost tipped

352

over, but Mark stopped the fall and held her in a bear hug.

"Sorry about that," he grinned at her. "I've been looking for you, Firestarter."

Becky could barely speak. Admitting to Karen that she had feelings for this impetuous pilot suddenly made her nervous around him. That and almost taking another fall sent her pulse racing.

"What are you doing here, Mark?"

"Our flight has been assigned to this area of operation. They're sending a shuttle tomorrow to take Karen to the Delamie for treatment. Our job is to make sure any curious Huntas in this part of town never makes it back to their base. Idaho is the best hope for humanity on the ground right now. Don't want the Huntas knowing about it."

It must've occurred to Mark then that Becky was leaning precariously on her crutches. "Hey, you up for something to eat? I can fill you in on what's been happening."

"Just where I was headed," she smiled. "I'm glad to see you're still in one piece."

He began walking, and Becky step-crutched alongside her flight leader. "Not everyone is in one piece, Becky. Things haven't been going so well. We've lost seventeen wasps in total already."

"And the pilots?"

"Nine lost," he replied, and the corners of his mouth dropped into a grimace. They turned a corner into a Mermot-filled cafeteria. Because Mermots didn't speak out loud, the only sounds were the clanking of trays and the shuffling of chairs. "You grab a seat, and I'll bring you something. Any preferences?"

"Just bring me whatever's edible."

Becky studied the Mermots as she waited for Mark. As always, they were unfailing polite. One Mermot had rushed to her aid as she was trying to juggle her crutches and sit. Each Mermot that she made eye contact with spoke a greeting into her mind. They arrived, ate, and departed with the same efficiency that they accomplished everything else. No wasted squabbling or bustling slowed them down. She wondered what humans might achieve if they could be so cooperative.

Mark jolted her out of her Mermot musings by slamming a tray in front of her. He grinned and noisily pulled out a chair across from her. "How is it, Mark, that you can be so elegant in a cockpit and like a bull in a china shop anywhere else?"

"Talent," he said. "Are you ready to get back in a cockpit tomorrow? We could really use you out there. I've been using your copilot in wasp four, but he's struggling without you, and I worry he's going to get himself killed."

Becky nodded. "Yeah, he was one of the last pilots to be qualified, and they didn't get much simulator time. He isn't ready to fly solo. As to your question, I can't wait to get back up there."

"Outstanding!" Mark hollered, causing several Mermots to look up from their eating task."

Becky asked, "Candidly, how has the war been going?"

"First you. How did you break your leg, and how did Karen end up in a coma?"

Becky bit her lip. "I think we're both lucky to still be alive." Becky gave the short version of their narrow escape from the exploding wasp, her roll down the hill, the storm, the subsequent Ranger attack, and finally, their rescue by Trent and the Earthpeople.

"If I didn't know better," Mark mused, "I'd say you just made that all up."

"I know! I feel terrible for Karen, but honestly it's dangerous to hang out with her. She's like a calamity magnet. In fact, I gave her the callsign Calamity, which she loved. She's funny, though. Like a wise and wacky old woman who doesn't care what anyone thinks. If she wasn't so prone to disaster, I'd strive to be just like her when I grow up. Now you, Mark."

His expression became serious. "Short answer, we're losing. Little by little, the Huntas' greater numbers of Earth-side ships are wearing us down. Our big ships in space are sitting out there doing nothing. Meanwhile, the Huntas have dispersed their forces across the planet. We have plenty of good targets on the ground, but we can't see them in space.

"If that isn't bad enough, the Huntas have begun operations to eliminate the humans that survived their initial bombings. Dammit, if we'd have just known the enemy had cloaking capability, we could've shored up New Washington. Then, at least our airfield and the people living there would've been safe. As it is now, we don't have access to our wasp base, and the town's people are imprisoned by the Huntas."

The color drained from Becky's face. "Wait, what? New Washington was captured? What's happened to my family?"

"I have a list of those captured. I'm sorry, Becky, but your parents and your brother weren't on that list. I don't know what happened to them. No one knows what happened to anyone not in captivity. Hopefully, they got out and they're hiding. I have no idea what's happened to my family in Louisiana, either."

Tears filled Becky's eyes. "I'm going to keep on believing that they're somewhere safe."

Mark nodded. "That's what we're all doing. Admiral Mike is coming here soon to command a ground battle. Until the scientists find a way to locate Hunta ships in space, someone needs to coordinate on Earth and try to organize the folks left alive around the world. Whatever happens, we can't let the Huntas know about this facility. Right now, Idaho is our last best hope to keep a foothold on Earth. That's why I need you with me tomorrow."

"You damn well bet I'm in. My foot should be good to go by the time I eat desert. Regardless, I could fly with just one foot!" She paused to look into Mark's eyes and felt her heart beat faster. "I'm glad you'll be leading us. I've missed our conversations. I've even missed Tammy."

Chapter 37
No Fail Flying

Tension was palpable as a large group of prisoners gathered just inside a forty-foot-wide tunnel opening, built by Mermots to accommodate the movement of people and supplies. A team of doctors surrounded Karen, who was resting peacefully on a stretcher. Brodie, Trent, and a handful of Mermot technicians lingered at the entry, shivering in the crisp fall day and anxious for the shuttle arrival. Behind them was the backbone of the operation: Earthpeople ready with forklifts to rapidly move supplies and equipment from the shuttle to the facility.

Meanwhile, at a protected underground hanger in another location within the facility, Mark, Becky, and fourteen other pilots climbed aboard their wasps waiting for takeoff. A wide tunnel to the surface allowed the spacecraft to fly single file to the surface.

Eight wasps would depart prior to the shuttle arrival with the objective to patrol a massive swath of land from the Washington/Canadian border to Northern Colorado, almost a half-million square miles. Tammy greeted Becky the minute the pilot got comfortable in the familiar gel seat of her wasp. "Welcome, Becky. You have no idea how much you've been missed. By Mark most of all."

"Tammy!" Mark cautioned on his communicator. "We've talked about this. We have a critical mission this morning, and I need your total focus to pull it off."

Tammy's sexy voice dripped with sarcasm, "Yes, Mark, my lord and master." Mark could already hear the laughter of the other pilots.

"I merely wanted to welcome Becky in the manner that she deserves. As an AI, I'm quite capable of walking and chewing gum at the same time." Tammy giggled. "Well, technically, I can't walk, but I'm sure you comprehend my meaning. Might I inquire about the health status of the delightful and wise Karen?"

Mark sighed, "Go ahead, you will anyway. Pilots, three minutes to finish pre-flight checks."

Becky answered, "I think she'll be fine, Tammy. She's still in a coma, but I'm certain the Ardinians can fix her. I gave her the call sign Calamity."

"Wonderful! How appropriate. Although, if her biological responses to flight are any indication, I'm not at all sure she will fly wasp airlines again."

Becky asked, "How do you know, Tammy? You weren't with us."

"Silly pilot. Everything that happens in a wasp is recorded. Once we are back in communication range, the data is transferred to me."

"Hmmpf. Didn't know that."

"Let's get serious now." Mark commanded. "Remember, stay in pairs in your sectors. We don't know what the Huntas will have in the air. Call for backup if you encounter four or more Hunta ships. I'll decide if other wasps can be diverted. Our mission is to ensure that any Huntas flying in our sector are unable to reach the facility. Make no mistake, today there will be no running to fight a battle tomorrow. I trust each of you to make the calls necessary to achieve victory. Any questions?"

One of the pilots asked, "Gameboy, won't the Huntas see the shuttle on their sensors and pinpoint the facility's location?"

"Negative. The Ardinians will be jamming any tech that might see the shuttle. We must ensure there are no visual sightings."

"Roger."

"Tammy, report any Hunta ground movements you detect immediately."

"Roger, Gameboy."

"Good flying! We Endure!" Mark shouted. "On my mark, now."

Mark was already flying forward through the tunnel as the other pilots in his flight yelled, "We Endure!" in response.

He shot into the sky and smiled for the first time that day. The weather report indicated low cloud cover over the coastal area, but for now the skies in Idaho were clear and welcoming. Hopefully, there wouldn't be too many Huntas to screw up the day.

Mark was glad Tammy couldn't read his thoughts. At least he hoped she couldn't. When she'd mentioned how much he'd missed Becky, his heart had started pounding. Tammy's physical assessment module would most likely notice an increased heart rate. He didn't understand how he could be deadly calm when flying in the heat of battle, but feel his heart go ape shit at the mention of Becky's name. Very frustrating.

He wondered if all leaders struggled with having favorites, even when they wanted to treat everyone the same way. He cared about each of his pilots, but while he wasn't paying attention, somehow Becky had taken a special place in his heart. It could be he was just sexually deprived and she was the best looking woman around. Then again, he knew she was far more than the sum of her appealing physical parts. She was smart and brave and funny, and a real friend. And she did have a great —

Speaking only into Mark's communicator, Tammy interrupted his thoughts. "Mark! You need to quit pining for Becky and get your head in the game."

"I wasn't pining! I was…wondering how to treat all of my pilots equally."

"Okey dokey, anything you say. I sense four Hunta fighters that lifted off two-hundred miles to the northwest. Should you call for backup?"

"What do you think, Tammy?" Since Karen's admonition about making Tammy feel needed, Mark had begun asking Tammy her opinion. Thus far, this approach had been only marginally successful in taming a willful AI.

"I recommend that we go this one alone. We don't know what else the other pairs will encounter, and it's awfully early to begin yanking teams here and there. Also, you are the best pilot on Earth, and I am the finest AI in the fleet. We can do this."

"I couldn't have said it better, Tammy."

"Gameboy, it would seem they have spotted us and are now flying under cloud cover. This is the first time the Huntas have employed that technique. They may be learning, however poorly. I recommend we hit them from above rather than attempt a chase. We are still faster."

"Set a course." Mark opened his communicator to Jenny, his copilot, and the partner wasp. "Four Hunta ships flying nap of the earth on your view screens. We'll come in from above. Remember to maintain distance from me so they can't do their kamikaze ramming tactic. I'll take the first ship, and you target the last, then we'll swing around to take the other two. Any questions?" When no one responded, Mark gave the go order and accelerated.

The wasps made quick work of the first two Hunta ships. As they were looping back for a second run, Mark heard Becky's voice. "Gameboy, this is Firestarter. We have fifteen Huntas flying in formation in our sector. I need some help, soon!"

Mark's gut reaction was to finish off the ships he was currently targeting and speed to Becky's aide, but he knew he was the farthest away from her location. "Roger, Firestarter. Wasp Team Three, fall in on Firestarter. She'll be the lead. Keep a channel open in case I need to make further adjustments."

Tammy whispered, "Are you sure that's enough, Mark? Four facing off against fifteen?"

"No, I'm not, but if I pull in another team, that'll leave too much area left uncovered. Becky is good. I'll let it play out. Our target is in range," he said calmly. "Jenny, fire at will."

After Mark and his wasp teammate destroyed the four Hunta ships in their sector, he announced, "We need to widen our flight pattern to cover Wasp Team Three's area." Tammy made the adjustments while Mark listened to Becky command her wasp teams.

She used a similar strategy. Becky ordered the wasps to disperse and focus on leading or trailing Huntas—like how a pack of predators would take down prey from a larger herd. They whittled down the fifteen Huntas to twelve, but then the remaining enemy countered by splitting into two groups of six ships each to block and ram individual wasps. The free wasps targeted the six ship groups while the wasps under siege, dove, spiraled, and bolted to keep from being trapped. Mark thought if not for the impenetrable Ardinian shielding, this matchup would have resulted in a human slaughter.

Becky yelled, "We just lost Glam girl. I need help, Mark!"

He'd been so focused on Becky's situation, Mark hadn't checked on the last pair, patrolling the northeast section. "Update, Tammy,"

"I'm afraid the northeast team is moving now to engage a group of three Hunta ships, and we have two Huntas arriving to the west." Tammy added sadly, "There is no other backup available."

Tammy's communication was open, and Becky heard it. "Roger, Tammy. We'll do our best."

Mark calculated the odds. Becky still had eleven opposing ships to her three. Her battle situation was worse than when she'd initiated contact. Three ships didn't allow much flexibility to contend with greater numbers. His only option was to quickly deal with the Hunta ships to the west before speeding to Becky's location and mop up whatever was left.

For the second time in his short pilot's career, Mark felt like a complete failure. He'd promised himself after Budapest he wouldn't allow the Huntas to get the better of them. They were losing again, but this time he might lose the only woman he'd ever had real feelings for. He'd never even hinted to Becky that he thought she was remarkable. He was nothing but an asshole loser, and never the man or the pilot he thought he was.

Tammy came to the rescue. She said, "Quit feeling sorry for yourself and get your ass in gear! You need to stop thinking the world is spinning around you. Grow up, Mark, right now!"

That did it for him. There was nothing quite like the shock of a sexy AI voice suddenly transforming into an enraged football coach to pull him out of defeatist thinking. "Roger, Tammy. Thanks. Pedal to the metal," Mark howled.

He and his partner quickly dispatched the two unsuspecting Hunta ships in his sector and flew to Becky at speeds even Mark thought were unachievable in the atmosphere. He hoped (no, *prayed*) any sonic boom they loosened wouldn't draw more Huntas.

When he arrived, Becky was alone and fending off three Hunta ships attempting to encircle her. Mark and his partner swooped in, firing with the last of their laser energy to kill two Huntas while Becky used her payload to finish off the third.

Just then, Mark heard the signal that meant the shuttle had departed Earth's atmosphere for the Delamie. "Any Huntas left out there, Tammy?"

"None that I can detect. You are safe to head back to the Idaho Facility. Well done, Commander."

Chapter 38
All Bad Things Must Come to an End

Chrystel and Margo were up before daylight. Margo inventoried the goods the Mermots had delivered from the earth like the bounty of a harvest. Margo said, "Chrystel, you didn't mention the weapons and ammo. Are you sure that's the best idea?"

"Is anyone ever sure?" Chrystel mused.

"Point taken. They sent surgical glue which should speed up the surgical process, and there's also some medicine in a baggie that says, *to induce vomiting*. I don't know what that's for."

"Oh, excellent. The vomiting stuff was my request. I must convince Herman I'm sick this morning, so he'll leave me here. I want to be ready with the laser in case we're discovered. Whatever happens, we must make sure we get the kids out. If I'm not as good an actress as I hope, it'll be up to my mom." Chrystel gave Margo a meaningful look.

"True." Margo answered. "I'm relatively certain that leaving it to Amelia wouldn't be the best idea."

Chrystel wanted one last review of the timetable with Margo before clavers began to wake. "My mom will give the children pills immediately after breakfast. They should all be asleep by 9:00 a.m. Aki has volunteered to take some puke medicine too. He's one of the oldest kids, and I think losing his twin made him grow up quick. Between me and Aki, Sara and Katie will rush to the children's tent to help the sick.

"When I'm sure the Huntas have bought our story, Sara and Katie will begin removing tags. As each tag is removed, my mom and I will pass the children to the Mermots to be transported through a tunnel. By 10:30 all the children should be safely away.

"Margo, you should begin to remove tags on the sneak as soon as you arrive in the greenhouse. At 10:30, greenhouse workers will need to make their way to the Mermot tunnels one at a time. Try to keep them from rushing the doors. That would be a sure fire way to get caught. You have a map of the departure points?"

"I do. And if the Huntas figure it out? Chrystel, they're brutal, but they aren't stupid."

"Then you'll have to improvise, thus the weapons. Just keep imagining the look on Cleo's face when she realizes we've sneaked away in broad daylight."

"Improvise and imagine. Got it," Margo smirked, imagining Cleo's face when she was notified the humans were gone. She then pulled Chrystel in for a surprise hug. "We can do this.

And just so you know, Chrystel, I like you a lot. We make a good team."

"Oh, God, Margo. Don't make me sentimental right now. I respect the hell out of you, too. Now go."

After the incident between Herman and the toddler, Chrystel began her mornings waiting for Herman in the common area of the park. She wanted to make sure he was kept as far away from the kids as possible. Today, she purposely stayed in the tent to draw Herman to her. He peeked his ugly mug inside the tent flaps and clicked.

Chrystel was lying in a cot and called to him that she was sick, her stomach already a churning, roiling lava pit from the puke inducing medicine. True to form, Herman entered, scowled, and hissed, and then he yanked Chrystel by the arm from the tent. As per the plan, Aki was positioned just on the outside and was already regurgitating breakfast, making a show of how loudly he could upchuck. Chrystel swallowed bile and gagged, fighting back the sympathetic urge to join Aki in his release. Herman gave the boy a disgusted Hunta expression, which wasn't entirely different from his happy face, before pulling Chrystel forward.

It was at that moment Chrystel quit fighting the need to expel her demons. With a velocity that astounded even her, breakfast surged forth, landing with steaming, acid-drenched repugnance on Herman's hand, his side, and down his legs to his feet. Chrystel believed her consumption of several glasses of water had been a marvelous inspiration. Herman shoved Chrystel away, sending her ass sliding into the mud. He frantically tried to scrape off the stinking mess with his forearm. Finally, achieving little reward from his ministrations, the Hunta monstrosity hissed, clicked one last time, and with great haste, left a retching Chrystel lying in the dirt.

Katie, Sara, and Sara's son jumped to the rescue. They helped Chrystel to her feet and moved her and Aki into the children's tent for treatment.

Chrystel beamed at her waiting mother, a wad of rice clinging to her chin, "So far so good. Let's get to work."

Some of the smaller children were already asleep. Amelia shook a young girl to determine how deeply she slept. When the girl didn't wake, Sara moved to the innocent child's side. "Let's hope these sleeping pills work."

Sara's tag removal procedure was flawlessly performed, and the little girl didn't bat an eye. "This little angel will be the first claver to escape," Sara proclaimed proudly and handed the sleeping child to her son. After the initial success, the children's tent became an assembly line of tag removal, wound gluing, and transfer to the Mermot's waiting hands. It was nearly ten o'clock when Chrystel announced, "Sara and Katie, we need to speed it up. We're running behind."

Sara huffed in frustration. Amelia glanced through the tent flap and said, "There's someone coming!"

"Can you see who it is?" Chrystel asked, as she handed over another child and then gathered the laser.

"It's Ted!"

"Good lord, what's he doing here? Hide your knives and cover the children you're working on. Mom, slide a cot over that hole! Try to act normal and be ready with a good story."

Chrystel studied the laser in her hands. The weapon was almost as large as a rifle, and there didn't seem to be any way to conceal it if she intercepted Ted outside. Keeping Ted from viewing their escape was the immediate priority. She sat the laser on a cot where it would be easily assessible and slid through the opening to greet him.

Chrystel called, "Hey Ted, to what do we owe the honor of your presence in this neck of the woods?"

Ted stopped and leaned slightly to look around Chrystel into the tent. "Cleo sent me to check on you. We heard you and some of the kids were sick."

"I'm feeling a little better. Might have been something bad in our food. Sara isn't sure if it's food poisoning or a stomach virus. She's seeing to the kids now."

"Clavers don't get stomach viruses," he retorted with a frown. "And I've never heard of food poisoning."

Damn, that didn't work well. Now what? Chrystel thought. "Sara thinks the bad nutrition and stress of being imprisoned could have weakened our immune systems. I'll come to you with an update as soon as she figures it out."

Ted's eyes narrowed. "I want to see for myself. Let me pass, Chrystel."

She jumped in front of him. "I wouldn't do that if I were you. If it's a virus, Sara says it's extremely contagious. I've vomited all morning. Believe me, you don't want to catch it."

"The fact that you seem to give a damn about whether I become ill tells me you're bullshitting me. Now move aside."

Chrystel's heart was beating hard, and she knew with a certainty her face was engorged with blood. In a fraction of a second, she weighed her two choices: take him out or convince him to join the escape. Logic said Ted should want to leave too, but as Chrystel had learned the hard way, logic didn't always win the day. Her powerful right hand was already in motion to jab the bridge of Ted's nose.

Chrystel's Seiken fist was within a hairs breath from its target when an electrical shock spasmed her body. She sank to the ground, every nerve ending and muscle reeling in uncontrolled panic.

The women inside the tent had heard the commotion. Katie was waiting with the laser nestled in her shoulder when Ted emerged inside. "I'll take that stunner now, Mayor Ted," Katie growled. "Set it on the ground in front of you. There isn't any need for violence, and I really don't want to hurt you. We can get you out of here. The Mermots will take you."

His forehead creased in a frown. "Who said I want to go?" He held up his hand. "Just an FYI, this little gadget in my hand controls your tags. You'll be toast with just a point and click. I believe I have the advantage here, so why don't you put down that damn laser?"

Katie smiled. "Hate to disappoint you, Ted, but we've already taken care of our tags."

He pointed at a sleeping child near him. "I won't ask again. Put down the laser."

The shock waves stabbing Chrystel's body were beginning to recede. She climbed to her knees and crawled inside toward Ted. "Why, Ted? Why would you do this?"

He stared down at Chrystel as if she were a beaten dog. "You really don't get it, do you, Chrystel? They've won. Even if you do escape, there'll be nowhere to go. You have no idea how many Huntas and ships are here. Cleo has promised me an enclave of my own as soon as the world had been cleansed of vermin like the Mermots and Ardinians. A place where humans can live in freedom."

"And you believe her? It's you who doesn't get it, Ted."

Ted held up a finger and then spoke into something that wasn't visible near his shoulder. "You were right, Cleo. I've got the situation under control here. Send word to the guards at the greenhouses that they're making an escape. Oh, and get some extra guards here too."

Chrystel pictured the spot behind Ted's knee where her toe needed to land. She flexed her leg muscle to ensure it was working. *Close enough*, she thought. With her hands on the ground, she shifted weight to the stabilizing side and kicked Ted so hard his knee folded.

He tried and lost the battle for balance, crumbling to the ground in slow motion. Chrystel sprang to her feet and jerked his outstretched clicker arm backwards. The bone snapped with a wince-worthy crack, like the branch of a dead tree.

Not yet defeated, Ted scrabbled forward to collect the clicker he'd dropped when his elbow was broken.

"Oh, hell no!" Chrystel shouted. She stepped on Ted's back and plucked the device before he could get his hands on it.

Sara's son, a large muscled man, jumped on top of Ted and started pounding his head with his fists. Katie had to intercede before he killed the unconscious mayor.

"We haven't got much time," Chrystel shouted. "Slice those tags out of the kids and don't worry about gluing them up. The Mermots will have to take care of them."

There were only two children left in the tent when Amelia shouted, "The guards are coming!"

"Grab one, Katie. I'll get the other. Let's shove them down the hole and hope the Huntas don't decide to set off all the tags."

When Chrystel offered the final child to Mermot rat hands, she yelled, "The last two have tags. Go as fast as you can. The Huntas are here!"

Chrystel was making her final plea to the Mermots when Herman followed the business end of his ray gun inside the tent. He surveyed the devastation and blood in the enclosure, kicked at Ted's prostrate body, and clicked something to the Huntas outside.

He gestured for the women to leave the tent. Chrystel glanced at the hole wondering if there was any chance to dive for it, but there were too many of the enemy. She saw a guard move in with a cannister attached to a long hose as they were pushed outside. It looked like gas of some sort.

"No, not the kids," Katie whispered.

Chapter 39
The Hunta

An hour after Moon Base Victory received the devastating news that only a third of New Washington prisoners had escaped, the Huntas finally responded to one of the Delamie's continuous hails. The Huntas' message was succinct: Be prepared to accept live video from the Hunta people at 1800 hours, New Washington time.

Members of Space Fleet filed into the largest of Moon Base Victory's conference rooms. On Earth, those who had the means to stream video were also gathering to hear the voice of their enemy for the first time. Mermots at the Idaho facility hung a giant screen from the ceiling of the production center. Humans, Earthpeople, Mermots, and dogs sat or stood waiting for the grim news.

Admiral Mike was the last to arrive for the Hunta video message. He walked down the isle of an auditorium, feeling as if a thousand pounds of pressure rested on his shoulders. When he arrived at his seat, he mechanically intoned, "Please sit." Shakete glanced at Mike, and he was glowing gold in sympathy for the human man who had never wanted such great responsibility.

The room was eerily silent. Normal start-of-a-meeting jocularity and optimism were replaced with long sighs and throat clearing. It was as if a phantom funeral dirge was playing in the background, a song of sad endings that could be felt but not heard.

The dark screen flickered on, and Cleo's arresting and unnatural, brilliant green eyes captured the attention of all viewers. She smiled broadly into the camera and said, "I am Cleo, the leader of Earthbound Huntas, and I have total authority to speak for my people. I come to the beings of Earth tonight to inform you that you have lost the battle for this planet. We have easily prevailed from your short and impotent efforts to retain this world.

"The Huntas have watched you for some time. What we witnessed were beings unable to do what was necessary to create stability from chaos. Given a few hundred more years, humans would undoubtedly destroy their own species and quite possibly damage this unique planet. We could not allow that to happen.

"However, the Huntas are not as cruel as the Ardinians would have you believe. We have among us some of your kind. A few of them are here with me now. The Hunta people will allow a means for your species to survive, something my ex-partner, Shakete, refused my people.

"We demand that you vacate the moon base and remove your fleet from this solar system, never to return. In exchange, we will return your kind to you.

"A Hunta ship carrying our prisoners will meet the Delamie escort, at a location to be provided, and there, we will transfer them to you. Do not send escort ships with the Delamie, or your people will be exterminated.

"We understand that humans will fight to the death to protect their tribes and wish to provide evidence of the futility of such resistance." Cleo turned away from the camera and clicked in Hunta language to someone off screen. Her visage blacked out and in its place was a distant view of Earth. Tiny pinpoints of light winked on in near atmosphere, lighting the planet like a Christmas tree ceremony. The number of lights grew and congealed until the green-blue orb called Earth appeared as a hazy shadow beneath a brilliant cover.

Terrified moans and cries came forth from the audience. Cleo spoke in the background as the twinkling lights flashed out of existence. "The Hunta armada is far greater than you imagined. Each flash represents the unveiling of a cloaked ship. This is no trick. At your leisure, you may verify the truth of my claims by recordings."

The horror of Cleo's presentation sucked the air from the room. Mike felt like his lungs wouldn't expand. Cleo was back on the screen, but this time, the camera angle moved away from her face to a scene of Founders Statue.

Mike noticed Amelia and Chrystel first and then Thomas, Katie, Rachael, Mabel, and Sara. Almost half of the New Washington Founders were on their knees and bound in front of a statue that honored their sacrifices. The new Mayor, Ted, held a prominent place in the center and was the only person held down by a Hunta soldier. He was also the only human fighting the humiliation. Twisting and crying, Ted yelled, "They lie. Don't believe Cleo!" The guard backhanded him with a massive gloved hand. Ted quit squirming, hung his head, and wept.

Looking straight into the camera, Cleo strode to Ted's side. "We felt you might need further encouragement to leave."

She pressed something in her hand, and Ted began to jerk. "This man, your designated leader, is a coward and a traitor to your people. I felt he would make the best example."

Froth began to seep from Ted's lips, and blood streamed from his eyes and his nose as he continued to spasm. "The Huntas have no use for traitors, even our enemy's traitors. Please know, we will kill every prisoner, one at a time, if you do not follow our instructions. Some humans in league with the rodents have disposed of the poison that is now taking the Mayor." She scowled, "But do not fear, we have other means of ridding the planet of your kin.

"You have twenty-four hours to decide. After that time, I will kill your people slowly, each facing a more gruesome death. There is no reason to remain here on Earth. Find another home and save your species. That is all." The screen became black, just like the emotions cascading through the moon base and the entire planet.

Chapter 40
Mike

Mike's hands were shaking. He fought back the weakness and solemnly stood to face the brave beings who had given everything to defend their home. "There are no words I know that can soothe the pain and fear engendered by what we just saw. I ask that you seek out those closest to you and find strength and support from them. I will never leave you, but I must take time to gather myself and think."

On rubbery legs, Mike strode from the room. Jack was at his side and Shakete behind them. When he exited, Mike turned to an Ardinian so gold Mike wondered if he hadn't hardened completely. "Shakete, we'll talk, but I said alone, and I meant it. I know you're as appalled and frustrated as I am right now. I'll be at the sun deck with Jack."

"I will tell the XO to ensure your privacy there."

"Thank you." Mike hurried away. The sun deck was the best place on the moon base to think. Spacious, adorned by greenery, and featuring a spectacular view of a magnified Earth, the deck provided a respite from the confines of a sealed habitat on an airless rock.

Mike gazed at the sight, a view that normally inspired him. Bone-chilling fear welled up inside when he considered a universe where humans, flaws and all, were replaced on this beautiful, awe-inspiring planet by a savage band of aliens.

He breathed deeply and muttered to himself. With Earth on the line, he needed straight thinking right now. Somehow, he must forget about the pain and the fear to make the best possible decision. Maybe if Cleo had chosen his daughter or his granddaughter for death by poison, he'd be blubbering like Ted. As Karen had once said, crying in moderation was therapeutic. Unfortunately for Mike, only those he loved on an individual level were an impetus for tears.

"Jack, I must make a choice. Even that sounds wrong to my ears. I was never elected to this position. I was never granted the authority to speak for Earth on a decision of this magnitude. I didn't even want this damn job, but there was no one else better to do it. And, there's no one else in a better position to decide. How's that for being boxed in?"

"Jack says Mike good man."

"Thanks, Jack. I'm glad you think so. If only it were that simple. Mike thinks you're a good dog too and a very special friend."

With a sigh, Jack dropped to the floor. Mike surmised Jack had seen enough of his protracted self-debates to know they might be here a while.

How could he even consider leaving the people on Earth to fend for themselves against the Huntas? He grabbed his face in his hands and moaned through his fingers. "Goddammit!"

What the hell kind of choice was it when your options are to fight an unwinnable war and lose the people you care about most or to skip town, resigning the people left on Earth to a terrible fate and hope to get a second crack at it later? As Shakete had said, Mike had no magical hares or golden nuggets to solve this dilemma. And unless a heavenly entity dropped some technological breakthrough from the sky in the next twenty-four hours, there would be no good solution.

Sometimes, retreat allowed victory in the end, but this situation didn't add up to one of those times. Once the Huntas were dug in and organized on Earth, taking it back could be an insurmountable task. The enemy had planned their siege well.

Undoubtedly, the Huntas' cloaking technology had allowed them ample time to easily gather intelligence. They knew the Ardinian shield made it impossible to degrade the fleet or take out the human command structure, so they identified the next best target: New Washington and the airfield.

New Washington was the key. It was the headquarters for the Earth-side wasp fleet, the science center, and the only training base for new pilots. Couple that with the fact that nearly all of Space Fleet had relatives or close friends located in that Pacific Northwest location, and the Huntas had a recipe for success.

If only Mike had known about the cloaking, he believed he'd have seen the possibilities in this deadly game of chess. The Huntas' strategy was impressive in its simplicity. First, they'd created worldwide chaos by interfering with communication systems, and then, systematically destroyed as many human enclaves as possible, which included a good chunk of the world's meager population. Simultaneously, they'd shattered New Washington's ability to put up a fight. By taking New Washington survivors as hostage, the Huntas had also succeeded in impairing Space Fleet's will to fight. The enemy's strategy was a Trojan Horse of a different kind.

The Huntas' plan had left the humans on Earth leaderless and running for their lives, with little means to regroup. If only they'd had a little more time to prepare. Mike had known they lacked redundancy in Earth's defense; in just six more months, they'd have finished their own plan to decentralize ground-based wasps, but perhaps the Huntas had known about that too.

Thank God, one of the first things they'd done was to create a secret weapons manufacturing plant in Idaho. The point of keeping it secret was to keep knowledge of a weapons plant from other humans, but in this case, it worked for more important reasons.

If he agreed to the Huntas' terms, the human species would survive, travelling through space in search of a new home just like the Ardinians had done for so long. His family and close friends from New Washington would be among the spacefaring survivors. But then there were the dogs. Would they be eradicated? No one was quite sure why the Huntas believed dogs to be a threat, but Mike knew from gathered intelligence the alien criminals killed any they found. The Earthpeople, a new species that deserved a chance at life, might cease to exist too. Only the Mermots could be counted on to keep an earthly foothold.

Mike thought when making a critical decision, it was always important to consider the worst possible outcome and weigh the odds. He'd known of an equation once that helped analyze worst case scenarios, but it had been so long ago, he couldn't remember it.

Instead, Mike played it out with his dog. "Jack, worst case is that we say 'Screw you' to the Huntas. They in turn carry out their threat to kill everyone in New Washington. We throw all that we have at the Huntas' significantly more capable forces and lose. The Huntas will then mop up the battlefield, destroying enough of humanity, Earthpeople, and dogs to ensure extinction. End of story. We're all gone for good.

The odds of events unfolding in this way are far better than fifty/fifty."

Jack looked up at Mike concerned. "Is that Mike's plan?"

"If, on the other hand, we leave, humanity has a shot at survival. Maybe Shakete solves the mystery of his energy weapon. Maybe the Ardinians will find a method to detect a cloaked ship or the technology to cloak their own ships. The Mermot moon is far away and unknown to the Huntas. The Ardinians, humans, and Mermots can build more ships and then come back and save anyone that's left. I'd give the odds on that as fifty/fifty.

"The biggest concern here is an impossible calculation of when they could come back. Everyone we know may be dead and gone by then, and perhaps at that point another planet-wide war will no longer be an imperative."

"Jack like second plan better," the dog whispered into Mike's mind.

Mike nodded. "Would you go with me to Idaho to help those who are left behind?"

"Where man goes, Jack goes."

Finally, some tears leaked from Mike's eyes. He hadn't added Karen to his analysis. In her unconscious state, she would have to leave with the Ardinians, and he might never see her again. His wife of over a hundred years—his beloved wife and a part of himself that went so deep, he knew he'd never be the same man without her. He folded to the floor next to Jack, grabbed his neck, and pressing his face into the fur of Jack's ruff, Mike found a safe place to release his grief.

Chapter 41
Chrystel

Chrystel busied herself helping her mom gather what few belongings they had with them in prison. In just a few hours, the Huntas would ferry New Washington clavers to the Delamie. The entire camp was in an uproar for fear the Huntas would somehow renege on their deal, but there was absolutely nothing anyone could do. The decision had been made. Space Fleet would leave in exchange for their living, breathing souls. Chrystel imagined any number of things that could go wrong with this bargain, not the least of which involved turning tail and running from Earth, but once again, the decision had been made and it was out of her hands. She hoped her grandfather had a plan. He had to.

Kismet was play growling in the corner as Margo teased her with an old shirt. After Amelia firmly demanded they stow away her little dog on their galactic travels, Margo had hatched a plan to make it happen. They all agreed, even though ultimately only the children and a few adults had escaped, Kismet had done her part and more. They wouldn't leave her here alone at the whims of Huntas or Rangers.

Chrystel slipped outside. She didn't know if or when she'd enjoy another day like this and wasn't about to waste what little time she had left. The clouds had lifted enough that a few cracks of blue were visible between the wispy white clouds. Inhaling the fresh air deeply, she turned into the cool breeze to allow the wind to massage her skin. *May I keep that feeling inside, and may I someday return to my home.*

Her face twisted into a scowl when she noticed Herman emerge through the gate. What the heck could he want with her now? Since Ted was no longer with them, she'd been forced to become Cleo's liaison. Herman beelined to her location and grabbed her arm. "Just don't, Herman. For Pete's sake, there's no need to harass me now. I will come with you!"

He allowed Chrystel to follow but glanced back several times to be sure she wasn't trying to trick him. When he exited the compound, instead of turning right to the courthouse, he veered left toward his ATV. He pointed for Chrystel to get in. When she was seated, he reached to grab and secure her restraints, but she blurted, "No! I'll do it." His plump eyes went wide, but he backed off and allowed her to restrain herself.

They took off in the direction of the greenhouses. Chrystel thought that Cleo must need something, again. Since Space Fleet had agreed to leave Earth, Cleo seemed to be spending all her time gleefully inspecting the poopueater harvest. As far as Chrystel was concerned, this drive was one last chance to create a photographic memory of her home to sustain her. Granted her home recently was a prison, but the ground they travelled was rightfully hers. Always would be. A home that had been conceded to these creeps.

When he turned right away from the enclave, Chrystel grew concerned. "Herman, where are you taking me?"

He drove and clicked. Chrystel sensed he was trying to explain something to her, but she had no idea what. Was Herman going to kill her for all the trouble she'd caused? As a prelude to snuffing her out, was Herman just now providing an itemized list of her infractions and misdeeds? She studied the key device on his belt, the one that unlocked the restraints, and wondered if there was even the slimmest chance she could get to the key, unlock herself, and run away.

Nope, not even a microscopic chance in hell.

When he turned off a dirt road to a rutted path, she became even more worried. Five minutes later, he applied the brake and turned off the ATV. He sat, staring straight ahead as if he'd decided today was a good day to ponder the meaning of the universe.

"What's going on, Herman? What are you doing?"

Was he planning to rape her? None of the Huntas, other than Cleo, had displayed even a smidgeon of sexual interest. It was odd that

Herman would consider something like that now. But what else could it be? Chrystel's heartrate soared. She tensed and readied herself to fight for her life.

Pulling the restraint key from its clasp, Herman clicked a statement to Chrystel and handed her the key. Then in the strangest accent she'd ever heard, Herman painfully stammered his first English word, "Go."

"Go?"

He nodded. Chrystel didn't spend a moment pondering why, at least not then. Unaccustomed to how the belts worked, she fiddled with the lock until a resounding clack indicated there was nothing left to keep her captive. Leaping from the ATV, she took two long strides and stopped.

She turned to Herman, realizing the jeopardy he'd placed himself in. If Cleo was willing to kill Ted, a traitor of her enemy and her sex slave, then it was unimaginable what she might do to Herman for setting her free.

No, Chrystel don't do it! Before she could grab ahold of reason, the words were already springing forth from her lips. "Do you want to come with me, Herman?" She pointed to him, patted her chest, and performed a sweeping gesture toward the forest.

His bulging eyes took in the wilderness beyond. Chrystel noticed a shifting in the stoic Hunta features, almost as if he was wistful for something that could never be. Something inside herself shifted as well, a recognition that even among a ruthless species of aliens, it was possible for a single individual to see things differently. Whatever his motivation, Herman's act was one that demanded courage.

Finally, Herman shook his head no.

"Thank you, Herman. Truly, thank you!" She waved to him, and he waved back with his giant hand. Like a freed gazelle, Chrystel steaked into the forest, heading east.

Running after being trapped for so long felt almost as good as sex. Her tight muscles loosened and relaxed with every mile. Her feet seemed to soar above the ground. It wasn't until she'd reached the outer edge of the enclave that she asked herself where she was going, or whether she should be leaving at all.

The people from New Washington needed her, but the people left behind on Earth might need her more. If the exchange went well, clavers would be safe aboard the Delamie, but the people left here would be far from safe.

Was she trying to justify abandoning her fellow prisoners because she secretly wanted to stay? To stay and find Brodie? To stay and fight with everything she had left to keep a foothold on Earth?

Probably. She slowed to a walk, even knowing every second she delayed was one more second for the Huntas to find her. She breathed in the smells of the wilderness around her. She listened to the birds enjoying a day without rain. Unlike her grandmother, space travel had never held any interest for her. What she loved, had always loved, was this place. Her place.

She jerked and dropped to the ground. Only seconds later a dog snout was sniffing her hair. Chrystel looked up into the blue eyes of a skinny dog, each of its ribs clearly defined. "You scared the crap out of me, dog! What're you doing out here?" Its mangy tail beat madly in response. "You got left, I guess. You're a survivor though, you poor thing."

And then she knew. There would always be a place where people like her were needed. The big dog on the porch—a warrior like Thomas. There was no shame in being needed in the place she wanted to be. Besides, Herman's courageous act had to count for something.

"Let's go, dog" She ran east and the dog, who she'd named Freedom in her mind, ran by her side.

Chrystel realized she would miss her mother most of all. In her heart, she felt immense gratitude that their time together as prisoners had finally released them both from the cage of their past. Her mother would be fine.

Chrystel was also glad Margo and Thomas would be with the survivors in space. She knew that neither would ever quit working to come back and save them. They were remarkable people: Margo, a master of organizing worldly things, and Thomas, her friend and mentor, a protector just like her.

She wondered again why Herman had freed her. Maybe Herman respected her strength. Maybe it was just another act of defiance against Cleo. A more hopeful thought tickled the back of her mind—that maybe the Huntas weren't entirely cruel monsters. Maybe there was hope that a connection between Huntas and humans was possible. Chrystel doubted that was the case, but she could never be sure what lurked inside a heart, human or alien.

Whatever Herman's motivation, she was just thankful. Her place was here, to do on Earth what she could for those who were left. Brodie came to mind then, and she grinned as she ran. "I'm coming, Brodie," Chrystel yelled. "You'll finally get that chance to convince me that you've changed. I might even be willing to give you a second chance."

Chapter 42
Mike and Karen

Mike gasped when the doctor led him inside the restorative cubicle where Karen was being treated. Machinery encased her body from under her arms to her knees. How that might cure a brain injury, Mike wasn't sure. Her feet, clad in Ardinian slippers, touched the floor but held no weight.

She looked so peaceful. Her beautiful face serene, as if she were Sleeping Beauty taking a long nap until her prince came to wake her. Her hair had grown out and flowed alongside her face in shimmering auburn. Highlights of gray were conspicuously missing as were the laugh lines beside her eyes.

Something caught in his throat. This was the same woman he remembered from the time right after the change, but now Karen was young again and he was an old man. The Ardinians had been busy restoring her body, but would they be able to restore her mind? Mike stopped the Ardinian doctor moving from the cubicle to give him privacy. "Can she hear me?" Mike asked.

"We can't be sure. Her brain activity has increased, so there's some chance."

"Thank you. I know what to do."

Mike drew Jack to Karen's side and placed one of her hands on top of the dog's head while he held the other. "I know you can do this Jack. I saw it first hand when you almost died in Idaho. Do your thing."

Jack panted in the affirmative.

"Karen, my sweetheart, it's Mike. I wanted to see you before I left. A lot has happened since your injury. I'd like to tell you all about it, but your first concern should be to get better.

"People on Earth need my help. Jack and I are going to Colorado and plan to make our way to Idaho. Your job is to stay here and get well. When you're up to it, help Shakete and the other misfits work together. You know Shakete needs one of us around to keep him oriented."

Mike breathed through his mouth. It wouldn't do to worry Karen by losing control of himself. "Amelia is here on the Delamie. So are Thomas, Mabel, and the twins. They promised to take care of you, but once you're well, they'll need you too.

"I just wanted you to know how much I love you. No matter how far apart we are, you're always with me." Mike's voice wavered, and he gritted his teeth.

"When you get out of here, Shakete has promised to give you a Jill. It won't be the original Jill, but trust me, you won't know the difference." He gazed at Jack with affection.

"Find a way to save us, Karen. I know if anyone can, it's you. I wish I could promise you I'll be waiting when you arrive, but you'd know that would be a lie. All I can promise is my best effort. Shakete has given me his word that he'll return to Earth to reclaim our home. Make him keep his word.

"My life has been made worth living because of you, Karen. You've given me more happiness and contentment than I have the words to describe." Mike inhaled.

"I also know that if you were in my shoes, you'd make the same choice to return to Earth. It'll help me in the time to come to know that you're safe here and that you'll help lead the effort to save us. Be well, my love."

He stepped to Karen and kissed his wife one last time.

To my readers: Thank you for reading Stolen World. In case you didn't know, there are two ways to publish. The first is to find a publisher who will do it for you, and the other made possible by Amazon is to self-publish. I've made the choice to self-publish because I can sell my novels at a lower price, and after a long career, I have no interest in a publishing company telling me what to write or when to write it.

I hope you'll consider taking a moment to leave an honest review for Stolen World. Reviews help authors get read, but someone must read an author's novels to get reviews. Self-published authors like me struggle with this conundrum. Anyway, if you have the time, I'd be extremely grateful for your feedback. Below is the link on Amazon to leave a review. The review section is at the bottom of the page:

https://www.amazon.com/Stolen-World-Endangered-Book-3-ebook/dp/B07QQMC7SX/ref=sr_1_3?keywords=stolen+world&qid=1555783960&s=digital-text&sr=1-3

Other Stuff

I know readers might feel like I've left the people of New Washington and their alien friends in the lurch, because I did. There just wasn't anyway to conclude the Endangered Series with only three novels. I'm working on the fourth and final novel in the series right now. My original intent was to release Book 4 within two months of Stolen World. I'm sighing here because a family emergency got in the way. The last novel will be published in 2019, but it probably won't be until near the end of the year. Just know, I'm doing my best to get er' done!

If you've read every book in the Endangered Series, I'm sure you've surmised I'm a dog lover. There are moments when I'm writing where I struggle to find my groove, and then there are talking dog herds. From the moment a dog exodus popped into my mind, I smiled. I smiled all the way through writing those scenes. I could smell it, see it, hear it, and feel it. Truly, I could have written a whole book on their journey with Trent, but that probably would've been too far afield of the series. I only hope the image of a doggie horde made you smile too.

My group of editors and betas is small but powerful. I'd like to thank each of them for their contributions to the finished product: Kel Crist, Sara Sakora, Jo Delano, Christel Taylor and David Matteri are each amazing beta readers and add a perspective I do not have the capacity to see alone. Thank you for doing what you do!

And then there are those brave souls willing to wade through my draft manuscripts to correct my multitude of errors. Thank you Adele Brinkley from Pen in Hand, and David Matteri for editing my scribblings. Even though I may never have a firm handle on comma placement, I've learned much from you both.

Finally, and most importantly, thank you to every reader willing to give my novels a look! It's most exciting to get emails from readers on my website or comments on my Facebook page. Please feel free to contact me by either method. I love hearing from you and promise an answer in a day, two days tops.

Here are the links:

Website https://www.nsaustinwrites.com

Facebook
https://www.facebook.com/nancyaustinauthor/notifications/

Made in the USA
Las Vegas, NV
02 January 2022

40117809R00233